Heaven and Hell

Heaven and Hell
Published by The Conrad Press in the United Kingdom 2016

Tel: +44(0)1227 472 874
www.theconradpress.com
info@theconradpress.com

ISBN 978-1-911546-19-1

Copyright © Michael C. Doyle, 2016

The moral right of Michael C. Doyle to be identified as author of this work has been asserted in accordance with the Copyright, Designs and Patents Act 1988.

All rights reserved. This book is copyright material and must not be copied, reproduced, transferred, distributed, leased, licensed or publicly performed or used in any way except as specifically permitted in writing by the publisher, as allowed under the terms and conditions under which it was purchased or as strictly permitted by applicable copyright law. Any unauthorised distribution or use of this text may be a direct infringement of the author's and publisher's rights, and those responsible may be liable in law accordingly.

Book cover design and typesetting by:
Charlotte Mouncey, www.bookstyle.co.uk

Cover Image *Les Oréades* (1902) by William-Adolphe Bouguereau, held at the Musée d'Orsay, Paris, France.

The Conrad Press logo was designed by Maria Priestley.

Printed by Management Books 2000 Limited
36 Western Road
Oxford
OX1 4LG

Heaven and Hell

Michael C. Doyle

To my wife Sharon,
without whom this book could never have been written.

By way of a preface:

If you believe in Heaven,
There is a Hell -
And no human ever wants to be there.

1

It was the beginning of Easter. Rumours of war were spreading throughout the Middle East.

Israeli soldiers crouched behind a wall, rifles aimed at the ready, as Arab youths hurled stones from the top of the Eastern wall surrounding Jerusalem.

The stones smashed onto the cobbled pavement below, narrowly missing the soldiers. They looked nervously at each other. Several more youths appeared at the top of the gate, overlooking the holy city.

Suddenly a shot rang out.

The scream of the bullet pierced the silence of the night as the bullet ricocheted off the top of the Lions' Gate, the entrance to the Muslim quarter of the Old City of Jerusalem. The youths fled at the sound of gunfire, but moments later they re-grouped, and returned to hurl more rocks at the soldiers.

This was not the greeting that Michael Cohen, a freelance journalist from England, had expected. He was thirty-three, clean-shaven with short dark brown hair, brown eyes, and an inquisitive, wide-awake look about him. Long before arriving in Israel he had doubts over his profession, even more so now when he considered the frightening repercussions of what could happen to the Middle East if he wrote a story. The nature of journalism often stressed him, but he liked writing. He also liked drawing and painting with oils; painting was one of his favourite ways to relax, along with chess, which he played to club standard. His degree was a BA in Art History. He'd studied at the Slade; it had been one of the happiest times of his life. He hoped passionately for a peaceful solution to the Middle East crisis. He had an idealistic view of humanity that people could live in peace and harmony.

2

Cohen profoundly believed in the possibility of peace and harmony between people, even though he knew it was an ideal only rarely achieved. He sought heaven but had all too often found hell in his life. For him, heaven was friendship, a good book, a beautiful landscape, a stunning painting, an exquisite piece of music… and of course women. He adored women. He found them infinitely attractive, beautiful even, yet also puzzling and a permanent enigma. Cohen knew that many men, of course, saw women more or less as he did. There was a difference, though, and he knew it from a lifetime of experience with having women as friends, and also as lovers. The difference was that women so often tended to adore him too. He had never really understood where this adoration sprang from, though he knew he was reasonably good-looking.

Cohen had been brought up in a liberal Jewish home in Finchley, along with two younger sisters, by an affectionate but not excessively doting mother, and a father who ran a lucrative hedge fund and who, leaving early in the morning to go to work and only returning at night after the young Cohen had gone to bed, had been absent from most of his childhood.

When Cohen was twelve years old, he and his family had gone on a summer camping holiday to a large, luxurious campsite near Hastings with tents that had two or three rooms. One evening, when dusk was falling and Cohen was returning alone from swimming, he mistook the tent and peered inside to see a complete stranger, a woman, completely naked, standing in front of him.

He was too young at the time to have any clear idea of how old the woman was, but later in his life he assumed she was about twenty-five. She had long, straight black hair that reached down to her waist. Her breasts seemed to him then, and always in his subsequent memory, very large and wonderfully womanly, yet what captivated him most was her face. Her eyes were dark brown, very bright and seemed to twinkle at him.

She smiled at him, her mouth half-open. He was so astonished by her appearance and so shocked by her nakedness that he didn't know what to do. He froze to the spot, the sight of her engraved on his mind.

It was the closest the twelve-year-old Cohen had ever experienced to heaven, and later in his life he was only too aware that, somehow, he had never experienced such a heaven again, not even when he lost his virginity at the age of sixteen to an eighteen-year-old French au pair. She was looking after the family of one of his school friends in a large house in Golders Green and, during a sleepover that featured about a dozen boys, she furtively and excitedly whispered to him, him alone, that she wanted him to *'couche avec moi'*. Cohen had been studying French at school by that time for five years. He had known what she meant. By the time he was sixteen numerous girls had wanted him to kiss them.

But he was still a boy at the campsite that day at the age of twelve, and desperately nervous. He just stood there, frozen with fear and excitement, until a man, who was, Cohen supposed, her husband or boyfriend, emerged from another, smaller, room in the tent.

The man saw Cohen and instantly threw himself at him. He bent him over his knee and smacked him so hard on his backside it really hurt. Cohen's heaven had become hell. Yet what he remembered even more than the smacking (which he was too ashamed about to report to his parents), was that the naked woman had tried to pull the man away from him.

'It was an accident!' she said. 'The boy just got lost.' But the man was having none of it. 'Don't talk rubbish!' he shouted at her. Finally, after delivering about a dozen excruciatingly painful final slaps, the man threw Cohen onto the floor, though not before telling the women to '*kick that little Peeping Tom bastard out*' before going back into the room he'd emerged from.

Cohen started to cry. The woman gently lifted Cohen to his feet. 'I'm sorry,' she whispered. 'I know you came in here by mistake. It's getting dark, after all. Look, you'd better go. I'm so sorry he spanked you.'

The woman, still completely naked, took Cohen's hand and started leading him towards the entrance of the tent. On the way, she stopped, put her arms around Cohen, bent down towards him (she was about six inches taller than he was) and kissed him. It was a real kiss; she opened her mouth and kissed him for perhaps ten or fifteen seconds, long enough for Cohen to be completely aware what was going on, then she probed her tongue into his mouth and French-kissed him. Her heavy, firm, breasts pressed against the top of his chest.

Cohen, even though his posterior still stung, was so excited and disturbed at the woman kissing him that he wondered if he might be going crazy with the thrill of what was happening. 'Don't ever forget me,' she whispered.

Cohen never did.

There were three more days of the holiday left and every time Cohen left the tent for the rest of the holiday his heart was thumping in case he saw the woman again. What would he say to her? What would he do? And if she saw him, what would happen then? But he didn't see her again.

The beautiful naked woman filled Cohen's daytime thoughts and night-time dreams for all of his teenage years and for all his life to come.

3

The soldiers stood up and approached the gate, their rifles aimed at the top of the wall, ready to shoot anyone who moved.

'Are you trying to kill them?' asked Cohen, surprised at what he'd witnessed.

'Of course,' said one of the soldiers, matter-of-factly, 'they're trying to kill us.'

'But they're just kids,' snapped Cohen.

'Welcome to Jerusalem,' said the soldier sarcastically. He then turned and fired another shot in the direction of two youths, who hid between the ramparts. The other soldier looked at Cohen's contemptuously. 'Whose side are you on? You'd best move away before you get hurt,' he warned. An angry crowd had gathered, mainly elderly Arab market traders returning home, gesticulating at the soldiers and spitting in their direction. The soldiers retreated cautiously, their rifles on their hips, away from the taunting crowd.

It was Cohen's first trip to Israel. The incident alarmed him to such an extent that he decided to go back to his hotel and order a stiff drink. One thing he was sure about, as he sipped his brandy in the relative safety of the King David Hotel, that he knew he wasn't cut out to be a war correspondent. The story he was on had nothing to do with the recent outbreak of fighting in Jerusalem and the West Bank.

Nevertheless, Cohen knew that if the information was true, and the Arabs got wind of it, all-out war could erupt and he'd be caught in the middle of it. No, he wasn't a war correspondent and he had no intention of putting his head in the firing line if he could help it. He hated war. To him war was madness. His sympathies lay with the poet John Donne who wrote: 'Any man's death diminishes me.'

The assignment Cohen was on was historical, dating back thousands of years to the time of King Solomon's reign. He'd been sent as a freelance journalist, mainly because he was a Jew, to confirm a tip-off from an English rabbi that Israel was planning to rebuild Solomon's Temple. When Cohen was given the tip-off he didn't rate it newsworthy.

He knew that the Jewish people had been planning to rebuild the temple, ever since it was destroyed by the Romans in A.D 70. But the more information he uncovered, the more he began to understand the full implications of what was at stake. The problem was the plans involved the rebuilding of the temple on its original site, Temple Mount, where it was built by King Solomon more than 3,000 years ago. That was where the Aqsa Mosque – the Dome of the Rock – now stood, considered by Muslims to be the holiest shrine after Kaaba in Mecca and the tomb of the prophet Mohammed in Medina.

According to Judaic prophecy the temple had to be rebuilt on the very same site as the mosque before the Messiah would come. And until it was rebuilt on Temple Mount, the Messiah would not appear to Israel. As it was written in the Book of Daniel and Haggai in the Old Testament; 'The new temple will be more splendid than the old one and there I will give my people prosperity and peace when the Messiah comes.'

4

Cohen knew he was fortunate to have arrived in Israel when he did. Only a few months earlier tanks had surrounded Bethlehem and Hebron. There had since been a lull in the fighting due to renewed peace talks, although a ceasefire was still not in place.

Cohen poured out another brandy and looked at the contacts in his notebook. He had been given the name of an architect who had drawn up plans for the rebuilding of the temple. The architect's name was Isaiah Rubens, a renowned municipal architect and town planner of Jerusalem. Highly respected in the Jewish international community, he had lectured on architecture in the United States. But there was other information from other sources which had begun to alarm Cohen and give him reason to believe Israel was determined to rebuild the temple. The right-wing Israeli government was taking over parts of East Jerusalem by requisitioning property belonging to the Arabs, and not only in East Jerusalem but in the Muslim Quarter of the Old City, where the Dome of the Rock stood. Cohen knew that if these sources were right, the Israeli government was preparing to take over the Muslim Quarter of the holy city and rebuild the Temple of Solomon on the same location as the mosque.

Recent reports claimed Arabs were being forced from their homes as part of the Israeli government's continuing purge in East Jerusalem to one day seize complete control of the holy city. Not that Cohen any sympathy with the Palestinian cause, but what was happening in Jerusalem, and what he witnessed, with soldiers shooting at young Arabs, left a mark on his conscience. For shootings and forced evictions reminded him of what his grandparents suffered under the Nazi occupation in Poland during the Second World War. The Nazis dispossessed them of all their property and businesses, and moved Germans into their homes. The Jews were rounded up and sent to the Warsaw ghetto and later moved to the concentration camps, where they would perish.

The Jews believed that Jerusalem, the holiest of cities, the home of the world's three great religions, was theirs by right, a direct inheritance from Jehovah through Abraham. In fact, it is their Promised Land, as Torah says.

Cohen knew that any attempt to rebuild the temple in the Muslim Quarter of the Old City would lead to all-out war. The Arabs would declare a holy war – 'Jihad' – overnight. He felt sure that if the mosque was destroyed to make way for the temple, this would lead to nuclear Armageddon in the Middle East – World War Three. The war would not be a conflict over land, but a conflict of three great religions, a conflict which has raged for centuries across continents, ever since Islam vowed to spread the word by the sword.

Cohen knew he was on a dangerous assignment and that he would have to get his facts right before he even began writing anything about it. He was only too aware that any error on his part would not only destroy the fragile peace progress, but also send panic throughout the whole of the Middle East. However, he knew it was also possible Israel had no intention of taking over Temple Mount, for there had been no mention of any plans to build the temple in the Israeli media, not in the *Jewish*

Chronicle nor in the *Jerusalem Post*, which published planning applications.

Cohen had thought of approaching the Israeli government, but dismissed the idea. It was far too politically explosive for the government to comment on the temple being rebuilt. His only hope would be to find someone within the Planning Department who was prepared to talk. Cohen also knew he would have to forgo his planned sightseeing trip around Jerusalem, for this story was too urgent. He had been looking forward to spending his first day in Jerusalem on a tour, visiting the Western Wall, King David's tomb and the Holocaust Museum. But witnessing the shooting incident had unnerved him, and he'd do another tour another time. Right now, he had to contact Isaiah Rubens as soon as he could. He gulped down his brandy and left the hotel. On his way, it dawned on him there would be no point approaching Rubens directly for he would very likely deny the story, especially when confronted by a foreign journalist.

It might have helped, thought Cohen, if he himself could speak fluent Hebrew, but he only had basic conversational Hebrew which he'd learned at an evening school in London. His parents had spoken English at home, but they'd taught him a few Hebrew words.

He hailed a cab and asked to be taken to Ein Karem, a village five miles outside Jerusalem. He'd been told where Rubens lived, but he didn't have the address.

On the journey, he took out press cuttings and was surprised at what he read. There was a story about Jewish women in Israel already designing and sewing robes for the temple priests, while a farmer was ready to give a prize heifer to be sacrificed when the temple was consecrated. Surely, thought Cohen,

Israel wouldn't take on all the Arab nations, for that would be war. Israel was, after all, surrounded by Arab states, with their backs to the Mediterranean Sea. Cohen knew that was what Palestinian terrorists had vowed to do – throw every pregnant Jewish woman and child into the sea, until no Jews are left.

The taxi headed west, through the market and out through the suburbs, past the upper-class white houses in West Jerusalem, and along the dual carriageway until it headed down a steep valley, surrounded by olive groves and cedar trees. In the distance Cohen could see the Judean hills, where he knew the ancient Israelites once took refuge from invading Roman armies. Descending further down the valley, the taxi rounded a steep bend and entered the village of Ein Karem. Despite the village's Arabic name there wasn't an Arab in sight when Cohen stepped out from his cab. It was only later he was informed that the village, once populated by Palestinians, had been overrun during the 1967 Arab- Israeli War, when the Palestinians fled their homes in fear of their lives.

The driver dropped him off at the only place offering accommodation, which turned out to be a backpackers' hostel. He had planned to spend the night in Ein Karem, but he hadn't reckoned on sharing with a group of students on tour. After tipping the driver, he headed into the hostel where a group of long-haired students were lounging about the reception area. He asked a petite dark hair girl behind the desk for a room for the night and she politely told him that there were no rooms at the inn. 'But you may find a room at the convent across the street,' said the receptionist. 'The nuns rent out rooms to tourists.'

Cohen, while not a practising Jew, thought it would be inappropriate for him to stay at a convent, especially Catholic.

Not that he had anything against nuns. He mulled it over and decided to stay overnight as he didn't want to go back to Jerusalem. So he headed down the pot-holed road until he saw a sign directing him to the Convent of St. Joseph and the Sisters of Charity. But he began to feel apprehensive again about staying there. He stopped and sat down on a wall to reconsider, and he suddenly heard a noise, a scraping noise, that sent shivers down his spine. He looked around and noticed he was sitting beside some garbage bins. Among them were several feral cats scratching through the garbage in search of scraps to eat. He couldn't believe that so many cats had been left to fend for themselves in such an affluent village. Didn't the Jews care about animals? He got up and approached the cats with a bite of his sandwich he had bought along with him, but they hissed and disappeared inside the garbage bins. Perhaps the villagers were right not to care for the cats after all, he thought. The cats wanted to be left alone, to fight among themselves for scraps. Not unlike the Jews and Arabs, he thought, fighting over scraps of land.

Following the path to the convent along a narrow path, he was led to a wrought-iron gate with a high wall, surrounded a large white-stoned mansion, set apart from the village. A notice on the gate requested that visitors ring the bell, which he did so, waiting patiently for someone to come. Had the nuns retired for the night? The gate was eventually opened. A nun, dressed in a white habit, glanced suspiciously at Cohen looking him up and down. 'Do you know what time it is?' she asked, admonishingly, looking at her watch.

'I'm sorry, I know it's late,' he apologised. 'Do you have a room?'

'We're very busy this time of the year. Are you here for the celebration?' she asked, breaking into a soft smile.

'Celebration?' queried Cohen.

'It's Holy Week next week, didn't you know?' she asked, surprised at his ignorance. 'Are you a Christian?'

'I'm Jewish. I'm visiting on business and the hostel is full up. I'm sorry to trouble you. I can go back to Jerusalem and stay there tonight, if it's inconvenient.'

'Well,' she said, 'we don't wish to be inhospitable to our Jewish neighbours. But do you know anyone in the village?'

'No, I don't know anyone. It's my first visit to Israel. I'm from London.'

'Well, you best come in and we'll see what we can do,' said the nun. 'We have a sister here from England,' she added, as she locked the gate. 'Do you attend a synagogue?'

'I haven't been to a synagogue since my bar mitzvah, I must confess,' said Cohen. 'I'm not very religious.'

'More is the pity,' the nun sighed, turning the register. 'Strictly speaking there aren't any rooms available, but I'll make an exception in your case. You can stay in the priest's room. He will here next week over Easter. You seem a nice Jewish boy, but you'll have to be very quiet when the nuns are at prayer. The sisters' cloisters are opposite the priest's room.'

Cohen didn't know that the nuns were next door.

'Now, I'll need you to register, what's your name?' asked the sister.

'Michael Cohen,' he said, quietly, so the nuns were not disturbed.

'An auspicious name,' she remarked, writing it down.

'What's suspicious about it?' said Cohen. He was tired and hadn't heard.

She smiled. 'Not suspicious, but auspicious. Your name is the same name as the archangel Michael. He defeated Satan and cast him into hell,' she added, in an authoritative voice. 'I'm Sister Ruth, welcome to Israel.'

'Thank you, sister,' said Cohen, shaking her hand. 'Wasn't it Ruth who saved Israel from invasion?'

'My, you certainly know your scripture.'

'When I was at school, we all had to read the Torah,' he explained.

Sister Ruth was most impressed and beckoned Cohen to follow her along a passage through to the cloisters. 'I will show you to your cell, I mean room,' she said, apologising.

'You had me worried, Sister. Israel is still a free country, isn't it?'

'Supposedly,' she said, curtly.

'Do I detect a note of Palestinian sympathy?' asked Cohen wryly.

'I sympathise with suffering. Surely you do too,' she said.

Cohen nodded in agreement, but he sensed an air of disapproval in the nun, as if some way the Jews were responsible for the troubles in Israel. But such a reaction wasn't new to him. He had come across anti-Semitism from Christians before. But he didn't expect to find it in a contemplative nun. On reaching the end of the corridor Sister Ruth took out a bunch of keys and opened the door to his room. 'You must be quiet, please, for the sisters are in prayer. If you wish to join them in the chapel, you'd be welcome.'

'Kind of you to offer but I've got a lot of work to do,' answered Cohen.

'That's the trouble with the world,' she sighed, 'everybody too busy to pray. I don't wish to sound patronizing, but we spend a lot of time praying for the Jews.'

'I'm glad to hear it,' said Cohen, with a faint smile.

'Why?' she asked.

'We need all the prayers we can get,' Cohen said.

'Indeed, but we also pray that the Jews will come to know Jesus as their true Messiah,' she said, with conviction.

'He was a prophet; that's all I know,' replied Cohen. 'Despite what people think, the Jews didn't nail him to the cross – the Romans did.'

Sister Ruth entered the stark room and looked at the crucifix on the bare wall. She turned to Cohen and looked compassionately into his eyes. 'Christ was much more than a prophet,' she said calmly. 'He is the Saviour of the world. If only the Jews had faith, they too would know him as the Messiah.' She gave a sigh. 'But all will be revealed in God's time.'

He looked into her clear blue eyes. The conviction in her voice, the peace and calm she radiated, made a deep impression. It was as though she'd pierced his soul.

'Christians have had their fair share of suffering and persecution too,' Sister Ruth added, raising her voice. 'In fact,' she insisted, 'ever since Jesus Christ was crucified. The Jews don't have a monopoly on suffering.'

Cohen couldn't help but start to feel annoyed. He looked out of the window and tried to collect his confused thoughts. He hadn't come to the convent for a lecture on Christianity. But when he turned to Sister Ruth and she wasn't there. She'd disappeared. He glanced at the window and spotted her in the cloisters, with her white habit shimmering in the silver light of the moon like an angel.

5

Cohen looked around the room and unpacked his case, forgetting his confused thoughts. It was a sparse room, painted all in white, and plainly furnished with a table, chair and a bed with a washing basin. The walls were bare, except for an icon of the Madonna and Child, and above his bed hung a stark, solitary crucifix. He studied the tortured Christ hanging from the cross. It made him uncomfortable, worshipping a dead man hanging from a tree. It was almost incomprehensible to him.

He believed that the Messiah would one day come and free the Jews from all their persecutors and restore Israel's greatness to King Solomon's glory. But before the Messiah could come, he knew from reading the Torah, the temple had to be rebuilt in Jerusalem on the very same site Abraham sacrificed his son Isaiah, on Temple Mount.

Israel would be prepared to risk all-out war to fulfil scripture, and rebuild the temple. For then, according to the Old Testament prophets, the Messiah would indeed come!

6

Cohen decided to have a fortifying drink in the bar before making enquiries about the architect's address. It turned out to be full of young Jewish men and women, chatting amongst themselves in Hebrew. He understood something of what they were saying.

He took his drink, a vodka and orange, to an empty table in a corner and thought about the interview, and how he should approach the architect. He knew that if he was to present himself as a journalist, Rubens would most likely deny that he himself had anything to do with the temple, let alone plans to rebuild it. Cohen knew he would have to come up with a different approach, namely someone who knew the architect, a friend, who could introduce him as a student of architecture.

A beautiful waitress, in her twenties, with shoulder-length black hair and an elegant face, came up and asked him in Hebrew if he wanted to order some food. Instantly, he thought how much she reminded him of the woman in the tent when he was a boy. Apologizing for his poor Hebrew, he ordered another vodka and orange and said he wasn't hungry, but if she'd ever heard where the architect Isaiah Rubens lived in the village.

'No, I no hear of him,' she replied in broken English this time. 'Want to ask the manager?' she said, smiling.

Within a few minutes, a swarthy Eastern European – most likely Jewish, Cohen supposed – approached his table. Cohen explained he was in Israel studying architecture and asked if he had heard of the architect Isaiah Rubens, and where to find him. The manager stared at Cohen suspiciously, as though the question had caught him off guard, then he broke into a broad grin.

'Of course everyone heard of him,' he grinned. 'He comes at weekends for lunch, sometimes. He's a great architect.'

'Do you know how I can contact him?' asked Cohen.

'Why don't you phone him?' said the manager.

'I tried, but his number is ex-directory.'

'Then go see his wife, she has a shop in the village,' he said.

'And where is the shop?' Cohen said, finishing up his vodka.

'She has an art shop in the village, selling ceramics, tiles. You can't miss it.' Cohen thanked him, and offered to buy him a drink.

'Thanks all the same, I have customers coming in. Maybe later, shalom,' the manager replied.

'Shalom,' responded Cohen, enjoying uttering the Hebrew word for peace. How ironic that such a word should be used in greeting and farewells amongst Jews, when there was so little evidence of peace in Israel. Cohen picked up his briefcase and made his way through the crowded tables and laughter, leaving the young Jewish men and women to enjoy their freedom while it lasted. For an ominous war would break out soon, Cohen thought.

He made his way back to the convent, relieved that he wouldn't have to press the bell again and disturb the nuns. He entered the gate and made his way quietly to his room, creeping past the nuns asleep in their cells.

The following morning, after a somewhat restless sleep, Cohen headed back into the village to look for an art shop. He passed the garbage bins and noticed the cats were still there, ferreting through the rubbish. He passed a few bungalows and was then confronted with a six-foot wall with barbed-wire fence. Standing beside the gate was a female security guard, a hand on her revolver.

It was the entrance to an infant school. The children frolicked in the playground, oblivious to the security surrounding them. The fact that kids as young as five had to be protected by an armed guard and a wire fenced distressed him. Would the children of Israel live as normal kids do in the West?

He approached the security guard. As he came near her, she put her hand on her revolver. She peered at Cohen, looking him up and down, to reassure that he posed no threat to the children. 'You're not an Arab?' she asked, abruptly.

'Do I look like an Arab?' he retorted. 'I'm as Jewish as Jehovah.'

'Then you shouldn't use his name in vain,' she snapped. 'What do you want?'

'I'm looking for an art shop,' Cohen said. He looked at her. She was barely twenty years old. What has made her so bitter, he wondered, at such a young age? And why, in such a rural village, was the school in need of such security? 'Is all this necessary?' he asked, looking up at the wire fenced.

'This is Israel,' she said, pointedly.

'But there are no Arabs here,' said Cohen, 'this is a quiet and peaceful village.'

'Right now it is,' she snapped. 'This school was attacked quite recently, didn't you hear about it?'

'I've just arrived in Israel. I didn't know. I'm sorry.'

'Count your blessings,' she shrugged.

'Do you hate Arabs?' he asked, bluntly.

'Sure, I hate them. They killed my brother. He was nineteen years old. He was in the army, called up a few months ago.'

'Can you forgive them?' asked Cohen.

'I'll never forgive them,' she said, and turned away into the playground to check on the safety on the children.

Cohen shrugged and headed in the direction she'd pointed. Maybe she was right, who can forgive terrorists who slaughter your family and murder schoolchildren?

He approached the centre of the village and he noticed a grocery store, next to it an art shop. He peered into the shop window where an array of colours confronted him, with an arrangement of floor tiles, bath tiles and wall tiles dancing before his eyes. It had a calming effect, the colours almost like a kaleidoscope. He entered the shop, glancing at the various tiles and ceramics. Then a tall, elegant blonde woman appeared and greeted him in an American accent. 'Hi there,' she said. 'Are you looking for something in particular? I'm sorry to have kept you waiting. I was working on a new design.'

Cohen was couldn't help but think how strikingly beautiful she was for a middle-aged woman. She had a voluptuous figure, with a smile so endearing that he felt at ease in her presence.

'Actually, I was wondering if you could help me,' asked Cohen hesitantly, unable to avoid being taken aback by her ample bosom. 'I'm an art student, but I'm also studying architecture. I'm looking for an architect, Isaiah Rubens. He might be able to help me.'

'Well, you've come to the right place,' she said proudly. 'He's my husband.'

'What a coincidence,' Cohen exclaimed, hoping his surprise sounded convincing. 'Is it possible I could meet him?'

'I'm sorry, but he's very busy working on an important project,' she said, sensing Cohen's disappointment. 'Say, you're from England, right?' she asked with a smile.

'I'm from London, for my sins,' Cohen joked.

'Gee, well you must come to visit us sometime!' she said. 'Are you staying long in Israel? My name's Jane, by the way.'

'I'm pleased to meet you, Jane. I'm Michael Cohen. I'm here for a while. I'm studying in London.'

'I have some friends in London,' said Jane. 'Say, we're having a dinner party tomorrow, just a few friends. Why don't you come round? If he's not too busy, perhaps you can meet my husband.'

Cohen couldn't believe his luck.

'We don't live far from the shop,' said Jane, writing the directions down. 'You can't miss it. Our house is the third on the right.'

'What time should I come?' he asked.

'Say, seven o'clock. We'll have a few cocktails before dinner. You'll find my husband quite helpful. He knows what it's like to struggle as a student. Are you for studying for a degree?'

'Well, a PhD actually,' said Cohen, coughing.

'Then you'll get along with my husband. He'll want to know all about your thesis.'

Cohen was concerned that Rubens would want to know about his thesis. He'd have to wing it, as the Americans say, and make something up. He'd have no choice if he wanted to befriend Rubens. But he knew that any slip up could mean the end of his assignment, if not the end of his career. But he wasn't a journalist by accident, for he'd learned to talk his way out of many a crisis. Jews were survivors. But setting himself up as an expert on a subject he knew next to nothing about left him with a sinking feeling in his stomach.

'Actually, it's more to do with art than architecture,' Cohen corrected himself. 'But it does involve architecture.'

'Hey, well you had best talk to Sarah, my neighbour. She loves art. She'll be joining us tomorrow.'

Cohen picked up a ceramic from the display, and anxious to change the subject, asked how much it cost. 'Oh, you can have it as a gift,' she said. 'I insist.'

'Well, that's very kind of you. Tomorrow then,' said Cohen.

'Yes, and don't worry about bringing a bottle, we have plenty to drink.' That was music to his ears, for he loathed sober gatherings and was always partial to a few drinks.

Cohen picked up the ceramic and said goodbye, headed out of the shop back to the convent, passing the school and the armed guard, who was looking at him suspiciously. He walked on past, preferring to avoid any further confrontation. The fact Cohen had made contact with Rubens's wife and would meet the man tomorrow gave him reason to relax a little.

At least he'd been given the chance to question Rubens and challenge him on whether he'd be designing the new temple, and if it was on the same site as the Dome of the Rock. Until that was confirmed, there was little more Cohen could do to fulfil his assignment. It meant that he had the day to himself. As he entered the convent grounds, he decided he would return to Jerusalem and spend the rest of the day sightseeing in the holy city, a blessing for tourists.

As he walked through the cloisters, Sister Ruth appeared: 'Are you staying for lunch?' she asked, in a rather hesitant voice.

'Not today thank you, sister. I've decided to take a pilgrimage into Jerusalem.'

'Such a blessing,' she remarked, giving a sign of the cross. 'No doubt you'll be going to the Western Wall to say a few prayers?'

'I will,' Cohen said. 'Where can I find a taxi?'

'A taxi?' she repeated, aghast. 'Pilgrims walk in the Holy Land, Mr Cohen, but I understand you're in a hurry. There is a regular bus service to Jerusalem though. You'd save a few shekels.'

'Thank you,' replied Cohen. 'I will.'

'What is that you have in your hand?' asked Sister Ruth, inquisitively.

'It's a ceramic. I got it from an art shop in the village. It's for you,' he said, offering the gift.

'How wonderful, I like the colours,' she said, admiringly. Just then another nun approached and was about to walk past when Sister Ruth beckoned her over.

'Just a moment, sister,' she said. 'I'd like you to meet Mr. Cohen from London,' she added. 'This is Sister Sharon, from Kent.' Cohen politely shook her hand and looked into her clear blue eyes. He was stunned by her beauty. Her eyes were like sapphires, radiating purity. She looked so young, virginal, like a child. She did not speak, but bowed graciously as he shook her hand, before quietly disappearing.

'You must forgive her, Mr. Cohen,' said Sister Ruth. 'She's shy and modest.'

'She's an angel,' remarked Cohen, mesmerised. 'Is she from Canterbury?'

'I see a prophet in our midst,' declared Sister Ruth. 'Enjoy your pilgrimage.'

Cohen said farewell, went to his room and sorted through his papers and notebook before heading out of the convent.

As he waited for the bus, he thought of Sister Sharon and why she'd left England to come here.

A bus journey took in the affluent parts of the city, reminding him of postcards sent from Israel by relatives. He was looking forward to his first pilgrimage to the holy city.

He just hoped there would no more shootings or war.

7

As the bus approached the outskirts of the city, an elderly woman reached across the aisle and offered him a piece of bread. He gratefully accepted the offering.

She gestured to him to eat it, lifting her frail hands to her mouth and giving him a toothless grin.

Cohen knew that almost Jewish mothers doted on their sons, and that sometimes this extended even to men who weren't actually their sons but of a similar age. On a crowded bus such mothering seemed a little embarrassing to him, though endearing.

When the bus arrived in the Old City at the Jaffa Gate, he helped the lady off the bus and thanked her. Cohen stood nervously at the entrance gate. Much to his relief there wasn't a soldier in sight, nor any hostile youths on the rampage, which was even better. He later realised the Jaffa Gate was not in the Muslim Quarter of the city, where most of the uprising occurred. He reached for the holy sign above the gate, the mezzuzah, containing the holy words of God, before entering the gate, kissing his hand, and heading for the Christian Quarter. He strolled through an open courtyard, passing the Anglican Church, Christ Church, and entered the Via Della Rosa, a narrow cobbled street bustling with bazaars and market traders on either side. It was along the Via Della Rosa that Christ carried his cross to his crucifixion on Good Friday. As he walked further, Arab merchants accosted him, eager to sell their goods. They invited him into their bazaars, offering him carpets, sandals and assortment of beads, souvenirs and trinkets from the East, but he wasn't interested. Exploring the Old City, he passed the Holy Sepulchre, the place of Christ's crucifixion, the holiest shrine in Christendom. It meant little to him at the time, but little did he know that one day he would return to the sepulchre a changed man. He left the Christian Quarter and entered the Jewish quarter, where he felt more at ease. The shops were avant-garde, classy, and an air of affluence permeated the mall. He stopped at an art gallery and asked directions to the Western Wall.

'Are you sure you want to go there today?' asked the gallery owner, a middle-aged Jewish lady, elegantly dressed.

'Is there a problem?' asked Cohen, apprehensively.

'Yesterday, Jews praying at the wall were stoned by Arabs from the other side. It may be safe now, but I'm warning you in case,' she said.

He thanked her for her concern and left the shop in the direction of the wall. Entering another cobbled street, he walked a few more blocks before turning into a courtyard. He crossed the courtyard and went down another narrow passage, which led him into a huge open concourse, and there, standing majestically before him, stood the last remains of Herod's Temple, the Western Wall.

Hundreds of Jews thronged the square, most of them making their way to the Western Wall to say their daily prayers, the men gathering to the left of the Wall, the women separated to the right. Although the majority of them were Israeli Jews, there were Jews from all over the world, Russian Jews, French, Ethiopian, Romanian, Italian, Americans and English Jews.

Cohen had never before witnessed such a gathering of Jews in prayer at one service. It deeply affected him. There was an atmosphere of holiness, which penetrated his very being. As he approached the wall, he felt tears well up. He knew he was standing on holy ground and felt compelled, as if by some inner force greater than himself, to join the prayer group and humble himself before God. Jews were rolling to and fro, placing prayer slips of paper into crevices between the granite stones and reciting prayers aloud, while woman wailed in suffering. The holiness cut Cohen to the heart. He fell to his knees and then, to his surprise, found himself weeping, not only for himself but for all the suffering and the horror of the Holocaust and the loss of his relatives in concentration camps. Was there no end, he wondered, to the suffering of the Jewish people?

Had God chosen the Jews to suffer as some kind of penance for the sins of the world?

Cohen felt confused and angry. He had no answers. All he knew was that he was here, at the holiest Jewish shrine, sharing their pain and suffering. During his moment of angst, Cohen suddenly felt a tap on his shoulder.

It was a Rabbi.

'You aren't an Orthodox Jew?' asked the Rabbi.

'How could you tell?' said Cohen, perplexed.

'Because if you were, you would cover your head with a skull cap,' he said.

The Rabbi led Cohen along the wall to an entrance where Jews were gathered in an alcove, placing paper skull caps on their heads, which rabbis were handing out to tourists. Cohen apologised and placed the skull cap on his head. He felt embarrassed at his lack of reverence.

'Sadly it's a common failing these days,' said the Rabbi, smiling. 'But all is well now. At least you're not being stoned.'

Cohen thanked him for the skull cap and returned to the wall. He wrote prayers on a scrap of paper and placed it between the stones. The prayers were for Joseph and Anne, his grandparents, gassed in the Auschwitz concentration camp.

8

The long, winding road that leads to Ein Karem left Cohen weary and exhausted. He wasn't used to praying, and the events of the day had drained him. When the bus finally arrived that evening, he was in dire need of a drink and headed straight to the bar, instead of going to the convent.

Settling himself at the bar, he took out a Hebrew phrase book and decided to have a chat with the beautiful black-haired waitress.

'Please, speak English,' she pouted, 'then I understand you,' she added, wiping the glasses.

He tried chatting her up but she didn't seem interested, and after a few hesitant replies from her he gave up, ordered a beer and turned his attention to a group of men sitting at a nearby table. They were engrossed in a game which didn't need any language – chess. Two of them crouched over a board, gazing intensely at the pieces, while others gathered round the table, gesticulating to indicate the best possible moves. Cohen was no novice. He'd spent some of his teenage years studying chess books, though his study of the game never dampened his fascination with girls. He now saw a chance to impress the locals with his expertise, but he knew that Jews were usually highly knowledgeable about chess. He knew that some of the greatest players in the history of chess were Jews – Steinitz, Spassky, Kasparov and of course the immortal Bobby Fischer, to name just a few.

Suddenly, the game finished amid uproar and howls of laughter.

'Checkmate!' roared the winner. It was the owner of the pub Cohen had spoken to a previous day, who'd helped him track down the architect.

'Hey, English fellow!' he shouted, brushing aside others who wanted to play. 'Come and sit down. We know you Englishmen play this game – let's see if you're any good.'

Cohen took up the challenge. 'I haven't played for a while,' he said.

'Ha, they all say that,' mocked the owner. 'You English no fool me. Say, you find the lady in the art shop, the architect's wife?'

'I did, thanks to you,' Cohen said, setting up his chess pieces.

The manager extended a hearty handshake. 'May the best man win. I'm Stefan by the way, I'm from Romania, where we eat Englishmen for breakfast at chess,' he roared with laughter. 'Let's see if you can fight.' Stefan picked up a pawn had slammed it down in the middle of the board. Cohen was about to make his reply when the pretty barmaid appeared and asked if he wanted a drink.

'It's on the house,' said Stefan, banging the table impatiently. 'You make move, I no sit here all night.'

It was a tactic Cohen had encountered before - hurry your opponent into a mistake! Cohen took his time and thought about his next move when the barmaid appeared with his drink, and instead of her usual pout gave him the flirtatious smile. He watched her walk back to the bar, her hips swaying seductively in her tight skirt.

'You want to play chess, or play with pussy,' snapped Stefan, impatiently. 'It's your move.'

Cohen looked back at the chessboard, threw caution to the wind, and launched a brutal attack. Within a few moves he had Stefan checkmated with his queen and knight. Stefan sat in disbelief.

Admitting defeat, he looked at Cohen: 'You got lucky, Englishman, but next time I get you,' he said, and getting up, went to the bar.

Confidence restored, Cohen set about demolishing the other opponents with consummate ease. The alcohol flowed and the bar erupted with the shouts of English champion. Such was his acclaimed reputation that he forgot all about time. It was two in the morning when he finally got back to the convent, the worse for wear. He fumbled for his key and stumbled along the cloister, crept past the sleeping nuns, and back to his room at the far end of the convent. He collapsed onto his bed and the last thing he remembered before passing out was the crucifix hanging over him, the tortured figure of Christ gazing down at him from the wall.

Cohen awoke hung over the following morning to the sound of footsteps. He'd forgotten to lock the door in his drunken haze, allowing the nun to quietly enter. He looked up from under the sheets through half-closed eyes. It was Sister Sharon.

She stood smiling with a tray in her hands, like some modern Florence Nightingale. 'Reverend Mother was concerned you'd not been eating since you arrived,' said Sister Sharon, 'so she asked me to bring you breakfast.'

Cohen groaned and rolled over in his bed. 'Oh God, what time is it? Room service in a convent?' he said, flabbergasted. 'But you didn't have to go to all this trouble. I hardly eat breakfast.'

'But you must,' admonished Sister Sharon, in a motherly tone, 'otherwise you'll get ill and waste away.'

'I thought nuns fasted?'

'We do, but only on fast days,' she said, smiling. She placed her tray on the table and turned to leave.

'Just a minute,' said Cohen. 'Are you from Canterbury?'

'Yes, I left there a year ago.'

'What made you come here, to Israel?'

'I was called,' said Sister Sharon, with conviction in her voice. 'God called me to the Holy Land. It's a great blessing to follow our Lord in his footsteps, in the very place where he once walked the earth.'

'In Ein Karem?' asked Cohen, perplexed.

'Oh yes, he was here once, and still is,' she smiled. 'You must excuse me, it's time for prayer.'

'Did you consider getting married?' he asked, before she left. 'You're a beautiful woman. Men would die for you.'

'But I am married,' she answered, proudly.

'You're married!' he exclaimed. 'So what are you doing in a convent?'

'I'm married to Jesus,' she smiled. Then bowing reverently, she silently left.

Cohen was dumbfounded. He went to the window and watched her walk gracefully along the cloisters, her white habit flowing in the breeze like an angel.

Cohen turned and looked up at the crucifix again. Married to Jesus, is that she said? What did she mean, 'He's still here'? Do dead men walk? He couldn't figure out what these nuns were all about. They were from another planet, beyond his imagination. Yet here they were, feeding and accommodating him as if he was a brother. He got out of bed and glanced at the breakfast tray. The sight of food made him feel sick. But to please the sister, he ate some toast and finished off a pot of tea.

Cohen got dressed and sat at the table with his notebook, scribbling down questions he planned to ask the architect later. One question which intrigued him was how to rebuild Solomon's Temple if they didn't have the original plans, for they'd been destroyed several hundred years ago.

In the Bible, there was some evidence of the size of the temple, restored by Herod the Great, the same temple Christ himself preached in. It was colossal, more than three times the size of Solomon's original temple.

Was it possible that Rubens had delved into ancient scripture and come up with some approximate measurements taken from the Torah? After writing down several more questions, he decided to spend the rest of the day exploring Ein Karem and visiting some of the Christine shrines which Sister Ruth had suggested he visit.

Cohen's reaction to Sister Ruth and the nuns was apprehensive, to say the least, for they had they fallen under some sort of spell, a spiritual hypnosis.

They hardly ever spoke unless spoken to, and were so self-effacing one could hardly be blamed for thinking they were devoid of all personality and any sense of self worth. But deep down he knew they had something he'd been trying to attain all his life, a sense of inner peace, stillness and calm, so alien to the modern world. Perhaps they were not of this world, but a spiritual mission to bring peace to humanity, the message of Christ.

But why did Jesus allow people to kill him, to go the cross like a lamb to slaughter, when he was anointed by God? Surely he would have been given the power from above to save his life?

It was anathema to Cohen, being Jewish, that a Jew as powerful as Christ would lay down his life when the history of the Israelites was full of martyrs who had fought to their death rather than surrender. Even at Masada they preferred death by their own sword rather than to surrender to the Romans.

Jews believe in an eye for an eye and a tooth for a tooth so that their children could live in freedom, not as slaves in Egypt or in bondage under the Babylonians, or as captives under the Romans, or worse still, gassed in Nazi death camps. He felt confused and betrayed by Christ, who in the name of Judaism had allowed himself to be slaughtered like a lamb, without a protest, when he himself said he could bring down 'legions of angels' to save him. Perhaps the nuns were like him, and in a time of crisis and danger they neither would lift a finger to defend themselves. Like Jesus, they would turn the other cheek. Maybe they were mad after all, thought Cohen. For what woman, threatened with death, would not defend her life, and indeed her womb, the source of all life and creation, unless they were truly mad. The only time a woman would do that, to lay her life down, was to defend her children. These nuns had even sacrificed motherhood, God's precious gift of bearing children. He tried to understand their way of life, that renouncing was their way of embracing the whole world, and becoming mothers to all people, especially the orphans.

Cohen felt the need to get out of the convent and packed his bag, picked up his notebook and left through a side gate. He breathed the fresh air and felt the warmth of the sun and relief at being out in the open air. The children were playing as he passed the refuge bins and the cats, and headed for the fountain in the village. It turned out to be a well, called Mary's Well, a Christian shrine for thousands of pilgrims who visit the village every year to pay homage to Mary, the mother of Jesus. She drank from the well on her way to meet cousin Elizabeth. Both women were pregnant when they met and the baby Elizabeth was carrying was St. John the Baptist. Elizabeth greeted Mary with the salutation: 'Blessed art thou among women and blessed is the fruit of thy womb.'

But Cohen wasn't aware of how sacred the well was to Christians, nor did he much care, for he spotted a beautiful girl sitting by the well, a sketch book in her lap, drawing the fountain. 'That's very good,' Cohen complimented her. 'Are you an artist?'

She looked up from her sketch, her blonde hair made almost white by the sun. 'I'm an art student,' she said, smiling. Cohen was taken aback by this vivacious girl, with blue eyes and low-cut top. She told him her name was Fay, that she was twenty-one and a Christian from Copenhagen, with a broad-minded outlook on life, so he was to find out. He leaned over to get a closer look at her drawing, his concentration not helped by the fact she wasn't wearing a bra. He instantly turned away in embarrassment, for she'd caught him in an act of voyeurism, but she carried on sketching as if nothing had happened, as though it was the most natural thing for men to stare at her boobs.

Cohen tried to regain his composure, for it wasn't every day he was confronted by such a blonde girl with an ample figure. And besides, he'd just come from a convent, where nuns consider it a sin to expose their ankles.

Cohen asked if she was on holiday in Israel, changing the subject and forgetting his lustful thoughts.

Fay told him that she was visiting Israel on her own and that she didn't have a boyfriend. 'I want to be free to travel and not be tied down by a man,' she said, looking up from her drawing. Cohen nodded, agreeing with her need for freedom. He appreciated her youthful spontaneity and honesty, and sensing a rapport, nonchalantly placed an arm around her shoulder as he knelt beside her. He focused on her drawing. She attracted him, but while he wasn't a virgin, he was always shy with women. His shyness had stemmed from when he was twelve years old on the camping holiday and he saw the naked woman in the tent. Cohen figured Fay was surely about the same age as the naked woman he had come upon in the tent, he remembered her with renewed insight that day more than twenty years ago.

Somehow Fay seemed to sense he found her fascinating. She smiled at him, put down her pencil, stretched her lovely long arms for a few moments, then said; 'I can take a break from drawing for a moment. Shall we go for a walk?'

He smiled. 'Yes, I'd like that.'

Fay got up and adjusted her top, then led him up a steep narrow hill, sheltered by over hanging trees. He nervously followed her, staring at her long slender legs.

She wore a white mini skirt which accentuated her beautiful thighs. He studied her round hips, moving provocatively from to side. At the top of the hill she led him into a field behind a row of hedges, and without the slightest embarrassment began to remove her top. 'You like my figure,' she said coquettishly.

'They're magnificent,' he said, admiring her breasts.

Then, without the slightest bit of self-consciousness, she promptly removed her skirt and her lace panties. Coaxing him to join her, she laid down casually in the tall grass, stretching her long legs.

Cohen was shocked to see Fay's naked body writhing in the grass, the sun beaming across her perfect breasts. His experience of seeing the naked woman in the tent came flashing back. But this time he could touch her without being chastised. Cohen knelt down beside her, his hands shaking in anticipation, and reached out to fondle her breasts. This time there would be no rejection.

But suddenly he went limp, his erection lost in the heat of the moment, and collapsed onto her breasts, gasping for air. He lay prone in this suffocating position, for had no experience of being aroused, let alone foreplay, and waited for her to take the initiative. She tenderly stroked his forehead, as though nursing a child, then turning on her side offered him a breast. He grasped it with parched lips, like a man dying of thirst, and he melted in her arms. He was about to kiss the other breast when she suddenly got up.

'Do you like drawing?' Fay asked, abruptly.

'Ye-e-s,' he stammered, falling backwards and banging his head on a rock.

'Well then, you can draw me,' she said, proudly.

'What, now?' he gasped, in confusion.

'What's the matter, don't you like my figure?' she pouted.

'On the contrary, it's just we could make...'

'I'm not shy, if that's what you mean. I did some art modelling at college. So, sketch me then,' she insisted. 'What pose would you like?' she asked, placing her arms over her head, sticking out her tits.

Cohen picked up her sketchbook, stood a few paces back, and studied her. 'I would prefer a reclining pose,' he said, pointing to the grass. Although his arousal was still a cause of embarrassment, he managed to regain his composure. He held his sketchbook where the source of discomfort showed.

'My, you sound professional,' she said. 'You're an artist.' Fay spread her aching body in the grass, arched her back to accentuate her breasts and stretched out her slender legs. 'The reclining pose, it's more relaxing,' she said, smiling.

Cohen began sketching in earnest, for he was no amateur. At the Slade he'd spent much of his time studying the Impressionism. Within a few minutes he'd completed his sketch, a reclining nude drawn with masterful skill and simplicity of style. 'Can I see?' she insisted, the moment he'd finished.

He sat down next to her and showed her the drawing.

'Wow, that's fantastic,' she beamed. 'You really are an artist. Please let me have it,' she pleaded. 'I'll do anything you want.'

'Anything?' he asked, peering over his glasses.

'Anything, girl guides' honour,' she insisted, raising her fingers.

Cohen looked into her clear blue eyes, full of youthful energy and spirit.

She was serious and he believed her. He looked at her nubile body again as she lay offering herself like a wanton goddess.

Cohen had studied the French masters and their passion for the naked model, especially Renoir, portraying nudes in natural surroundings. But just then, like in Nabokov's Lolita, she teased him by turning on her side, abruptly abandoning her provocative pose and ignored him. She picked up the sketch and stared narcissistic at the drawing, admiring the reflection, as women do, of herself in the mirror.

'What are you doing?' asked Cohen. In his frustration he took the sketch out of her hand, and grabbing her arms, pinned her to the ground. She fell limp in his clutches, even if she wasn't in the mood, she didn't have the strength to resist him. She let go, abandoning herself to his lust like a wild cat on heat. She raised her knees and arching her torso, clawed and scratched at his back, aching for to him to take her.

Cohen lay on top of her poised but the effect of her screaming had the opposite effect on him. Her screaming frightened the life out of him. 'What's the matter?' she asked, frustrated.

'You screamed – did I hurt you?' asked Cohen, concerned.

'Don't be silly,' she groaned, 'I was just getting in the mood. Come here. I promise not to scream, if that's what you want.'

Cohen was still shaking so much so he began to hallucinate. Her sensuous body began to change and distort before his very eyes. She was no longer young but old, her blonde hair turned grey, her breasts began to sag and teeth were falling out. Her blue eyes grew dim, unfocused, a deformed old woman about to die. His hallucination was so real it had the effect of speeding up time, projecting him into a future where he saw that bonding with a woman was futile. Beguiled by beauty, men kill each other for a woman, not finding the right path to life, free of all possessions and material attachments, he thought. He could break free of the chains of the opposite sex. Such grief he could live without, for it was the women who perpetuated life and all its accompanying suffering.

'Come here,' she repeated, spreading her legs.

Cohen was looking up to heaven, trying to clear his head, but the sky kept moving around. Nothing had changed. She was still a deformed, decaying woman ready for the grave. He knew that the pursuit of beauty could only end in disillusion. For unlike Keats, who said 'a thing of beauty is a joy forever', he knew that it didn't last long, for beauty in the end turns to dust. Cohen was holding his head in despair.

'Are you all right?' she asked, leaning over him.

'I'm a bit dizzy,' he said spluttering. As he lay on his back staring up at the sky, fear gripped his soul. He felt he was dying, and indeed he was convinced of it, for his body began to slowly melt into the earth. He was the experiencing the death of his body and had no power to prevent it. But suddenly the fear that seized him began to fade and then disappear. And then the most amazing thing happened - he literally melted into the earth, his soul rising up and hovering above his body. All fear had gone, and in its place was an incredible feeling of bliss, an all encompassing love, like he was in heaven.

9

Cohen headed back toward the safety of the convent, a place of refuge, solitude and quiet.

He had encountered the fairer sex at her most sexually ferocious, a tigress playing with her prey. As he staggered down the hill on his way back to the convent, he passed the Well and recalls of how beautiful Fay was and how he'd abandoned her. He hesitated and looked back up the hill again if he could see any sign of her, but she didn't appear. He turned, and instead of going back to the convent headed for the bar, desperate for another stiff drink. He ordered a double vodka and sat down in a corner table, still shaking from the experience. He felt calmer but within a few minutes he began to hear voices talking about him, accusing him of sexual debauchery and depravity.

In a fit of paranoia he dashed out of the bar and fled to the safety of the convent. He had no idea what time it was, for to him time was suspended. The children no longer played in the schoolyard, even the cats had disappeared. The sun hovered in the sky; the clouds were motionless, the day stood still.

It was timeless.

Cohen felt not only disorientated but decidedly ill. He staggered to the convent and lay on his bed exhausted, full of fear. What was happening to him? The events of the day were like a dream, an experience so surreal he began to think that it was real. Could he have been so beguiled by Fay, so fearful of sex that the whole traumatic experience was nothing more than a hallucination? That the girl never actually went into the woods with him, that it was just a figment of his imagination, a subconscious desire to have his wicked way with her at the Well, that it was nothing more than a harmless sexual fantasy?

Surely if the girl had gone into the woods, he'd at least gone with her. But Cohen couldn't remember, and the more he tried the more it faded from his memory, like a phantom in the night. He began to question his sanity, and fear took hold of him again. What was real was the traumatic experience of dying, his soul departed from his body. The bliss and joy was all from heaven, but heaven didn't last long. No sooner had he encountered God than fear brought him crashing down to reality.

Cohen made arrangements to attend the dinner that evening with the architect, but he was in no mental or physical state to go. He had to cancel the engagement, but how? He may not get another chance to question the architect. A knock on the door startled him.

'Are you all right?' asked Sister Ruth, popping her head round the door. 'I thought I heard you groaning. Are you in pain?'

'I was praying,' said Cohen, 'I'm OK.'

'That's the spirit,' she smiled. 'God not only hears our prayers, but answers them. Why not come to chapel this evening?'

'Thank you sister,' said Cohen, 'but I have an engagement.'

'Pity,' said Sister Ruth. 'More work and no prayers. Are you sure you're alright? You look a bit pale.'

'I'm alright,' he said, 'though I had a bit of a shock this afternoon.'

'Why,' she asked, 'what happened.'

'I had an encounter with God,' he exclaimed.

'Praise the Lord,' said Sister Ruth. 'Lots of pilgrims have experiences of God when they come to the Holy Land. Consider it a blessing and a revelation, for God is merciful to those who seek him,' she smiled.

'But I wasn't seeking,' protested Cohen.

'He found you all the same,' she said, assuredly.

'What about you, sister? Have you met him?' Cohen asked, abruptly.

'I met him every day,' she smiled, 'in the Eucharist.'

'Eucharist?' queried Cohen.

'The Holy Communion we share each day in the chapel, the bread and wine. You should come sometime to the chapel. I have to go now.'

Cohen watched her silently close the door. He looked again the crucifix on the wall, tears rolled down his face. He fell to his knees and stared at the solitary figure of Christ on the cross, his arms outstretched as though he was welcoming him. He felt an overwhelming sense of peace flood his soul. The burden of this life seemed to float away, as though he no longer had a care in the world. Could this be what the nuns had experienced? Did the Spirit of Christ enter his soul?

Cohen got up and washed his face in the sink, put on a clean shirt and combed his hair. At least he could make himself presentable for the architect and was mentally ready to go to the dinner party now. The hour was approaching and Cohen, to fortify his courage, took time out for a drink before heading to the architect's home. But as he headed for the bar, he suffered another panic attack. He was afraid Fay might be in the bar. How could he explain his erratic behaviour, and his sexual misgivings? He thought of avoiding the bar and heading straight for the dinner party, but the thought of arriving sober brought on another panic attack. He plucked up the courage and ordered a double vodka. Looking around, he saw no sign of Fay. Knocking back his vodka, he asked the barmaid if she'd seen a blonde with big breasts that evening. 'I no see her,' she said, in broken English. 'I don't look at women breasts.'

Cohen felt confused. Surely an art student would be looking for a drink in a small village, with it being so hot in Israel and the temperature soaring to forty degrees. He ordered another double vodka before facing the architect. He looked at his notes and the questions he would have to ask. Staggering out of the bar, he felt it was time enough to confront the architect about the temple. After taking the wrong turn he arrived at the architect's house an hour later, the worse for wear. Leaning on the doorbell, he was met by the architect's wife, dressed elegantly in a party dress. Jane Rubens greeted him with a frown.

'You've finally made it,' she said. 'I'm afraid you've missed out on the cocktails. We're just about to sit down for dinner.'

Cohen straightened his tie and adjusted his hair as he was led through the hallway into the lounge where several guests were finishing their cocktails. They looked disapprovingly in his direction.

Jane introduced Cohen in a more cordial tone. 'He's here in Israel to complete his PhD in architecture.'

Cohen stood in silence while guests showed their approval, admiring his ambition. Isaiah Rubens, a stout middle-aged man with balding hair, stepped forward and shook his hand, but Cohen was reeling from the shock of his introduction, for he had no recollection of ever having said he was studying architecture, let alone a PhD.

'Art,' Cohen stuttered, 'it's actually art.'

'But I thought you said architecture?' said Jane.

'No, it's a misunderstanding. I'm an artist,' said Cohen, 'or at least I try to be one.'

'Either way you're most welcome,' said Rubens, 'for we have something in common, wouldn't you agree?'

'Yes indeed,' replied Cohen. Despite his one too many vodka's he was able to anticipate what Isaac Rubens was hinting at, which endeared him to the architect for the rest of the evening.

'We are both designers,' Cohen blurted out.

'Exactly,' exclaimed Rubens, 'and for that you deserve a cocktail,' he added, pouring a drink.

One of the guests, a Jewish lady purporting to be an expert at art, introduced herself. 'You're an artist, for heaven's sake,' said Sarah. 'I love artists; they can tell us so much, see into the unknown and open our eyes to the wonders of the world.' Sarah helped Cohen feel at ease, although he still felt under pressure to confront the architect about the temple. The guests were assigned their seats around the dinner table. Jane put Cohen next to Rubens, with Sarah alongside.

'Actually, your wife is correct, in one sense,' said Cohen, turning to the architect. 'I have been studying architecture as a subject for my paintings. I'm particularly interested in painting historical buildings, especially ancient monuments: synagogues, temples, that sort of thing.'

'Well, you've come to the right place,' said Rubens. 'Israel has more sacred buildings than any other country.'

'Is that so?' remarked Cohen, 'Are there any sacred buildings being constructed in Jerusalem at the moment?'

Rubens gave a wry smile. 'I do have something in the pipeline, but you won't be able to paint it, at least for a couple of years.'

'Why is that?' Cohen asked, inquisitively.

'Because we've only just been given planning permission and we still have to raise the finances. I'll show you the drawings after dinner.'

Cohen raised his cocktail, not believing his luck. Surely the drawings must be the plans for the temple. And if that was the case, it would confirm his tip-off and give him the exclusive scoop of the story. He was about to question Rubens when Sarah interrupted. 'Do tell us more about your art, Michael,' she insisted. 'You don't mind me calling you Michael? It's such a wonderful ancient Hebrew name. I'm not implying you're ancient my dear,' she chuckled, 'but tell me, what artist has influenced the most?'

Sarah's interruption came at the critical moment in his conversation with Rubens, which annoyed him. But instead he politely turned to her and said nobody had influenced him. 'But there were several masters,' Cohen said, in earnest.

'Such as?' said Sarah, pressing him.

'Well, let's see now,' said Cohen, pouring himself a brandy, 'I was first drawn to the Renaissance masters, such as Raphael, Rubens and Caravaggio, and of course Leonardo de Vinci.'

'But you left out Michelangelo,' said Sarah, surprised. 'Didn't you like his work?'

Cohen paused a moment, raising his brandy. 'Yes, of course, but he had difficulty painting the female form.'

'Then you don't just paint buildings,' she said, a twinkle in her eye.

'Well, at Art College we had to paint life studies,' Cohen remarked. He deliberately avoiding the term nude for upsetting the other guests, for although Jews were highly gifted in the arts, not all approved of nudity, especially those of religious disposition. 'You've painted nudes then?' asked Sarah, matter-of-factly. 'What's wrong with Michelangelo's nudes?'

The brandy now having an effect on Cohen, he made a major effort not to slur his words, as he explained that Michelangelo had difficulty painting female breasts.

'In what way?' Sarah persisted.

'He painted them all out of proportion, he stuck them on. You can't sit in the Sistine Chapel without noticing,' he said, slurring his words.

Rubens burst out laughing. 'That's one problem architects don't have to deal with, more the pity.'

'Do go on, who else inspired you,' repeated Sarah.

'Well, the Dutch masters: Rembrandt, Van Dyke, Vermeer and Van Gogh.'

'I adore Van Gogh,' said Sarah, beaming.

'But of all the artists the ones who influenced me the most were the Impressionists, such as Cezanne, Monet, Renoir, Sisley, and Pissarro,' said Cohen proudly.

'I love Renoir,' said Sarah. 'Now there's an artist who could paint nudes.'

Cohen poured himself another brandy, and taking courage, explained that any artist worth his salt couldn't ignore the modern movement. 'Matisse had a profound influence on me, as did Picasso and Modigliani, but then came the abstract painters, Pollock, Kline and Rothko, all from New York, and, may I say, all Jewish.'

'My, you do know your art,' smiled Jane, relieved that Cohen had redeemed himself. He no longer appeared dishevelled but had begun to impress the guests, among them Sarah.

'There you see, Isaiah,' exclaimed Sarah, 'I told you Jews were just as good as artists as they were in architecture.'

Cohen was about to ask Rubens about the temple when he suddenly felt Sarah's hand stroke his thigh under the table. He almost choked on his kosher meal.

'I'd love you to paint me,' Sarah gushed.

'What, in the nude?' chuckled Rubens.

'Why not?' Sarah retorted. 'There's nothing wrong with my figure, is there Michael?' she asked, still stroking his thigh.

'Your figure is fine,' remarked Cohen, coughing in his brandy.

'Now that's enough nudity for now,' said Jane, admonishing her friend.

Sarah removed her hand from Cohen's thigh, but not before giving him an intimate squeeze.

'A woman of your beauty, I couldn't possibly do you any justice,' said Cohen, blushing. 'There's a limit to every artist's skill.'

'Indeed there is,' agreed Rubens, finishing his dinner. 'Enough talk about posing in the nude. Come with me, Mr. Cohen. I want to show you some of my work.' He asked his wife to fetch some more brandy to bring to the study.

'Perhaps Mr. Cohen has had enough to drink?' said Jane, discretely.

'Nonsense, he is our guest, all the way from England. Let Michelangelo here drink as much as he likes.' Rubens led Cohen into his study, a large spacious room with an immense drawing board taking up most of the room. He went over to the filing cabinet and pulled out a large scroll neatly tied in the middle with a red ribbon. He untied the scroll and carefully rolled it out onto the drawing board.

'There now, can you tell me what it is?' asked Rubens proudly.

The scroll spread the entire length of the board and on it was a huge drawing executed with draughtsman-like skill in minute detail. Cohen couldn't believe what he saw – it was a detailed drawing of the new Temple!

'What you're looking at is five years of research and planning,' said Rubens. 'Solomon's Temple was recreated stone by stone from the original measurements.'

'But how is that possible,' queried Cohen. 'Surely the original plans went missing all those centuries ago?'

Rubens was about to explain the original measurements from the Torah, when Sarah came in with her cleavage showing, brandishing a tray of brandy and cigars. 'Gentleman, here is your brandy,' she announced, bending over to reveal her breasts as she poured them a drink. 'Is there anything else you wanted?' she asked, smiling at Cohen.

'That'll do fine,' said Rubens. He offered Cohen a cigar and returned to his drawing. 'There's more to come,' he said enthusiastically. 'Wait till you see this. Rubens went over to the cabinet, reached for the top shelf and held in his hands a model of the new Temple.

'Good heavens,' cried Cohen, 'it's amazing. It looks like the original Temple that Solomon built, not Herod's Temple. I thought you would have worked from Herod's measurements, with them being more recent?

'God no.' exclaimed Rubens. 'Herod's Temple was more than four times the size of Solomon's Temple. It would have been impossible to build it on the site we're proposing.'

'And what site is that?' asked Cohen, holding his breath.

'Why, it has to be built on its original site, King Solomon's Temple.'

'You mean on Temple Mount?' asked Cohen, incredulously.

'Of course, where else?'

'But the mosque is there.'

'Yes, but we're going to build it alongside the mosque,' declared Rubens.

'Alongside the mosque?' said Cohen, astounded. 'But that's in the Muslim Quarter of the Old City. Surely they'd never allow that.'

'We've already acquired planning permission. Jerusalem belongs to the Jews, not the Arabs.'

Rubens confirmed Cohen's worst fear. He knew that the Muslims, to protect the sacred mosque and safeguard their sovereignty, would fight to the death. To build a Jewish temple alongside the mosque would be tantamount to Third World War.

'We're already reclaiming parts of the Old City,' said Rubens, proudly.

'You mean that taking over properties and moving the Arabs out?' asked Cohen.

'What choice do we have,' said Rubens. 'Solomon built his Temple on Temple Mount thousands of years before Islam came, and until the Temple is restored on the same site, the Jewish Messiah will not appear. That is established prophecy. You should know that, being a Jew.'

Cohen poured himself another brandy and sank down into his chair to take in what he'd heard. What more confirmation did he need? Before him were the plans to rebuild the new Temple. Not only that, Rubens had confirmed planning permission had been already given. All the other sources were true as well, those women who'd been sewing robes for the Temple priests.

'You looked concerned, Mr. Cohen,' said Rubens. 'I thought you, of all people, as someone who appreciates architecture, would be delighted for Israel to restore its most sacred of all monuments, King Solomon's Temple, and bring back Solomon's glory.'

'Then it's true, the right-wing Israeli government is requisitioning Arab properties in the Old City?' Cohen said.

Rubens stubbed out his cigar, somewhat irritated by the question. 'It is our land, and has been the time of Abraham. We can do with it what we want.'

'What about the Palestinians?' Cohen asked. 'Shall we drive out of the country entirely?'

'Are you a Palestinian sympathiser?' retorted Rubens, contemptuously.

'No, I am a Jew, but I believe in justice,' Cohen said.

'Justice.' exclaimed Rubens. 'When they blow up buses and kill our children. Where is the justice in that? Didn't you know that terrorists want to throw all pregnant Jewish women into the sea?'

'I've heard,' said Cohen, who could see Rubens was getting hot under the collar and losing his patience. He tactfully changed the subject.

'Is that the Western Wall?' he asked, pointing to the model of the temple.

'I'm beginning to doubt you are a Jew at all,' said Rubens angrily. 'When did you last attend a synagogue? Don't you know we refer to it as the Wailing Wall, for obvious reasons?'

'Yes, forgive me,' he apologised, 'but that is the wall built by Herod when he restored the temple. Are you going to incorporate into the new Temple?'

'Now you're talking sense,' said Rubens, calmer. 'Yes, of course, we must keep the Wailing Wall. It is the most sacred shrine in the Jewish faith, and it won't be a problem incorporating into the building.'

'But it's quite a distance from the original site where the Dome of the Rock stands, don't you agree?' he asked.

'It's not so far. We will extend the area around the mosque,' said Rubens dismissively.

Cohen thought about the mosque and the new Temple practically alongside each other, and looked again at the model. 'It's very impressive. It's a magnificent structure,' he said, trying to placate Rubens. 'It will not only be a sacred temple, but fulfil the Judaic prophecy.'

He then paused and turning to Rubens and asked pointedly: 'And when is the Temple going to be rebuilt?'

Rubens paused a moment, and waving his hands, said: 'We don't know yet. We will have to raise the money, that shouldn't be a problem. If the government can't raise all the finances, I'm certain that Israelis can, not to mention private investors. But it shouldn't take more than two years to complete, that's taking into account extending the Wailing Wall around the mosque and laying foundations.'

Cohen looked closer at the model. 'Would it be possible to have a photo of the model?' he asked.

'I'm afraid not. These plans have only approved just recently. There'll be an official announcement in due course, when we've raised the finances. I wouldn't want the plans getting into wrong hands, a Palestinian sympathiser or the press, ha, ha,' he joked. 'Let us take our drinks to the lounge.'

Cohen followed Rubens back into the lounge, where Sarah sat on the sofa, the hem of her skirt rising provocatively above her knees as he she crossed her legs, revealing her long thighs. She beckoned him to come and sit down next to her, patting the sofa beside her. 'What have been up to all this time?' she asked. 'You haven't answered my question.'

'I'm sorry, have been busy with business,' said Cohen.

'So, will you paint me in the nude?' she asked, pouting.

Cohen, embarrassed by other guests, said: 'But I couldn't possibly do you justice.'

Sarah crossed her legs and looked at Cohen. 'Then you agree, I do have a nice figure,' she said, smiling.

'Very feminine,' he remarked.

'Then paint me,' Sarah said, teasing.

Cohen paused to reflect on his earlier attempt to sketch the Danish girl who had undressed without a care in the world and even offered herself to him. Had Sarah offered herself too? He looked at Sarah and, like with Fay, was tempted to touch her slender thighs. He was more so when she revealed her suspenders. He looked away, feeling uncomfortable with the guests milling around.

'Where are you staying?' asked Sarah, inquisitive.

'In the village,' he replied, not wishing to give up the true whereabouts of his accommodation, for the guests would not accept a Jew staying at the convent.

'Whereabouts?' Sarah said, pressing him. 'I trust you're not staying at that ghastly hostel.'

Cohen sensed her Jewish snobbery, ignored the question and changed the subject.

'How about me drawing you,' Cohen asked.

'I'd love that,' she gushed. 'Say, what about tonight, after the party?'

'I have some work to finish tonight,' said Cohen, 'but we could arrange it during the week.'

'I'm always free, darling,' she sighed, uncrossing her legs and taking a card from her handbag. 'Call me anytime, and if you want to draw me in the style of Renoir, I'm willing to take my clothes off,' she laughed.

Cohen looked at the card. It said Interior Designer.

'That's me. Keeps my body and soul together and pays for my gynaecologist,' she chortled.

'I'll give you a call,' said Cohen. He said goodnight to Rubens, wishing him well with the new Temple.

Sarah accompanied him to the door. She led him down the garden path then stopped suddenly to Cohen's surprise, kissed him passionately on the mouth.

Cohen knew she wanted him but he was tired and his shyness had reared itself up again with his mind. Also, it was past midnight and he had to get back to the convent to get up early in the morning. He took the path to the convent, leaving Sarah, alone and upset. As he walked back to the convent, his mind was beginning to race. It was too late to catch the early morning editions of the newspapers. He had doubts about the devastating repercussions if his story were to be published. He had doubts over his profession, prying into people lives and putting them at risk. There was something dishonest about journalism, which disturbed him: the underhanded methods to gain information, corrupt payments and bribes and hypocrisy, the sensational slanting of news, all of which led him to believe that his father was right when he branded reporters as 'parasites'. What did they contribute except fear, destruction and death? The bigger the headline, the more sinful it became. What the media reported was just a reflection of the times, a perverse and wicked world in which we lived.

He was glad to get back to the convent, away from the world, and appreciate the stillness and solitude of its confining walls. Before going to bed, he looked up at the crucifix and prayed for God's help to face the next day with courage. He felt strength from deep within, a spiritual enlightenment he'd never experienced before.

God not only existed, he whispered before falling asleep, but he answered prayers and took pity on a sinner like him.

10

Cohen awoke with another hangover, staggered out of bed, and gazed forlornly in the mirror at his haggard face. His hands shook as he tried to do up his shirt. He combed his hair and decided to go for a walk to clear his head. The events of yesterday came back to haunt him as he walked through the street and approached the fountain. There was no sign of Fay, and he breathed a sigh of relief. It crossed his mind that she could be at the top of the hill, tempting him with her precocious charms. He thought of lying in the tall grass, to make amends, and prove his manhood. The urge passed him and he banished her from his mind. Cohen was about to take a drink from the fountain, for he was dehydrated from having had too much alcohol at the dinner party, when suddenly he heard a voice. The voice did not come from a person, but was all around him. He looked around but saw no one. Then the voice spoke again, louder and more clearly:

'Do not touch this water for it is holy and you are unclean. Go up the mountain and enter the church,' said the voice.

Cohen stood in stunned silence. Was he hallucinating, was he hearing voices? Surely not, for there is something real about the voice, it was a distinctive voice and the words cut him to the heart, piercing his very soul. He sat down beside the garden seat, confused and afraid, his heart pounding, frightened to move. But then, as if compelled by a greater force, he got up and obeyed the command. He walked up the hill and taking a path for the church, he saw a steep flight of stone steps. He climbed the steps and entered the church, a 12th century Gothic building, his heart racing, not knowing why he was there. He recalled a previous recent visit to a shrine. Inside, Cohen nervously walked around the church for any kind of sign telling him what the voice meant. He entered the sanctuary and, looking up, saw an immense fresco of Mary Mother of God, greeted by her cousin Elizabeth at the well.

It had a sign painted in gold which read: The Church of the Visitation.

He studied the fresco and saw that it was the Well in Ein Karem, the very Fountain he had desecrated with the Danish student.

Shaking with fear, he felt his soul has been convicted, like a condemned man on the gallows. He had fornicated at the holy shrine and must pay the price – he must be stoned to death, according to the Torah.

He fell to his knees and wept. Suddenly, the voice commanded: 'Stand up. Your sins are forgiven. Go forth and sin no more.'

Startled at what he'd heard, Cohen looked around the aisle and then, peering up, saw the giant cross with the tortured body of Christ gazing down at him. Tears of repentance rolled down Cohen's cheeks, banishing fear. A feeling of deep inner peace overwhelmed him, so profound that he was transported to another world. He stood transfixed, gazing up at the crucified Christ in awe and wonder. 'This man is the truly the Son of God,' confessed Cohen aloud. 'He died for my sins and the sins of the world. My heart is no longer heavy. I feel free, liberated,' he exclaimed joyfully. He raised his arms to heaven and began to praise the Lord out loud: 'Thank you God for being merciful to me, a sinner, setting me free of my chains of bondage.'

Bursting with joy, he ran from the church back down to the village. He ran past the bar, no longer tempted to indulge in his wayward past, and headed for the convent, anxious to convey his conversion to the nuns.

Cohen had no doubt in his mind that it was Christ himself who had spoken to him, both at the well and in the Church of the Visitation. He explained it to Sister Ruth on returning to the convent.

'Bless my soul,' exclaimed the sister. 'It sounds you've had a Road to Damascus experience, like St. Paul when he was converted. It's a very special blessing. Few people have such a dramatic conversion. For most of us it's a gradual conversion, though many a trial and suffering, I might add. But you may have greater trials ahead. The motto is to undergo and not go under,' she said, smiling.

'What happened to St. Paul?' he asked.

'Well, he was on his way to Damascus to persecute the Christians, who fled there,' sister said. 'A blinding light knocked him off his horse, and the Lord said to him: 'Why do you persecute me?' St. Paul said: 'Who are you?' The Lord answered: 'It is me, Jesus, who you persecute.' Paul, blinded for three days, was taken to Damascus and healed. His conversion was so profound that the Christians, who fled persecution in Jerusalem, accepted him as a disciple and he later became an Apostle to the Gentiles.'

Cohen was impressed by Paul's conversion. 'But what shall I do to follow Jesus?' he asked, urgently.

'Well, first you must be baptised by a priest,' said the sister. 'Then read the Bible and obey the Lord's commandments.'

'What commandments are these? Surely not the laws we follow as Jews?'

'Heavens no, our Lord Jesus knew what a burden those laws were for the people. He has set us free from the law. The Lord's commandments are this – to love God, and thy neighbour as yourself.'

'What about the commandments given to us by Moses?' Cohen asked.

'We must obey them for they came from God. You know yourself what trouble the Jews brought upon themselves when they disobeyed the commandments during the Exodus.'

Sister Ruth opened a drawer and took out a Bible. 'Have this,' she said, passing it to Cohen. 'Be sure you read it every day. It will protect you and strengthen your faith. You can be sure the devil likes nothing better than to attack new Christians and remove all hope and faith. He is like a devouring wolf, but the Lord will protect you if you remain faithful to Christ.'

'And where do I find a priest?' Cohen asked, impatiently.

'At the monastery at the top of the village, not far from here,' said the sister. 'Ask for Friar Claudio, they're Franciscans.'

'Franciscan?' he queried.

'It's an order of friars named after St. Francis. Haven't you heard of him? He was considered to be the greatest of all the saints. St. Francis had a miraculous conversion and saw Christ bleeding from the cross. He literally followed Jesus, gave everything to the poor and became a beggar.'

'A beggar?' exclaimed Cohen.

'Yes,' said Sister Ruth, 'but don't forget, Christ was homeless, an itinerate preacher. Jesus said: 'Foxes have holes and birds have nests, but the Son of God has no place to lay his head.' It's all in the New Testament. You can start by the reading of the Gospel of John.'

Sister Ruth paused for a moment as she walked to the door. 'The finger of God reached down and touched you, Michael. I must go now. Make sure you say your prayers.'

'What's the name of the monastery?' Cohen asked.

'It's the Monastery of St. John the Baptist. St. John was born in Ein Karem, in a house where the monastery stands. May God bless you,' Sister Ruth smiled and, making the sign of the Cross, departed.

Cohen sat down and pondered everything the sister had told him. It struck him that Ein Karem was more Christian than Jewish. That was evident from the number of coaches arriving that summer with hoards of pilgrims visiting the shrines. It began to dawn on him just how holy the village was, with the convent and the monastery, and how in his spiritual ignorance he'd trodden underfoot all that was sacred and holy through his irreverent behaviour.

He picked up his Bible and began to read the Gospel of John 3:16, which had a profound effect on him: 'For God so loved the world He gave his only begotten Son, that whosoever believes in him would not die but have eternal life.'

He read further the passage of Christ's commitment: 'Sell all you have and give to the poor, then take up your cross and follow me.'

Cohen closed the Bible and fell to his knees before the crucifix.

He prayed to Christ to become his disciple, to be given grace to follow him and renounce the world. He would give up journalism and forget his assignment and the rebuilding of the temple. He would forget the world and all its distractions and temptations.

All that mattered now was Christ and eternal life and becoming his disciple. Cohen would no longer serve the world, but God. For the next three days he remained in his room praying and fasting, night and day. He kept up a strict vigil in preparation for his forthcoming baptism. He wanted to purge himself of worldliness and all that was self-seeking, to repent of his sins and prepare for his calling, his discipleship, for whatever the Lord asked him to do. His life was no longer his own, he belonged to God, and had been bought at a price ransomed with the blood of Christ. In his baptism he would become a new creature in Christ, as a sheep among wolves, to spread the Good News and to continue Christ's work of reconciling a fallen world through evangelism. After finishing his vigil and ending his fast, he said goodbye to the sisters and set out to find the monastery and the priest who would baptise him.

He followed the directions given by Sister Ruth, along the path leading to the monastery, a twelfth-century Gothic building. At the entrance he was greeted by an emaciated friar dressed in a brown habit, who invited him inside.

'The holy father is not here at present,' said the friar. 'He is in Jerusalem but should be back soon. If you wait in the chapel he shouldn't be too long. Are you a Catholic?' he asked, curiously.

'I'm a Christian,' said Cohen.

The friar gave him a wry smile, and led him to the chapel. Cohen was surprised to see two nuns praying in the chapel, dressed in blue habits and praying in French, reciting prayers on the rosary. He sat nervously at the back and opened the Bible, which Sister Ruth had given him.

'Then shall they deliver you up to be afflicted and shall kill you, and you shall be hated of all nations for my name's sake.'

The scripture so alarmed him, he was tempted to flee the monastery there and then, forgoing baptism by the priest. Was this the price of discipleship? Cohen thought. Fear and loathing took hold of him as the French nuns passed by. They bowed gracefully, acknowledging him with smiles, as they left the church. So why was he so fearful in God's house? Already he was starting to have doubts and he hadn't met the priest yet, let alone been baptised. What was happening to him? Why should one passage of scripture have such a devastating effect on him? He felt the Bible was speaking directly to him, warning of the danger if he became a disciple.

Cohen thought seriously about the scripture and felt it best he waited for the priest to return. He would be able to allay his fears and lead Cohen back to the right path. He would hope that after his baptism fears and doubts would go away and he would be at peace with God.

But how could that be, peace, when Christ was nailed to a Cross? Where was the peace in that? Cohen asked. Yet this was the price Christ paid to reconcile us to God. Isn't what Christ wants to go through with discipleship, the same trials of self-sacrifice, to offer oneself like a lamb to the slaughter as Christians have for centuries, ever since they were thrown to the lions in the coliseum?

Cohen thought back on his life. All the sins he had committed made it feel like he was carrying the cross all the way to Calvary. Suddenly he heard a voice at the back of the chapel. 'Did you want to see me,' someone asked gruffly with an Italian accent. It was Father Claudio, Father Superior of the monastery, beckoning Cohen to follow him. 'Let's go to my study. We can talk there,' he said abruptly.

Cohen followed the priest up a flight of winding stone steps, along a wide arched passage overlooking the sanctuary. Huge paintings of martyred saints and popes going back centuries hung on the walls as he was led to the priest's study.

'What is it you wanted to see me about?' Father Claudio asked, puffing a cigarette.

'Sister Ruth suggested I come and see you about baptism,' he said.

'Is your family Catholic?' said the priest, coughing.

'No, they're Jewish,' replied Cohen.

'Jewish?' repeated the priest, dismayed.

'Yes, my parents are from Poland, but they live in England.'

'Why do you want to be baptised?' asked the priest, astounded.

'I got converted,' said Cohen. 'Can you do it today?'

'Ha, ha,' the priest laughed, 'it's not that simple. You need instruction and to undergo catechism.'

'I don't understand. What is catechism?' questioned Cohen, puzzled.

'Exactly, you don't understand, that's why you need instruction,' said Father Claudio, stubbing out his cigarette.

'But this is a monastery, named after St. John the Baptist. Didn't he baptise hundreds of Christians on the same day?' Cohen asked.

'Yes, but its different now. People couldn't read or write in those days. You need instruction in the faith so you understand the meaning of baptism and what is expected of you when become a Christian,' said Father Claudio.

'And how long would that take?' Cohen protested.

'Six months,' replied the priest.

Cohen looked disappointed. How could he wait six months after the Lord had called him to renounce the world? Jesus called him today, not next year.

'Why are you here in Israel?' asked Father Claudio, abruptly again.

'I'm a journalist. I was working on a story,' Cohen said.

'Saints preserve us, a journalist. What's the story about?'

'It's not that important now, believe me. What's more important is I need to be baptised,' said Cohen.

'Then you best go back to England, and join a church there and receive instruction,' Father Claudio said dismissively.

'But I don't want to go back to England. God wants me here.' protested Cohen.

'How can you be sure?' said Father Claudio, lightening another cigarette.

'Because I am a Jew, this is my land,' said Cohen. 'Jesus was a Jew and he wants me here. My heart knows it.'

'How old are you?' asked the priest.

'I'm thirty-three, the same age as Jesus when he died,' said Cohen, modestly.

'Have you thought about being a Franciscan?'

'No, I don't know anything about them, except that St. Francis loved Jesus.'

'Well, we have friars from all over the world,' said Father Claudio, matter-of-factly. 'We train them here at the monastery, which was built by the friars in the twelfth century. You have much to learn, my son. Reading the life of St. Francis would help. Where are you staying?'

'With the nuns,' he answered, hesitantly. 'They have a guest room.'

'And how long have felt this need become a Christian?' asked the priest.

'For a week,' said Cohen, apologetically.

'Just a week!' exclaimed Father Claudio. 'Well, Rome wasn't built in a day, you know. Come and see me in two days' time, and I'll let you know if you can stay at the monastery.'

Cohen got up and left the monastery with mixed feelings. He was happy that they would accept him at the monastery, but disappointed he would not be baptised for six months. It was a long time. What if he died in that time? Would he be saved or taken to hell, where souls were tormented eternally? He felt confused and fearful of what lay ahead. Cohen walked through the Judean hills, dejected and alone. He wanted to be close to nature, to feel Mother Earth, feel the sand under his feet and to experience the harshness of the desert, to suffer as Christ did in the wilderness.

He climbed the peaks and gazed at the vista of the Holy Land, as far as the eye could see. He stood still in awe of its beauty and splendour, and he made a vow of silence, praying in his heart throughout his vigil. He gazed in wonder at the stars, staring into infinity, and for the first time he experienced the breathtaking sight of shooting stars hurtling through space at lightning speed. He even saw the star the three kings from the Orient followed, heralding the coming of Christ. He fell to his knees in adoration, just as the three wise men did in ages past.

In the morning, he awoke tired and irritable, having been bitten by mosquitoes most of the night. He continued walking the hills, which grew in size and statue, until they formed mountains so majestic he stood in awe.

Climbing a peak, he gazed across the landscape, and looking back he could see in the distance the village of Ein Karem and the monastery he'd left behind. The village from a distance seemed peaceful, serenely nestled in the valley, but Cohen had reservations about returning to the monastery, for his heart was not there. Despite his new found faith, he wasn't at peace. He was anxious about the monastery. What would it mean to live in a Christian community? He was Jewish and Jews never lived in monasteries, only Essenes, who followed a strict law of Moses lived apart from society in caves. What if he wasn't meant to live in a religious community? After all, it was an alien way of life to the Jews. Jesus had never lived in a monastery. He was an itinerant preacher and spent most of his life preaching and wandering from town to town with 'no place to lay his head'.

Doubts suddenly began to overwhelm Cohen about joining the Franciscans, but he was anxious to be baptised, even if it mean waiting six months. At least that would give him time to know about Christianity, to study the Bible and to live among Christians.

Sitting in a yoga position on the mountain summit, he mediated on what Christ would mean to the Jews if he was the true Messiah. The Messiah the Jews were waiting for, thought Cohen, would be Christ when he returned for his Second Coming, as promised in the Book of Revelation. And what a shock this would be for the Jews who rejected him. They would have to bear the guilt for his death, his crucifixion.

But Cohen reckoned the Jews were foremost in his mission, for they were God's people. Jesus came to the Jews so that men's sins would be forgiven - that was how much God loved the Jews. He sent his Son for their salvation, the Jews first, the Gentiles second.

Cohen now believed that Christ was the Messiah they had been waiting for all along. Jesus had promised to return, to restore the Kingdom of God on earth, and create a new heaven and a new earth and that all things would be made new. So the Pharisees got it wrong, tragically and prophetically. They put their trust in Moses and when Jesus said he was the Son of God they tore their garments and accused him of blasphemy. Then they delivered him up for death and the Jews cried out:

'Crucify him, crucify him; let his blood be upon our heads.'

Cohen grieved for the Jews. They were stubborn. Still they rejected Him. Even in their synagogues they named him the 'minor prophet'. In their ignorance they waited for the Messiah to come. He was with them the whole time. And so, who would take this saving message of Christ to the Jews, blinded by materialism and lack of faith in God? Where was the modern day John the Baptist, who shook the synagogues and the Pharisees to the very core with his preaching of hellfire and damnation unless the people repented.

And who would take the saving gospel of Jesus to the Jews? He hadn't thought to be a missionary, certainly not in Israel, for it was against the law to proselytise. It wasn't something he had been thinking about ever since he was converted, but the idea of witnessing for Jews certainly appealed to him. But surely God was not asking him to preach to the Jews? For anyone caught proselytising could be thrown into jail and deported.

So what? Cohen thought. How many of Christ's disciples were arrested and put in jail. The history of Christianity was full of the blood of martyrs who died for their faith.

Is that what God was asking him to do – be a witness for the Jews? He would try to be obedient to God's calling, but would the Jews listen? The Pharisees would denounce Cohen as a traitor, a Jew who sold out his heritage.

In preaching to the Jews, there'd also be the risk of public humiliation, rejection, being stoned to death, like St. Stephen, the first Christian martyr. Cohen had no stomach for confrontation and violence. He would be best suited to propagating the faith by continuing to write, to show that the pen is mightier than the sword, and leave the front line battle to Christ's soldiers, preachers of courage who fear no evil.

Perhaps the nuns had it right. At least the walls of the convent provided some protection from persecution from the wicked world. It was an act of heroism to be deported for the faith, but quite another to be stoned on the street.

Cohen was not ready to be a martyr, and besides he hadn't been baptised. He would take on Sister Ruth's advice, become baptised first, then strengthen himself in prayer and spiritual reading before taking on the material world and converting the Jews. For how many men have fallen at the wayside, unprepared for the spiritual warfare ahead? And does the scripture not warn us that it is folly to go into battle with only half the soldiers of one's enemy?

Cohen decided it would be spiritually prudent if he accepted the invitation of the monastery and prepared for baptism, which would change his life forever.

11

Cohen met the Father Superior of the monastery at his office in Jerusalem the following morning. The priest seemed more amiable than when they first met, and he asked if he still wanted to join the monastery.

'Yes, I would dearly like to be baptised,' said Cohen. 'I've been greatly looking forward to joining the monastery and meeting the friars.' On the drive to the monastery, Father Claudio brought up the subject of Cohen being a journalist and asked about the story he had been working on. 'I hope you're not of those reporters who wants to write scandals about the church,' he said, joking. 'What story did you say you were writing?'

Cohen he did not want to tell his story, but he felt it necessary if he wanted to please the priest. 'It was about the Jewish temple, Solomon's Temple, and plans to rebuild it. Have you heard about it?' Cohen asked.

'My dear boy, the Jews have been going on about since the dawn of time,' said Father Claudio. 'There's nothing new in that.'

'That's what I thought,' replied Cohen, wishing to drop the subject. He hadn't thought about his assignment for several days. He would have phone his agency and get them to take him off the assignment. It seemed totally irrelevant to him now whether the Jews built the Temple or not. Even if they did, it would be meaningless.

The Messiah had already come.

'There are far more interesting subjects to write about,' said Father Claudio. 'Take our monastery: we've just been given the status by the Pope to train friars for the Holy Land, to be custodians of the holy shrines. You should write about that.'

'I may well do so,' said Cohen, 'but I imagine the Catholic press would cover it.'

'The Catholic press!' scoffed the priest. 'They don't even know where the Holy Land is!'

Cohen laughed. He'd never heard of such a put-down of the media in all his life. 'Why are you laughing?' asked the priest. 'It's true. They never write about my monastery and all the work we do here. Maybe the Catholic press believe all Franciscans live in Italy and nowhere else.'

Father Claudio drove like a maniac, weaving in and out of traffic as though he was a racing driver, tearing down the mountainside towards Ein Karem like a priest possessed. Pulling up outside the monastery, he was greeted by one of his friars.

'This is Brother Thomas,' said Father Claudio, introducing him. 'He used to be a nurse, so he'll look after you,' he grinned.

'Let me take your bag,' offered Brother Thomas, taking it from Cohen's hand and leading his way up the steps to the monastery.

It was the last act of courtesy from the friar, for after Cohen entered the monastery, the brother did not speak to him again. In fact, the friar went out of his way to avoid him. It wasn't the only rejection would experience, for within days it became clear that some of the friars were treating him as an outsider. He was not a Franciscan, or a Catholic, and wasn't even baptised. The rejection hurt Cohen deeply to the point where he spent of his time after Mass visiting the ancient sites and holy shrines in Jerusalem. What hurt Cohen most was that the one of the brothers, who had totally ignored him, was an English friar. He even carried his suitcase into the monastery. Such indifference from a friar, training to surrender his life to serve others, could make a saint turn in his grave. But because Padre Claudio had given Cohen free time during the day, providing he attended Mass and Vespers, he was virtually free to come and go from the monastery as he pleased.

The freedom was to detach him from the friars and ignore them, hardly the Christian brotherly love he had hoped for.

Padre Claudio was, Cohen learned, seventy years old, wiser and more hospitable than the friars. He showed Cohen the shrine of St. John the Baptist, upon the site of whose birthplace the monastery was constructed. He explained some of the history of the monastery, built by in the twelfth century by friars who had sailed over from Italy.

When the padre had shown Cohen to his room he apologised as he had given him a cell on the floor above the novices where the nuns lived.

'They cook for us,' Father Claudio explained. 'They have separate quarters at the end of the cloisters. They won't disturb you. I'm sure you're used to living with nuns,' he chuckled. 'They are French because of their cuisine, as we have some friars very fussy over their food, especially the Americans.'

Cohen found the room was more than comfortable. It had its own en-suite bathroom, a writing desk and chairs, and a large bed overlooking a garden with orange and lemon trees in neat rows.

'I'd like you to settle in for a few days, then come and see me and make your confession,' said the priest.

'Confession?' queried Cohen.

'Yes, anyone who stays at the monastery must make regular confessions,' said the padre. 'Vespers is at half past five this afternoon, in the chapel.'

Cohen sat at the desk overlooking the garden. He had never seen orange and lemon trees before, the brightness of their colours gleaming in the sun captivated him.

Cohen then found a prayer stool in front of an icon of Madonna and he knelt down and began to pray. He felt in his heart that God had forgiven him when he experienced his conversion. What more was there to confess? On second thoughts, he would have to tell his parents about his conversion and that would hurt them, which he'd bound to confess. But he wasn't about to tell them just yet, at least not until he'd been baptised.

Should he reveal the plans to rebuild the temple? It dawned on him that revealing plans wasn't really a sin, at least judging by the priest who'd said the temple was insignificant. Frustrated with not knowing what to confess, Cohen got up from his prayer stool and decided to explore the monastery. He went into the corridor and walked down the arched cloisters, glancing at the huge icon paintings which hung either side of the walls. The paintings were in a dilapidated state with some of the canvases were peeling, while others were torn and frayed at the edges. Cohen thought that if Father Claudio gave permission, he would restore them to their original state. As he was studying one of the paintings, St. John the Baptist baptising Jesus, a young woman approached. Although she was not a nun, she had the appearance of being religious, a long robe with a black skirt with a navy blue cardigan, her hair tied neatly back in a bun.

'Bonsoir,' she said in a soft French accent, 'you must be the new aspirant. I'm Lucy, my room is next door.'

Cohen was taken aback. He didn't expect a woman living in such close proximity right next door to him in the monastery, for heaven's sake.

'You like art?' said Lucy, looking at the painting. Cohen felt her brush against him, as she looked closer at the canvases.

'I love art, but these paintings are in a sorry state. Are you staying with the nuns?' Cohen asked.

'I'm helping the nuns do the cooking. Before, I was in the Carmelite convent for two years, but it didn't work out,' said Lucy. 'Are you going to be a friar?'

'It's a possibility, but I'm here to prepare for my baptism,' said Cohen. 'Where are you from? I noticed your accent.'

'I'm from Quebec, just outside Montreal. Before I came to Israel I was in a convent in France,' said Lucy. 'You'll have to excuse me. I have to go to the kitchen now.'

Cohen watched her disappear along the cloisters her nimble feet moving like those of an angel without a care in the world. Women tend to slouch as if burdened by the worries of this world. Nuns are the opposite. They move with such grace and purpose as though they are spiritually energised.

Such was Lucy. She had been well trained by the Carmelites.

Not so surprisingly, Cohen fell under her spell and waited for the moment to see her again. He went back to his room and waited for the bell to ring for supper.

In the refectory, friars sat in tables next to the wall facing each other. A short prayer was followed by grace said by the Father Superior, before the friars sat down to tuck into their generous portions of roast beef served by the French nuns and, of course, Lucy.

When Lucy approached Cohen's table, she smiled affectionately. The gesture embarrassed him and made him feel uncomfortable in front of the friars, even more so as she heaped lots of potatoes on his plate, far more than he could possibly manage. The ample helping did not go unnoticed by the friars, in particular the English friar, who gave him a disapproving look. Feeling it would be a sin to leave food on his plate he forced himself to eat the entire meal, whereupon at Vespers he felt sick and excused himself from vigils.

Gluttony came to mind as a sin, although he'd never before been tempted with food. Drink and women were his vices, sins he should be confessing.

Lucy was flitting from the refectory to the kitchen as she served the friars hot meals. She changed into a blue skirt and sandals and wore a white veil. She reminded him of the sister at the convent, Sister Sharon, an English nun. Lucy, however, being French, she had an air of chic about her, feminine, and graceful.

Later that evening, she would shock him to the point he nearly fled the monastery. It happened quite unexpectedly, and by pure chance.

After Vespers, he took a walk in the garden admiring the oranges and lemon trees, and decided to go back to his room, when he heard the sound of running water. It came from Lucy's room and he noticed that the door was ajar. Out of curiosity, he could not resist peering into the room. The running water came from the shower in the far corner of the room and stark naked was Lucy, washing her buxom breasts.

Cohen stood transfixed, not daring to breathe for fear she might start screaming. But his fears were unfounded, like when he saw the woman naked in the tent in his youth.

'I forgot to close the door,' Lucy said, rinsing herself, and she carried on with her shower.

Cohen took a hasty retreat to his room. She was French, after all, no different all those Scandinavian girls when it came to sex. They had no inhibitions. He was hoping that no one had spotted him entering Lucy's room. But was he really to blame? Why on earth did a woman choose to live in a monastery surrounded by men who had taken vows of chastity? How could he confess such a sin on seeing the nun naked after a week in the monastery? What would the priest think of him? He would show him the door.

Cohen was not familiar with religious scruples and how they tormented monks but he came close to it that night, tossing and turning in his bed over a sin. He had committed lust over Lucy. He began wondering whether he should flee the monastery and forget his confession with the priest, something he was now dreading.

He tried to get to sleep, but all he could remember was the curvaceous Lucy standing naked in the shower, wanton and ready.

After a good night's sleep, having dreamt about the naked woman in the tent making love to him, Cohen made a point of using the stairs at the opposite end to the nuns' quarters to make his way privately to the chapel for the Mass. After the Mass he remained in the chapel, preparing himself for his dreaded confession. His hands began to sweat as he opened the Bible and began to search for some comforting words to allay his fears: 'All who look upon a woman with lust in their heart commit adultery.' He shuddered at the words. Then he came across a passage that leapt out: 'Thou shall call no man father, for thou hast only one Father, the Lord God.' It confirmed what

Cohen thought: there is one Father and you should confess your sins directly to him, for God forgives all the sinners.

No one should call another father, for God is the Father.

And as for the so-called 'sins' he'd committed in the monastery, it fell under religious scruples, forgotten the next day. He was no more a glutton than the friars and as for Lucy, he'd come across her by chance and walked away.

No, he would not take confession, but trust in God. He had been forgiven all his sins on the day he made his conversion. Later that day, Father Claudio summoned him to his study and Cohen explained to him the reasons for not wanting to take confession. Father Claudio told Cohen if he wanted to be Catholic he was duty bound, prior to being baptised, to give a full and frank confession as the Holy Church decreed.

'Don't worry about it now, my son,' said Father Claudio. 'You will see the wisdom and sanctity of confessing your sins before a priest later, for only a priest can give you absolution. It is the authority Our Lord gave to the church. Now, I want to go to Father Paulo for instruction in the faith.'

Cohen was confused by Father Claudio's teaching of confession. He went to his room pondering the mystery and sanctity of the Sacraments, for it was all new to him as a Jew.

He spent the next few weeks studying under the tutelage of Father Paulo, a black American priest, who had joined the Franciscans in the United States to train the novices. Whereas Cohen was expecting to learn from the Bible the life of Christ, Father Paulo was teaching something else. It was all about St. Francis and the life of the Franciscans. This not only confused Cohen, but gave him great consternation when he was informed by Father Claudio that he would be expected to learn Italian. Then the priest delivered what was even more of a bombshell.

He would have to go Rome before he entered the Franciscans, for his novice training.

'Rome?' he repeated, astonished.

'Why, yes. All friars serve two years in Rome before they come here for their final year,' said Father Claudio. 'That's how they speak Italian.'

'But I'm a Jew.' Cohen protested. 'Israel is my home.'

'If you become a friar, you go where the church sends you,' retorted the priest. 'We are here to serve, not to do as we please.'

Father Claudio lit a cigarette and offered one to Cohen. 'You have plenty of time to consider. There is no rush,' he said, reassuringly. 'You can stay for three months as an aspirant then decide what you want to do.'

'I would need time,' said Cohen.

'Well then, it's settled. You're staying here for a few months,' said Father Claudio. 'How are you finding life so far in the monastery?'

'Well, yes, except for the services. They're in Latin,' protested Cohen.

'That's why you'd need to go to Rome. Latin was the sacred liturgy for centuries in the church, but today most of the pilgrims that come to the Holy Land are from Italy, and the friars speak Italian, so you must learn Italian and Latin. And don't forget, the founder was St. Francis, and he too was Italian.'

How could he forget? That's all he'd heard since arriving at the monastery: St. Francis, the Life of St. Francis, the Rule of St. Francis and the History of the Order of St. Francis, the Little Saint from Assisi, who renounced everything in order to follow Christ. Cohen wanted to know about Jesus, and yet little was mentioned. He felt overwhelmed by the teaching of St. Francis, as though he was being indoctrinated into some form of cult to worship the Tramp of God, groomed into becoming 'Vera Sancti Francisci Effigies', made into the 'true likeness of St. Francis'. In a short time, he would even dress like St. Francis, in a brown habit and cowl with a leather belt strapped around his waist, flopping about in sandals. It was all too much for Cohen. He turned to Lucy.

She was not part of the Community. She was not a Franciscan nun, one of the Poor Clare's, but an ex-Carmelite, an outsider, one he could confide in and find the true Christ. There was no pretence in her, no church bureaucracy or pageantry. She was French, after all, and didn't care too much for the Italians for their ideal of patriotism.

Yet isolated as she was for leaving the Carmelites, she had the two French nuns to talk to and confide in.

Cohen had no one to confide in, except her. While the English friar, Brother Thomas, continued not to talk with him, the American friar taunted him in the refectory about being a homosexual. While the brethren seemed to display a certain amount of irreverence, Lucy had a deep love for prayer, a piety he'd not experienced before. There was a stillness about her, an inner quite, which radiated a sense a peace and tranquillity which attracted him. One evening, she knocked on his door.

'Are you busy?' she asked. 'I want to show you something. Follow me.'

Cohen looked puzzled and followed Lucy along the passage, up a flight of steps, until they reached a sanctuary high above the chapel, a tiny cell sealed off from the rest of the monastery. Lucy quietly opened the door, urging him to be silent as she placed a finger on her lips. Slowly she crept inside the tabernacle, bowing her head, and fell gracefully to her knees, urging him to sit down next to her. Halfway up at the wall in a tiny alcove was the receptacle, containing monstrance holding the Blessed Sacrament. Cohen knelt beside her. The Eucharist had a powerful presence which overwhelmed him, suspending his senses.

'I come here most of the time to pray,' she whispered, 'especially when I'm hurting.'

'Are you hurting now?' he gently asked.

'We are all hurting,' she sighed, 'but the Lord hears us. Be quiet now, and let Him come to us.'

Cohen had no idea how long they remained kneeling together in prayer, for he'd lost all sense of time. He felt the warmth radiating from the Blessed Sacrament fill his entire body. His loneliness disappeared and he was filled with indescribable love. Tears rolled down his cheeks. He didn't bother to wipe them away, for the love of God was healing him. Tears of repentance were streaming down his face. God was in him and all his pain and anguish and loneliness was now gone, washed by Jesus and the Holy Spirit. God had given him a sister in Christ, Lucy.

Cohen reached out to hold her hand, but instead she wiped the tears from his face, and kissed him on the cheek before disappearing silently into the night.

12

The next day Cohen and Lucy caught the bus together to Jerusalem. Lucy had a job cleaning for a rich Jewish family. It helped to pay for clothes and expenses, although the padre gave the nuns an allowance each. 'Listen, Lucy,' said Cohen, 'I want to apologise for the other night, seeing you in the shower. I didn't mean to look, but the door was left open.'

'Forget it. It's not important,' said Lucy. 'I'm sure you've seen a naked woman before. I forgot to close the door.'

'Please don't be embarrassed if I tell you you've got a beautiful figure,' said Cohen, looking at her.

'Thanks, but compliments don't mean anything to a nun,' said Lucy, adjusting her skirt. She then told him that before coming to Israel, she had been in a relationship for ten years in Montreal. The affair ended when she found God. 'And that was it,' she said. 'Ooh-la-la, I quit my job, left my man and came to Israel, just like that. When the Lord calls, you have to go. I was a teacher, it was a responsible job.'

'And you became a Carmelite nun?' Cohen said.

'Yes, in France,' said Lucy. 'I did some cleaning in a convent before I joined.'

'So why did you leave the Carmelites?'

'It was an enclosed order, very claustrophobic,' she sighed. 'For two years I never went out, not even shopping. If a visitor from France came to see me, I had to speak with her through a grill, can you imagine? Some of the sisters didn't help. Women can be very bitchy and small-minded when they are together like that, very difficult, even spiteful sometimes.'

'Did you miss being with a man?' Cohen asked, curiously.

'It is the same for a woman as for a man,' said Lucy, pointedly.

Cohen felt embarrassed for having asked. 'Sorry, I didn't mean to pry.'

'It's life, c'est la vie, but that all behind me,' said Lucy. 'It's only God.'

'About last night, in the tabernacle,' he said, 'something happened to me.'

'Me too,' said Lucy. 'It was the Eucharist. It was pre-sanctified for those in the monastery who want to pray.'

'You mean Jesus is present in the sacrament?' asked Cohen, puzzled.

'Why, yes, you didn't know?' asked Lucy.

'I'm still to be baptised,' Cohen, apologetically.

'Then you are just beginning to start the exciting journey, but it will not be without trials. Many a night I've cried myself to sleep in a convent.'

'You cried in the convent?' Cohen repeated. 'You, of all people, seem so content.'

'We can never be content in this life,' said Lucy. 'Our home is in heaven,' her eyes lit up as she spoke.

'You have a deep faith,' remarked Cohen. 'I envy you.'

'Faith is for everyone. You only have to ask God,' said Lucy. 'This is where I get off. I'll see you at supper. God bless,' and she kissed him on the cheek.

He waved as she got off the bus, but she didn't look back. He watched her walk into the affluent Jewish suburbs, and wondered what she thought of him.

Cohen spent the rest of the day on pilgrimage, visiting the holy shrines. Later he climbed the Mount of Olives to visit the Ascension shrine. It was much steeper than he'd thought, taking him hours climbing the narrow road to the top.

He sat down exhausted by the side of the road and surveyed the spectacular view below, the City of Jerusalem in all its splendour and glory.

Olive trees cascaded down the mountain like waves rolling to distant shores, and in the distance he could see the golden temple, the Dome of the Rock. At the top of the mountain stood the shrine of the Ascension where Jesus bade his last farewell to his disciples and ascended to heaven. Several elderly Arabs sat outside the shop watching the youths playing football. He asked for directions to the shrine and an old man pointed the way. On reaching the shrine, he discovered it was built in the shape of a Muslim prayer tower, a minaret. It had an arched door and when he entered an Arab stopped him and asked him to pay an admission fee. It was the first time he'd ever been charged to enter a holy shrine. The Arab shrugged and took the money.

On entering the shrine, he was surprised to discover it was completely empty, a round twenty-foot stone wall with a roofless top, just bare earth to walk on.

Being without a roof was not without significance, for when Cohen stood in the middle he pictured Jesus ascending up into the clouds, as scripture described. How sad the disciples must have been to see their Lord taken up. Jesus had promised, however, that he would return – his Second Coming.

Cohen bowed his head close to the perimeter wall, the Jewish tradition of prayer, and prayed for Christ's return. For it was becoming clear the world would end soon, perhaps a Third World War, he thought.

There seemed to be no end to suffering: the shooting of children, Palestinian refugees, the displacement of the Jews, man's inhumanity towards man. When will suffering end? The Second Coming of Christ!

For then all things will be made anew. There will be a new earth and a new heaven, trumpets will blast and Christ in His glory will return triumphant, according to the Book of Revelation.

Leaving the Mount of Olives, Cohen made his way to Bethany, a village visited by Jesus. An Arab woman said it was five kilometres to the east of Jerusalem. He was anxious to head for Bethany because it was where Jesus raised Lazarus from the dead. It was the raising up of Lazarus that captivated his imagination. He set out on his pilgrimage along a narrow path, which ended in sand dunes that proved difficult to tread through. On his way he passed a church dedicated to St. Mary. Making a sign of the cross, he continued along the sand dunes to Bethany.

After a few kilometres he found the heat unbearable. He felt thirsty and had forgotten his sun hat, and the mosquitoes were biting him. The sun beat down on him and felt desperate for a drink of water. Reaching the top of the hill, he saw the village of Bethany, looming in the distance.

On entering the village he asked for a cup of drinking water from an old woman, and set out for Lazarus's tomb. An Arab girl in a headscarf and torn dress approached him for money. She held out her hand.

Cohen gave her a few shekels and asked if she could take him to the tomb. She led him to where the huge tomb was built, near the centre of the village.

Cautiously he poked his head inside and wondered if she'd taken him to the right place, as there was not another pilgrim in sight. He entered the tomb in reverence. There was a steep drop. It was pitch black and he held onto the handrail as he descended. It was so dark he could not see in front of him. He managed to hold on to a banister and edged his way down a never-ending staircase, so steep that he felt as though he was in the bowels of hell, but without the comfort of hellfire to see where he was going. Panic seized him, and not unlike Lazarus, he raised himself up and fled to the light at the entrance of the tomb.

In Cohen's desperation to flee back to the land of the living, he foolishly banged his head on the roof of the cave. Staggering back into the daylight, instead of welcoming the blue skies, all Cohen saw was a cluster of stars swirling around. Dazed, he had to sit by the entrance to the tomb until he recovered. He noticed there was a grocer's shop opposite and made his way across the dirt road. He explained to the shopkeeper the ordeal suffered in the darken tomb as he rubbed his sore head.

'You should have come to the shop first,' said the Arab. 'I switch the light on in the tomb from under the counter, only ten shekels.'

Cohen laughed. He saw the funny side of it. He made his way up the hill when he was met by an old Arab who asked if he'd like to see the Upper Room, where Jesus shared the Last Supper with his disciples. He was never expecting a second shrine in Bethany, and was more than willing to pay the twenty shekels. The Arab pocketed the money and led Cohen to his house, a rambling shack with two storeys. The Arab introduced him to his wife and took him up a flight of stairs to an upper room where thirteen cushions had been placed in a circle.

'This is where Jesus had his Last Supper with the disciples,' said the Arab man gleefully. His wife stood by proudly nodding. 'Jesus sat there, in the middle,' she pointed with conviction.

Cohen reverently knelt down and said a prayer, with the Arab couple joining him. He asked the Lord to bless this house and make it fruitful for it was sanctified with the Last Supper Jesus had taken here in this room. He got up and shook hands with the couple, thanked them for their hospitality and before leaving was offered a bottle of water for five shekels.

On his way back to the monastery, Cohen entered the suburbs of East Jerusalem. Some of the Arab youths picked up stones and hurled them at him as he walked past. He turned to confront them but they ran away, one looking about twelve years old. They could spot a Jew a mile away, or they simply took offence at his Western clothes.

Cohen had suffered enough for one day and made a hastily retreat into West Jerusalem, a haven for the Jews. Back at the monastery he related the events of the day to the friars, including his pilgrimage to Bethany, where the Arab told him Jesus had spent his Last Supper. Suddenly the friars fell about in hysterics, Lucy joining in with the chorus of laughter.

'The Last Supper wasn't in Bethany,' one of the friars said. 'It was in Jerusalem. How much did he charge you?'

'Twenty shekels,' Cohen said, innocently.

'Oh my God, he saw you coming!' laughed the friar.

'Maybe they're a poor family and needed the money,' said Cohen on reflection.

In the afternoon, after Mass, Father Claudio asked whether Cohen, with his journalistic background, could put the monastery library in some kind of order. It had been sadly neglected over the years, almost as much as the monastery paintings. The padre gave him permission to restore some of the dilapidated canvases and make use of the carpentry room in the basement. Cohen set about his new duties with great enthusiasm, surveying the paintings most in need of restoration and organising the materials to complete the task. Looking at the paintings in the cloisters, he picked out the most damaged. It was the portrait of Pope Gregory, dating back to the twelfth century.

The paint was cracked and the frame was falling off. He set about his work with a few splashes of burnt umber and burnt sienna, mixing it with of yellow cadmium. He stood back and admired his work.

Magnificent! The portrait was transformed.

But when he entered the library on the upper floor he nearly despaired, for it was a complete shambles. Books were left in disarray on the tables; other books were piled on the floor and dusty shelves were jammed and overflowing with manuscripts. It was a nightmare. It was heartbreaking work but it had to be done. Not only was it God's work, but he also wanted to please the padre.

It would take months to get the library in working order, and it didn't surprise him that the friars rarely used the library, preferring the modern study on the ground floor.

But the work gave him time to study some of the books, in particular some of the lithographs and drawings of Dante's Inferno, which fuelled his imagination. They were realistic lithographs, vividly portraying the terrors that people faced if they were cast into hell. Anyone seeing those drawings would have no hesitation in repenting in sackcloth and ashes, no matter how little they had sinned, he thought. Some of the lithographs frightened the life out of him and, seeing the shock value, he put the drawings on the table for anyone else to see. A few guests who ventured into the library were not to be seen again.

But one special guest Cohen he was fond off was Lucy, for she had a natural love of books, in particular devotional books. She was surprised at the progress he'd made at the library in terms of getting it into working order, namely the chronological order of books with indices.

'Do you have the Spiritual Dialogue by St. Catherine of Siena and Heaven, Hell and Purgatory by St. Catherine of Genoa, though I haven't read them for some time?' asked Lucy. 'And there's The Inner Castle by St. Therese of Avila. Do you have those books?'

Without hesitation he got the ladder, and promptly handed her the three books.

One evening, when Cohen was working late, she came into the library tearful, and to his surprise put her arms around him. 'What's the matter?' asked Cohen, embracing her tenderly.

'I've had a letter from my parents,' she sobbed. 'My brother is dead. He shot himself. He was an alcoholic. I prayed for him to stop drinking, but he couldn't.'

Cohen was speechless. He didn't what to say. He knew he was inclined to drink too much himself. He knew drinking was addictive, but was lost for words to console her.

'Why not go and pray, Lucy, in front of the Eucharist?' he asked.

'No, not now,' she said. 'I want you to hold me. I want to feel a man hold me. I want to be alive,' she blurted.

'Lucy you're upset. You're beside yourself with grief,' said Cohen. 'You don't know what you're saying.'

'I know exactly what I'm saying,' said Lucy. At that she kissed him tenderly on the mouth, and then with all the passion of a woman whose sexual desires had been repressed by living in a convent, she French kissed him.

'Please, Lucy,' he said, pulling her away. 'You're upset, come downstairs with me and we'll talk.'

Lucy followed him to his room and lay on the bed sobbing. 'Please hold me,' she pleaded, 'just for a minute.'

Cohen sat beside her and held her hand. But she turned towards him and threw her arms around him, revealing her bosoms. 'Please, Lucy, try and control yourself: we're in a monastery,' he pleaded, pulling away. 'The nuns are next door, they could hear us. Let's pray together, like we did the other night.'

'I don't want to pray,' confessed Lucy. 'I want you to hold me,' she moaned.

'Please, you'll only regret this later,' Cohen warned.

Lucy grabbed him again and pulled him closer. Just as she started to take off her bra there was a sudden knock on the door.

It was the Father Superior.

Cohen panicked, shot off the bed and adjusted his clothing. He grabbed Lucy and pushed her into the bathroom, flushing the toilet and closing the door.

'Sorry, I was in the toilet,' apologised Cohen.

'Did I hear another voice?' asked the padre. 'Do you have company?'

'No, I was practicing contralto in the bath,' said Cohen through clenched teeth. 'I used to sing alto in the choir.'

'In the choir? But I thought you weren't a Christian,' said Father Claudio.

'It wasn't a church choir,' said Cohen. 'It was what we call a Barber Choir.'

'Well, then we must make use of your talent and have you sing for us in the choir,' said the padre. 'Now, about that painting you restored of Pope Gregory…'

'You like it?' Cohen asked, eagerly.

'It's a mess.' he said. 'What have you done to it? I don't recognise it.'

'But I only retouched it with burnt sienna and raw umber and a splash of yellow cadmium,' Cohen said, apologising.

'I don't care about what you did to it. It's a mess,' said the padre. 'Wipe that paint off and leave the painting as it was. Can you manage that? And while I'm on about it, the library…'

'You approve?' Cohen asked, hopefully.

'It's a mess,' said Father Claudio. 'I can't find any books.'

'But there's a filing system now, books are indexed,' said Cohen proudly.

'That may be so, but it's all in English. I want Italian. Have not you been learning Italian? You have a phrase book, why don't you use it,' said the priest, appalled.

'I'll do it right away,' Cohen said.

Father Claudio raised his eyebrows to heaven and walked back through the cloisters with a sigh of resignation.

Cohen closed the door and breathed a deep breath of relief as he found Lucy coming out of the bathroom.

'Did you really mess up the Pope's portrait?' Lucy asked.

'I confess,' said Cohen. 'My position at the monastery is becoming more untenable by the day. It was one of those antiquated portraits. Who would recognise him now?'

'Obviously, the padre,' said Lucy, half smiling.

'I thought you were upset?' Cohen said.

'I am, but I can't cry forever,' said Lucy, wiping away the tears. She came up to him and put her arms around him, pouting her lips. 'Now were we, before we got interrupted?'

'Please Lucy, not again.'

'I want you just this once, you understand. I want to feel like a woman again, have a man hold me, please. I'm not a nun any more, not under vows.'

'Lucy, you're like a sister to me,' said Cohen. 'Let's not spoil that.'

Lucy got up from the bed and turned to Cohen. 'You English are all the same,' she scoffed. 'You are all so reserved. Why not be like the Frenchmen and have a bit of fun now and again? How can you refuse a woman, a French woman at that?'

Adjusting her blouse, she looked at him disgusted, and turning on her heels marched out of the room, slamming the door behind her.

'Women,' exclaimed Cohen, 'who can understand them?'

Cohen went into the hallway to study the portrait of Pope Gregory. On seeing the portrait a second time, he would obey the padre and get some turpentine and restore it to its original condition.

As for the library, Cohen felt his work was unappreciated. All the indexes were all wrong because the Italians didn't speak English. Why couldn't they learn English? It was the international language after all.

What really made him angry was the fact that he'd made the Spiritual Father upset. He felt an ominous cloud descend upon him, that his days at the monastery were numbered. Where would he go? He had no money, and he couldn't go back to England.

Later that evening, Cohen sealed his own fate when he went down to the wine cellar. He took two bottles to his room and drank to drown his sorrows. In the morning, still reeling from the affects hangover, he met the American friar in the refectory, the one who taunted him about being gay.

Cohen accidentally knocked over the coffee he was holding, spilling it all down the friar's habit. The friar had no hesitation in reporting the incident to the Spiritual Father, and that afternoon Cohen was asked to leave the monastery.

He had been there nearly three months and was on the verge of being sent to Rome for his baptism and to complete his studies in the Catechism.

It was a shock for Cohen when Father Claudio said he would have to leave the monastery immediately. He explained that the friars were his first responsibility, even though he agreed that some of them were difficult, especially the Americans. Father Claudio asked him to wait while went into his study and opened the safe. He took out some dollars and handed them to Cohen, for he was broke. 'I cannot send you away penniless; here is a gift from the church. Go with God, and remember that you are a child of God.'

Cohen thanked the priest and with tears in his eyes picked up the bag and headed out of the monastery for the last time.

At the entrance gate he saw Lucy walking to the bus stop. He explained to her what had happened. She hugged him tight and urged him to go the French monastery, a few kilometres in the Judean desert.

'I know the monks there. They are real monks and will look after you,' she said, reassuringly. 'Tell them I sent you and don't be afraid. God looks after his servants.'

Lucy kissed him, but this time it was a sisterly kiss on the cheek. 'I will come and see you,' she said, and turning away, she headed for the bus. He watched her go and then in desperation headed out for the Judean desert, where he spent some time praying. He wanted to be alone and gather his thoughts. He sat down and pondered his fate. Where was the Christian journey taking him? Why shouldn't he go back to the world and tell his story about the temple? Then he remembered the money the padre had given him. He took it out of the leather bag and counted it. To Cohen's amazement he found that the padre had given him more than $500. What would he do with all that money? Cohen wondered. Why had the priest been so generous? Did he feel sorry for him having to go?

But Cohen knew in his heart he was to blame. How could he, with aspirations of being a monk, accidentally spill coffee all over the friar, lie in bed with a woman and get drunk? It wasn't the behaviour of someone committed to the religious life. He contemplated whether he should go to the French monastery Lucy recommended, but his heart was not there. He had had enough of monasteries. He needed to think and pray for some direction in his life. He needed to discover God's will.

Cohen looked out over the Judean desert across the valleys and gazed at the mountains in the distance. He felt insignificant compared to the vast expanse of God's paradise on earth. And he felt alone. He longed for company again and realise that if he belonged to a Christian community it would help him grow in faith. He would have to take up Lucy's recommendation and apply to the French monastery. It was the only way forward. Otherwise, he would go back to the world. It was a defeatist thing to do, capitulation, in the face of all he wanted to achieve. He wanted God.

Cohen was well aware from studying the Bible that taking up the cross and living a Christian life would not be without its trials. But the last place he expected to face trials was in a monastery, especially temptations of the flesh. It was clear to him that he wasn't ready to join the French monastery, that if he wanted peace, he would have to go and find it for himself. For, like Jesus, he would have to go out into the wilderness be obedient to God, and defy the devil and all worldly temptations. But there was no point in living in the wilderness on his own, like St. Anthony the founder of the hermit life, who needed years of praying in order to venture out in the desert.

Temptation could be worse for the solitary. It would take the power of St. Anthony to live alone in the desert, for he resisted a naked woman lured to take his chastity, like the naked woman in the tent Cohen saw as a boy.

He felt confused. He could not take the loneliness of living a solitary life. There was only one answer – walk! Walking freed his spirit. It gave him a sense of purpose, striding into the unknown, like an explorer seeking mountains to conquer. It lifted his spirits and made him feel alive again. He had the good sense to buy a rucksack from the market, and strapping it on his back, set out across the Judean wilderness.

His only purpose was to be alone with God and to discern His will. Cohen was now convinced that without God's will, life had little meaning.

13

During the day the desert seemed to shimmer in the sun, sending ripples streaking across the valley. At night it was so cold. Cohen felt desperately alone in the desert, as was supposedly Jesus was during His forty days in the wilderness.

Leaving the monastery acrimoniously, he'd forgotten to bring food. He journeyed on undaunted by the pains of hunger. There wasn't a soul in sight, no sign of a village or an animal to keep him company, only the whistling of the desert wind. He knew it was not as though he was in the middle of the Sahara desert, for he was bound to come across a village soon. His only real concern was his sense of direction. For all he knew, he could be walking round in circles.

But after walking several kilometres he spotted a light in the distance. As he got closer he recognised someone camping out in the desert. Should he take the risk of approaching at night or just make their acquaintance in the morning?

But the hunger pains were getting to him and he decided to approach with caution, for he'd heard about bandits hiding in the hills and waiting to prey on unsuspecting tourists. He was not about to risk his life and robbed of his cash for the sake of a meal. As he turned to walk away he could spot several camels next to some tents.

It was a Bedouin tribe. It was too late to turn back, for they had already spotted him.

'Salaam,' greeted one of the Bedouin tribe, stepping forward. He led Cohen into their camp and invited him for a meal next to the fire. He gratefully accepted and sat down with the tribe. Cohen greeted them in English, not Hebrew, knowing their attitude towards the Jews. Some tribes were hostile to the Jews, but they seemed to be friendly. In fact, they seemed more hospitable than the Arabs he'd met so far. They were genuinely warm and in addition to the food they offered a drink and a blanket to keep him warm in cold night of the desert.

'You come from far?' asked their chief, in broken English.

'From Jerusalem,' said Cohen.

'Allah be praised,' the chief replied, then all of the tribe stood up and bowed in deep reverence towards the holy city. It struck Cohen that they were simple nomads roaming the desert, living in the extreme climate, yet they were the most humble men he'd ever met.

Cohen noticed the chief looking up at the stars that adorned the night sky. He pointed his finger at the stars, making a grand gesture across the sky.

'Allah is great,' the chief proclaimed.

Cohen nodded his approval.

The Bedouin hospitality overwhelmed him and he took money out of his pocket and offered to pay for the food. But the chief refused and took offence. It was an insult he could pay for their hospitality. Embarrassed by his ignorance of the customs, Cohen put the money back in to his pocket. The chief smiled then clapped his hands and in an instant several women came running out of the tent and began dancing. They were dressed in exotic coloured dresses and bedecked with jewellery and rings. They danced to a drum and pipes in an Arabic rhythm, their hips swaying to and fro and hands twirling above their heads around the campfire.

Cohen was entranced. He felt caught up in the atmosphere and ambience of the Arabian music. When the dancing was over, the chief offered Cohen a tent – only if he would chose one of the dancers for the night, as was the custom! He knew it would be wrong to refuse the chief's hospitality, and he bowed his head gracefully. Cohen said goodnight and entered the tent. A young Bedouin girl, in her teens, appeared before him, bowing humbly before him. The girl appeared to be happy that she was chosen, for it was considered an honour in the tribe to entertain the guest, to care for all his needs.

What contrast to Western women who had lost their humility and grace through pride and independence, Cohen thought. The girl undressed before him and lay down invitingly on the bed. She was indeed exceptional beautiful, with dark eyes and raven hair flowing down her shoulders and her well rounded bosoms. He leaned across her and stroked her hair and kissed her tenderly on the lips. She fell into his arms and opened her legs, urging him to take her.

Before he was about to possess her, he fell asleep in her arms, shattered from his exhausting journey.

He woke up with the Bedouin girl leaning over him with a cup of coffee. She flashed her dark eyes and smiled. 'I'm sorry, I fell asleep. I was exhausted,' Cohen apologised. 'I must have walked about thirty kilometres yesterday.'

He was thankful he hadn't slept with her. She could be the chief's daughter. He would force him to remain with the tribe and marry the girl to preserve the family honour; such was the customs of the nomadic tribes.

After drinking his coffee, the girl gently bathed him, washing his hands and feet and tenderly wiping his face. When she had finished, she kissed him on the cheek.

The girl then excused herself, saying she had to go and milk the goats. Cohen studied the gentle sway of her hips as she left the tent. She was a beautiful, graceful woman who would make a man very happy, invariably a Bedouin. But he couldn't help but be concerned by the fact that wherever he went in Israel, women seemed to follow him.

It was time to move on before he outstayed his welcome. For all he knew, his refusal to bed the Bedouin girl might cause offence if she complained. The chief might take that as a personal insult that he rejected her, that she wasn't good enough for him.

Cohen said farewell the chief and to the tribe before the girl appeared, thanking them for their hospitality, and set out again across the desert, heading back to Jerusalem. He decided after a long prayer and meditation that he would go to the French monastery Lucy referred to. Along the journey he came to the River Jordan, where St. John the Baptist baptised Jesus. Along the bank he spotted a group of young people being baptised.

Cohen approached them and spoke to a blond girl waiting to go into the water. He asked her if he too could be baptised.

'If you to believe that Jesus is the Son of God and died for our sins, you can be baptised,' said the girl, her faith evident.

'I believe,' said Cohen. 'You mean I don't have to wait six months and study the Bible?'

'Oh God no.' said the girl. 'Many people were baptised by John the Baptist the same day they repented, likewise here.'

'You don't say,' remarked Cohen.

'Why don't you to follow me into the water so you can be baptised by the minister,' asked the girl, wading into the river.

He needed no further encouragement. He stripped to his waist and followed her into the river. When it was his turn the pastor asked him his name, and with no ado he plunged Cohen headfirst into the water. He gasped for air as he came to the surface to hear the pastor announce proudly: 'I baptise you in the name of the Father, the Son and the Holy Spirit.'

Cohen stood up and wiped the water from his eyes and looked up to heaven.

'Praise the Lord,' said the pastor. 'You are now born again. Alleluia.' Cohen felt a surge of power run through his body; he began to shake and tremble. He staggered back to the bank of the river and tried to thank the blond girl but was unable to speak. His throat was chocked up and his tongue was numb. He tried to shout for joy, but nothing came out.

Then suddenly, out of nowhere, came a strange utterance from his lips: 'Shalom shada, shalom, shalom, shada.'

The words Cohen spoke were from God and joy filled his heart. His spirit had been set free. Suddenly, the girl told him: 'You are praying in tongues. Praise the Lord. It's a gift from the Holy Spirit. You are praying in the spirit. It is the purest form of prayer, straight from the heart. Make sure you keep praying in tongues, otherwise we can lose our gifts if we don't use them.'

Cohen was beside himself with joy. He was now a true Christian, in spirit and truth, and was now free to serve the Lord and to discern His will, free of all that dogma and religion. He had never felt so liberated in all his life.

By the banks of the River Jordan, he wept tears of joy and repentance, for he knew deep down in his heart all his sins had been forgiven – washed in the blood of Christ. When the pastor had finished baptizing, Cohen thanked him.

'Welcome to the Christian family,' said the parson. 'And what church are you from?'

'I was about to become a Catholic,' said Cohen.

'Now you are a Baptist in the Lord,' replied the parson, raising his hands.

'What makes a Baptist different from a Catholic?' queried Cohen.

'Baptists believe in the Word of God and total submersion in water, just like Christ when he was baptised by John the Baptist,' said the parson. 'We don't "sprinkle", no half measures. There's too much dogma in the Catholic Church. Best you join a Baptist church, my son, and hear the Word of God.'

Cohen embraced the minister, hugged the blond girl and departed. He didn't want to get into a theological debate about the different denominations. All he knew was that he was now a baptised Christian, filled by the Holy Spirit. His only concern was how he should serve God.

Despite his shortcomings, he was still drawn to the monastic life and living in a community with brothers who were prepared to consecrate their lives to Christ. Such deep and personal commitment, Cohen wanted to give all of himself to Christ, not to hold anything back, but to obey the commandments, to love God and love his neighbour as himself. But to love himself was all anathema to him. God's love encompassed all. He needed some time to pray in solitude, and away from the bustle of life.

Cohen left the desert and climbed the Mount of Olives, where Jesus prayed in the garden of Gethsemane, sweating blood the night he was arrested.

Kneeling beside an olive tree, Cohen prayed throughout the night.

Just before dawn, after praying constantly all night, a vision came to him. He saw heaven open up and a great multitude of angels praising and glorifying God. He walked among them, beside still lakes. They were dressed in white shining robes and their hearts were pure, completely open to one another. On the far side of the lake, he could see more people sitting still, their hearts becoming one. There was no separation, not like in this life, for all in heaven were free to enter each other's hearts at will. There was no barrier of sin, for their hearts were pure.

Cohen's heart was pure bliss as he watched all the worshippers beside the lake praising God, their Creator. He found himself beside these still waters of eternal life, and completely at peace. He was in God's love with a host of angels, and Paradise was his eternal home.

Then suddenly, without warning, the vision left him, only to be replaced by another vision, one of torment and hellfire. He found himself at the gates of hell, where demons screamed in rage, flames of fire shooting from their mouths. Their demonic tormented souls flew through the air attacking him from every direction. One of the demons had burning coals in his hand and hurled them at Cohen as fire raged throughout the cave. The air was filled with acrid smoke and hate. The demons were enraged because Cohen had drunk the blood of Christ, rendering them powerless to entice him in to hell. They screamed and raged, hurling molten rocks at him, but to no avail. They could not destroy him, and the more they tried the more enraged they became. They blasphemed and denounced Christ, calling on Satan to cast Cohen into hellfire.

Suddenly the vision left him, and he lay down on the Mount of Olives totally exhausted, his body trembling from shock. It was the most the traumatic experience of his life. What was Cohen to make of these visions, a revelation by God? They were so real, so vivid, he thought he'd actually been there, as though he was in heaven itself and had fallen into damnation.

The revelations not only confirmed life after death, but this awesome Judgement Day, when a soul could either enter the gates of paradise to live with Jesus or be cast down with demons into hell fire. It was up to the individual whether they wanted to be saved or not, to repent or perish. Every soul was precious to God. He wanted all men to be saved, but He didn't force them to come to Him, instead, giving them free will.

But many men chose the world and greed for riches, so they would perish like the seed falling on parched soil or being choked by thorns. You could not serve both money and God.

Cohen's vision told him that he had to become a missionary, to bring the souls to the Lord. Men couldn't believe in Christ if they hadn't heard about Him first, and how could they hear of Him if they weren't told?

In Israel the Jews would not turn to Christ, for they believed him to be a minor prophet, among other things, and put their trust in materialism and riches, turning away from God. Unless a prophet came, they would not return to the Lord, or hear the good news of salvation when it first came to the Jews. For God sent His Son to save the Jews first, then mankind. Was God asking him to preach to the Jews, to tell them about Jesus, their Messiah, the Anointed One they rejected, and that by believing in Him Israel would be saved? To tell Jews about Christ in the streets and the marketplaces, even in the synagogues was tantamount to being arrested, for proselytising for Jesus was against the law.

He would be openly attacked on the streets for preaching. For the Jews, to this day, are blinded by the fact that they failed to open their eyes and hearts with the love of Christ.

For nothing had changed among the Jews for centuries. They believed in an eye for an eye and a tooth for a tooth. The first Christian who tried to preach the name of Jesus was stoned to death outside the gates of Jerusalem. St Stephen looked up to heaven and saw Christ at God's right hand as they stoned him to death for blasphemy. They showed no mercy. Saul, who was later to be called Paul, stood there holding the coats of the executioners. Later, on his way to Damascus, he was blinded by lightening and fell off his horse. He saw Jesus and told him not to persecute Christians. For three days could not see. He was led to a servant of God in Damascus, St. Ananias, who restored his sight. He instantly converted to Christianity and went to become an apostle to the Gentiles.

How could Cohen know he wouldn't just be thrown in jail and deported as a madman? This was the thanks he would get for converting the Jews. Was Christ asking him to lay down his life, as He himself had done? Was He calling upon Cohen, who'd been a coward most of his life, to suddenly put his life on the line, to sacrifice everything in order to bring Christ's salvation to the Jews?

As dawn awoke on the mountain, Cohen opened the Book of Revelation and found consolation. In his vision St. John foretold in the Resurrection it would be the martyrs who had shed their blood in defence of their faith who would rise from the dead first and enter heaven.

Having discerned God's will to be a missionary in Israel, Cohen knew he would have to prepare himself for his ordeal ahead. He would need to become more knowledgeable about the Bible and to grow in prayer and the power of the Holy Spirit. He would need to put on the armour of God, the breastplate and shield, faith and hope, and be armed with the sword, the word of God, if he was to conquer his enemies.

Cohen would require the power of God to fulfil his mission, for the devil would try to thwart him at every turn, as he did Jesus in the wilderness. To try and win Jewish souls for Christ, he would not only contend with the Satan with but the state of Israel, for proselytising Christianity was a criminal offence punishable by jail and deportation.

As the sun began to rise over the mountain, he headed back to Jerusalem and to the French monastery. The monastery would strengthen him with prayer before he embarked on his mission.

And it would let him see Lucy again.

14

Cohen walked to the French monastery in the desert, about ten kilometres from Jerusalem, wading through the sand dunes and riverbeds in order to join the community.

His appearance was now more of an Orthodox monk with his beard and hair tied behind his head. As he walked across the harsh desert he was suddenly startled by a movement in a bush. Standing beside an olive tree was a gazelle.

Cohen had never seen a gazelle before, certainly not in the wild. He was struck by its beauty and sleek build with white stripes running down its back, and it stared right at him with large brown eyes glistening in the sun. Cohen stood motionless, looking apprehensively at its huge sharp antlers, and wondering whether or not he was on its territory, or if she was a mother defending her young. No sooner had it caught sight of Cohen than it took off and headed to the hills at lightning speed, bounding across the sand dunes and covering enormous distances with skipping movements. He was amazed at such speed.

The gazelle wasn't his only brush with wildlife that day. He made the mistake of laying his head on a large stone for rest when up popped a deadly scorpion he'd disturbed. Its tail was in the air, rattling and ready to strike, but like the fleeing gazelle, Cohen was up and gone before it could sting him with its deadly poison.

Climbing another hill he could see Jerusalem in the distance, and Mount Zion. Looking down across the valley, he could see the sheep and goats grazing on the hillside and the monastery he had left behind in Ein Karem.

Cohen was in tune with the perils of the desert, for death was never far away. He had grown to respect the desert, its climate and hazards from the Bedouin tribe. The harshness of the desert recalled how a priest and a party of about twenty pilgrims once went into the desert to experience solitude. All but one survived. They perished through dehydration, not having taken with them enough water bottles for the three-day trek, described in the holiday brochure as a wilderness experience.

Cohen's time with the Bedouin had taught him to respect the desert. Always carry sufficient water, if you were about to cross the desert. The young pilgrims who died had only taken a bottle of water with them, and few wore headscarves to protect them from the sun.

As Cohen climbed the hill he could in the distance the spire of St. John the Baptist, the monastery where the friars lived. The red roof of the monastery stood out from the white buildings like a beacon guiding pilgrims on their journey to Jerusalem.

Cohen edged his way down a steep embankment and crossed the dried-up riverbed. The dead fish were lying in the mud, the stench almost unbearable in the heat of the day. He climbed up the other side and hacked his way through thick undergrowth and brambles until he reached a signpost to the Monastery of St. John of the Desert.

He followed the path along a high ridge and could see the monastery built on the mountain, like the Greek monasteries on Mount Athos. It gave the appearance of hanging precariously over the cliff side, as though part of the monastery had been carved out of the side of the mountain. Not the place for any monk who suffered from vertigo, thought Cohen. It was something he was prone to throughout his life, but his experience of rock climbing in Israel had helped him as get over his fear of heights. As he approached the monastery, the building was perched on the side of a steep incline, and any lapse in concentration could result in instant death. Cohen stood outside the monastery gate, exhausted from his climb. It was now the middle of August, the temperature well over forty degrees, and sweat poured profusely from his body. He rang the bell and waited.

A tall bearded monk dressed in Orthodox robes eventually opened the gate. He looked at Cohen's dishevelled appearance, and mistaking him for a tramp, asked if he wanted any food. 'Thanks, but I've come to ask if I can stay at the monastery,' said Cohen. 'I've been staying at the Franciscan monastery in Ein Karem.'

'Come in,' said the monk. 'We are just about to have coffee in the refectory.'

Cohen followed the nimble-footed monk along a path as he tried to keep up. The monastery was built in three layers of buildings descending down the side of the mountain, each one connected by stone steps. The buildings were all painted white with red rooftops, which glowed in the sun. Glancing down the steps, he noticed a pond with large goldfish and water lilies. Cohen had never seen such an opulent monastery before. The sweet scent of multi-coloured blossom filled the air. It reminded him of *Lost Horizon*, a novel by James Hilton, about a monastery in the Tibetan mountains, where monks never aged. Cohen found it was spiritually enchanting, a fairy tale garden, and he felt at peace with the monastery and all its surroundings.

'Come inside,' said Father Samuel, entering the refectory. 'The brothers will be here in a few minutes.'

The refectory was simply furnished with a long wooden table with bench seats, a few icons on the walls, and a small reception for guests.

'Would you prefer tea?' asked Father Samuel. 'I can speak five languages and guess where you're from. You Englishmen are so polite,' he grinned, 'except when it comes to war. But let's not discuss it now – it will only lead to arguments.'

'Are you suggesting that the English are warmongers?' Cohen asked.

All of a sudden the refectory door and in walked several French monks asking what the padre was talking about.

'He's from England,' said Father Samuel, introducing Cohen to the monks.

'*Mon dieu*,' said one of the monks.

Father Samuel explained the history of the place, that the French monks came here twenty years ago looking for a monastery, inspired by Father John, the Spiritual Father, who wanted to break away from the Roman Catholic Church in France and form a French community in the Holy Land.

'He wanted to follow the Eastern rites of the church because he felt the West had been corrupted. Father John was disillusioned with the Catholics in France. He had formed a large community near Lyon and followed the Eastern rite. It was then he decided to come to Israel and discovered this monastery in the desert abandoned,' said Father Samuel proudly.

'Why was such a beautiful monastery abandoned?' exclaimed Cohen, incredulously. 'Where did the monks go?'

'Where did you say you had been staying?' Father Samuel asked.

'With the Franciscans,' replied Cohen. 'Why?'

'Before we came the friars were here,' said Father Samuel, laughing. 'They built this monastery because it's on the site of the cave where St. John the Baptist lived in the desert. The monastery was built as a shrine.'

'Heavens no!' exclaimed Cohen, flabbergasted. The monks sitting in the lounge drinking their coffee all laughed.

'It was too quiet for them, being friars,' said Father Samuel. 'They are used to being with people, with the crowd. So they leased it to us for a nominal fee. They were here for a good few years, but few pilgrims came to visit. It was too far out of their way. Tourists don't like the desert,' he said. 'So, why did you come to this monastery?'

'I'm on a pilgrimage to the Holy Land,' said Cohen.

Father Samuel looked quizzically at Cohen with his deep brown eyes. His appearance was that of an Orthodox monk, with his pronounced nose and beard and long hair tied behind in a bunch. 'How long did you to stay with the Franciscans?'

'About three months,' said Cohen.

'Who is the Spiritual Father there?' Father Samuel asked probingly.

Cohen felt he was being tested, for the priest must surely have known. The monastery was only a few kilometres away in Ein Karem. But the French had never trusted the English, thought Cohen, as far back as Napoleon.

'Padre Claudio,' replied Cohen instantly.

'Ah yes, I know of him,' said Father Samuel. 'He is a strong priest. Are you Jewish?'

'I am,' said Cohen, proudly.

'Shalom,' responded Father Samuel. 'Do you speak French?'

'I speak Hebrew.'

Father Samuel nodded and turned to the monks speaking in French.

Cohen gazed around the refectory, pondering his fate at the French monastery, the second monastery he had stayed at in the space of a few months. After the monks had finished their coffee, Father Samuel led Cohen to the chapel, a small white building next to the fishpond. Stepping inside, Cohen was reminded of a Greek Orthodox Church, resplendent with icons and candles, which he had visited on his pilgrimage to Jerusalem. There were pews either side of the chapel facing the aisle and bronze candle lamps hanging from the ceiling. As Father Samuel approached the altar he suddenly dropped to the marbled floor, prostrating himself. Astonished, Cohen hadn't seen a priest fall down in a display of faith before. 'Do you always do that?' he asked in a whisper.

'We follow the Eastern rite,' said Father Samuel. 'The monk always prostrates himself before the altar.'

'How is that different from the Roman Catholic Church?' Cohen asked.

'It is completely different. The Eastern rite has not changed since the time of Christ. It was how the early Christians worshipped, with true devotion and reverence,' said Father Samuel, again prostrating himself on the floor. 'It's also an act of penance. Now you try it.'

Cohen felt in need of penance. He dropped to the floor and stretched out his legs and arms. He felt the coolness of the marble floor against his skin, but little else. He prostrated again before following the priest out of the chapel to the courtyard.

Father Samuel turned on the hosepipe and began watering the plants around the chapel garden.

'How long were you thinking of staying?' Father Samuel asked, watering the evergreens.

'A couple months, if that's OK with you,' said Cohen.

Father Samuel nodded his approval, and carried on watering the garden.

'I would like do some voluntary work to earn my keep,' Cohen said.

'We always welcome volunteers,' said Father Samuel. 'There's a lot of work to do around here. We don't have many monks.'

'Thanks. What work would you like me to do?' said Cohen.

'Don't thank me, thank God,' said the priest. 'You can work tomorrow. Let me show you your room. It will soon be time for Vespers.'

Father Samuel led Cohen up a flight of steps where several monks' cells were nestled alongside a veranda. From there he had a breathtaking view of the valley below.

'This is where the monks' quarters are. You can have this room,' he said as he unlocked the door and handed Cohen the key. 'Vespers is at 6pm,' he said, before bowing and taking his leave.

Cohen remained outside, drawn to the view. He gazed out over the veranda across the valley and the expanse of the desert. In the distance he spotted an isolated cabin, possibly a hermitage of St. John the Baptist. He looked up at the sky, and saw an eagle soaring above the valley. He watched it glide in a wide arc looking for its prey. Suddenly the eagle swooped down for its kill, like the Nazis killed the Jews. He went to his room and lay on the bed, tired from a journey through the desert. He could feel the sand in his shoes. He looked around the room, which was Spartan with a washbasin and a few books. He decided to freshen up before Vespers and take a long, cool shower. One thing that struck Cohen about the French monastery – there were no women! Perhaps he'd come to the right monastery after all, where monks lived an ascetic life in an enclosed order, away from any temptations of the flesh.

At Vespers the monks sang in French in pews facing each other, taking it in turns to sing the verses of psalms, like in the tradition of the Greek monasteries. The monks had deep, resonant voices and their chanting was beautifully melodic. It reminded him of a medieval Gregorian chant he'd once heard.

Father Samuel, wearing a pillbox hat with a veil, began incensing the golden altar with the thurible in a slow and deliberate gesture. He then entered the chapel and swung the thurible before each monk, genuflecting as he did so. They, in turn, bowed reverently before the incense in a gesture of humility. The priest finished incensing the chapel, the triptych and the icons on the walls and returned to the altar. The chanting and the incense had a hypnotic effect on Cohen, but there was an air of joy to it, which elevated his soul and warmed his heart.

When the chanting had finished the monks suddenly prostrated themselves on the floor, their arms and legs fully outstretched on the marble. Some of the monks had difficulty getting back on their feet, as did Cohen. For it was not once or twice, but several times over that they repeated these prostrations in an act of penance. Cohen joined them in repeated prostrations. After several days of this form of worship it began to take its toll on his body. And it was not the only suffering he endured, for the French monks had further acts of penance lined up for him.

Cohen was ordered up on to the roof of the monastery to do some repairs. In the middle of summer it had soared forty degrees centigrade. He was given a tin of black paint and told to seal all the cracks on the roof. At first it didn't seem too arduous a task, but by midday the sun was blisteringly hot, and by the second day he had suffered sunstroke.

Cohen complained about the heat and the monks fell around laughing.

'What did you expect in the desert?' said one of the monks. 'You English have no backbone.'

Cohen stared at him indignantly. The monk looked to Cohen like a mad Viking with his red beard and long hair. He was surprised to learn later that he was the cook, a French chef, who served some of the most delightful cuisine.

The French monks loved their food, eating as many as five meals a day and their resident cordon bleu chef made sure they didn't go wanting, so much for fasting. The chef not only served choice starters and roast beef, but also trifles with strawberries and sliced oranges.

'You think it is hot?' the chef scoffed. 'The English are weak.'

'The English can cope with the heat,' Cohen retorted. 'We kicked Rommel out of out Africa, don't forget. We weren't called the Desert Rats for nothing.'

'How many times did Napoleon kick the English out of France?' the chef asked.

'We beat him at Waterloo,' said Cohen proudly.

On entering, Father Samuel intervened. He told the monks it was not the time for discussions of war.

It dawned on Cohen was more than just a coincidence that he was working on the roof of the monastery in the hottest months of the year. The monks had more work for him – dig the earth! His penitential task was to move tons of earth with just a spade and a wheelbarrow. It was a daunting task.

A mountain of soil had been delivered to the monastery, and had to be move to a trailer. The earth was spread out into a garden, deep enough for the plants and flower beds to be planted – all for the sake of a nun arriving from Bethlehem!

The great pile of earth had been dumped at the gate and had to be taken in the wheelbarrow to the trailer along a plank to negotiate stones. The stones were to be removed, stone by stone, before the earth was spread around the trailer.

By the second day Cohen felt exhausted.

Despite feeling that there was a French conspiracy to work him to death, Cohen saw the tasks as him getting his body in shape, and more importantly, an act of penance. Until he became a Christian he'd felt like he'd squandered most of his life drinking and carousing. Not the sort of life one would expect from a middle class educated Jew. But such is the distraction of youth.

Help came one day in the shape of a Russian immigrant, a stocky peasant from Siberia, whose wife had left him because of his drinking. He didn't speak English but while he was helping Cohen dig the earth he offered him a hat to shield him from the sun. Another day in the sun without protection and Cohen would have suffered sunstroke again.

After a few days of digging, he asked Father Samuel why the nun would stay at the monastery. 'She was living in Bethlehem as a hermit but she was attacked by an Arab youth with a knife. So the bishop felt it best if she came and stayed with monks who would protect her,' said Father Samuel.

'Someone attacked the nun with knife?' said Cohen, astounded.

'It wasn't the only attack. Here the monks have been threatened,' said Father Samuel. 'Come with me, I'll show you something,'

He led Cohen to the refectory and pointed to several splintered holes in the wall.

'Bullet holes,' he exclaimed. 'We were attacked here one night. Two men dressed in combat jackets climbed over the monastery wall. One of them grabbed me by the throat with a knife and held me up against the wall. He wanted to know where the other monks were. I pushed him away and ran to the refectory to warn the brothers. As I was running I tripped and fell. I heard a shot and the sound of a bullet whiz past my head. If I hadn't slipped, I wouldn't be here now. When I got to the refectory the monks had come out to see what the noise was. Then one of the gunmen stood at the top of the steps and started firing. He had a machine-gun and was spraying bullets at the refectory where the monks were. See, here, and there,' he said, pointing at the bullet holes in the wall. 'The Father Superior came out and ordered all the monks back inside the refectory. The gunman aimed his rifle to shoot him, but it jammed. It was a miracle. His life was spared, and no-one was hurt.'

'Who were these gunmen?' Cohen asked.

'Zionists, Jewish fanatics,' said the priest. 'They want all Christians out of Israel. We called the police but they weren't interested, even when I showed them the bullet holes,' said Father Samuel. 'They even tried to make out it was our fault.'

Cohen could not believe Christians were in such danger in the Holy Land.

'It's been like that for some time,' said Father Samuel, resigned.

'But why do they want Christians out?' Cohen asked, 'they've been since here since the time of Christ.'

'Fanatics don't want other religions here, just Judaism,' said the priest. 'Most Jews don't bother us. In fact, many come to visit us on Shabbat, the Jewish Sabbath.'

'Where is Father John now?' Cohen asked.

'He's in France, but he will be here next week,' said Father Samuel.

He took out an envelope from his pocket and handed it to Cohen. 'I've been asked to give you this.'

Cohen opened the enveloped. Inside were 300 shekels. 'It's from Sister Marie,' said Father Samuel, 'for the work you've done on the garden.'

Cohen was beginning to admire this nun especially after all she had been through in Bethlehem. It was rewarding to be paid for one's work.

'When is she arriving?' Cohen asked.

'Tomorrow afternoon,' said Father Samuel. 'Be on your best behaviour.'

His remark left Cohen somewhat uncomfortable. He wondered whether or not word had got back to the monks about his behaviour at the previous monastery.

Could Lucy have said anything about the affair, since she often visited the French monastery? He thought he'd put the incident behind him, but paranoia was beginning to mount as to whether the monks knew.

If Lucy had said anything it would be curtains. It would make his position at the monastery untenable, for he wouldn't be allowed to remain if they knew of his infidelity.

The week before, Father Samuel had given him permission to wear a robe in the chapel. It had given Cohen a renewed purpose for being there. 'You can go to Ein Karem this afternoon if you want,' said Father Samuel. 'But you can't wear the robe outside the monastery.'

Wearing the robe in the monastery had encouraged him to join the Community. It was more to conform to worship: the robe would blend in with the monks better than the dishevelled clothes he'd arrived in.

Cohen had become attached to his robe and was allowed to wear it in the chapel as well as in the refectory and the monastery grounds. After several weeks he'd grown a full length beard and his hair was longer, so he tied it in a bun behind his head, like the Orthodox monks. He now looked like part of the community to such a degree two Ethiopian women attending the Mass reverently bowed to him as they walked past. Such veneration by two beautiful women was making him feel important, a feeling of power - and all because of the robe!

He came down to earth when he read a Bible passage in which Christ warned the Pharisees of the vanity of parading in fine robes around the markets for attention.

However, Cohen felt upset that he wasn't allowed to wear the robe outside the monastery, especially when the women bowed again in front of him as they left the chapel. He felt the robe would give him some protection from the darker forces lurking outside the monastery.

Cohen went back to the monks' quarters and took a shower, ready to go to the village. He took the robe and hung it on the door and changed into his jeans and shirt. He would visit the bar this afternoon as it was hot and he needed a stiff drink.

It was the Jewish Sabbath and the pub was full, mostly with families enjoying the weekend.

A Jewish band was entertaining them outside on the lawn with Hebrew folk songs. Cohen found himself a quiet table and ordered a beer. He deserved it after the sweat and toil of working in the monastery. As he sipped his beer the bar boss came over and greeted him.

'Hi Mike,' he grinned, slapping on the back. 'Are you still playing chess?'

'No, I've been staying at the monastery,' said Cohen apologetically.

'What? You'll be lonely there – no women,' he chuckled. 'Listen, I want you to do me a favour. One of my waitresses, a Romanian, she can't get a visa to stay here. If you'll be willing to go ahead with an arranged marriage, she'll get a British passport and then she can stay in Israel. What you say? I'll send her over.'

Cohen was about to protest when a petite, raven-haired woman came over to his table and sat down. He had seen her before, serving meals in the restaurant. 'I'm Nina,' she said, her dark hair falling down to her slim waist. She brushed it from her face and, lowering her eyelids, leaned forward and whispered in his ear: 'I'm desperate. I have no visa to stay here and I won't go back to Romania. The country is poor. Jobs pay hardly anything, not enough to live on. If you help me get an arranged marriage I'll give anything you want.'

Cohen looked into her beautiful eyes, her soft raven hair falling onto her breasts. She had a certain gypsy quality to her looks, certain wildness in her black eyes, but he sensed her unhappiness. He didn't want to add to her misery by refusing an arranged marriage.

'Let me make some enquiry to the British embassy,' he said, holding her hand. 'Maybe we can arrange something. I can't promise.'

'I'd do anything if you got me a visa,' said Nina, in earnest.

Cohen gazed at her cleavage. Her breasts were large for a petite woman. 'You like?' said Nina, sticking out her boobs. She took his hand and placed it on one of her breasts.

'Very nice,' he said, touching her, but then promptly removing his hand for fear someone may have spotted his indiscretion.

'We can go up to my room, if you want?' Nina said, beckoning.

'Let me make some enquiries first,' said Cohen, rejecting her offer. He felt genuinely sorry for the poor girl, for he knew that Romania was facing hard times.

Nina got up to leave, the top of her stockings showing. He wondered if she was wearing suspenders, an item of lingerie Cohen always admired. If he married her, she was all his, he thought. But the idea of a *femme fatale* climbing into his bed made him fearful. He had to put all such temptation behind him. He now planned to be a monk and as such had to treat all women as either sisters or mothers.

Cohen never blamed himself for being tempted, for all men were tempted and it wasn't every day he got a proposal from a Romanian beauty. He paid for the bill and decided to explore further up the hill where he'd spotted a Russian convent a mile from the village.

It was a steep climb up the hill and the road was shrouded by overhanging trees. He passed an open field where he'd once met Fay.

He thought of her body lying next to him, naked and wanton in the grass, but the temptation passed.

Further up the hill he came to a gate, the entrance to the Russian convent. Cohen could hear in the distance the sound of music, the choir singing in Russian. He felt drawn to the music for he'd never heard a choir angelic as the nuns chanting the Russian Orthodox liturgy. He entered the convent grounds and walked along a narrow path past several white buildings with red turrets, a picture he'd seen in the Russia tourist guide. It was as though he was walking back in time to medieval Russia. In the distance he saw two elderly nuns, dressed in black and wearing veils. He approached them and asked where the chapel was.

'*Nyet,* no English,' said one of the nuns, pointing in the direction of a young nun walking towards the chapel. Cohen caught up with her and asked if he could visit the chapel.

She greeted with him with a warm smile, revealing two gold teeth near the front of her mouth. She spoke with perfect English and invited him into the chapel. She was strikingly beautiful, in her twenties, with high Slavonic cheekbones and dark brown eyes, a Russian woman that men would dream about. She went into the chapel, bowing, took a candle and crossed herself and said a prayer before the icon of the Mother of God. She nodded to Cohen and he felt compelled to do likewise. She handed him a long thin taper and lit it from her own candle. He bowed reverently. 'You can say a prayer before the icon,' she said, pointing.

Cohen picked up the candle, placed it next to the icon and said a prayer for his mother. He gazed in awe around the chapel. Such was the beauty and splendour of the building. Golden lamps hung from the ceilings and entire walls were covered in icons of silver and gold. The sweet smell of incense filled the chapel as he listened to the nuns in the choir chanting. He felt the presence of God as they sang soprano in perfect harmony, repeating choruses of Alleluias.

He felt a divine presence as the music transported him towards heaven, enraptured his soul. Amidst the congregation, Cohen was the only male present. The priest came in later and he envied the man's job. The thought of hearing nuns' confessions, all those intimate sexual fantasies, drove him mad. It was one of the arguments put forward for the ordination of women priests, that they shouldn't suffer the humiliation and embarrassment of having to confess their sexual needs to a male priest.

After the service, Sister Natasha introduced herself and invited Cohen into the refectory for tea. Several elderly nuns were sitting round a table and politely bowed their heads. Cohen wished he'd been allowed to wear his robe, for when the priest made his entrance all the nuns stood up and bowed to him before serving him the largest portion of cake.

Cohen told Sister Natasha that he was from England and had been converted in Israel that he was now at the French monastery. Sister Natasha said she was from Moscow, where she had first entered convent life. She was one of two sisters had been sent to the Holy Land to replace nuns who tragically died.

'What happened?' Cohen asked.

'They were mother and daughter who were sent to this convent by Moscow,' said Sister Natasha. 'Many years they stayed at this convent praying everyday in this chapel. But one morning, walking arm in arm to the chapel, they were attacked. A Zionist got into the convent and stabbed them in their backs.

It was awful. They both cried out to God to forgive him. They were buried side by side in the chapel cemetery.'

'My God,' exclaimed Cohen. 'How could such a wicked thing happen in a convent? Was he caught?'

'Yes. He was a Zionist from New York. He hated everyone who wasn't Jewish, especially the Christians,' said Sister Natasha. 'But he had mental problems.'

Cohen told Sister Natasha that the French monastery had suffered similar attacks from Zionists. 'Surely you can't feel safe staying here after what happened?' he asked.

'But we're Christians, we must learn to live with persecution,' the nun said. 'A wall has been built around the convent since then. The Holy Metropolitan Father in Moscow ordered the wall to be built. It cost a lot of money and it took a year to build. It's very high, as you can see. Christians have always been persecuted, even by the Jews, and still are to this day, as our martyred nuns bear witness,' Sister Natasha said.

Cohen felt aggrieved at the persecution of the nuns by the Jews.

Why this crime against Christians by the Jewish nation, Israel, God's chosen people?

Sister Natasha looked frail and vulnerable as she spoke. He wanted to reach out and touch her, tell her everything would be all right, that all things work out for the best for those that love God. But he felt anger and rage that such an evil person could do such a thing, destroy the lives of two innocent nuns, mother and daughter, at a convent. It was unspeakable that such wickedness could prevail in the Holy Land. But look what they did to Jesus.

Was the world going mad? Cohen asked. Why these acts of wickedness, and savagery, carried out in a convent, of all places? It made him question why God would allow such evil acts against his servants.

Later, when Cohen met a holy man from Russia, a starets, he came to understand some of the ways and mysteries of God. The starets told him: 'In a world where people are not taught the way of the cross, patience in times of adversity will decrease, and frustrations and outbursts of violence will increase. God does not spare his people from tribulations, which the world brings upon itself through the sins of disbelief and disobedience to the commandments of Christ. Be warned, my son, we are approaching another age of martyrdom and we must prepare for it, to die for Christ. These nuns who were martyred knew the dangers of coming here. They did not die in vain: they died as martyrs in the Christ. Martyrdom means witnessing. We must as Christians be ready for it.'

Cohen meditated over the words of wisdom of the starets. One feeling pervaded in him, his desire to pray for the nuns!

'Can you show me their graves?' he asked. Sister Natasha took him into the garden and across the courtyard. At the back of the convent there was a small cemetery. She led him to the graves, mother and daughter buried side by side. Cohen knelt beside the graves and began to pray. He glanced up at the headstones and repeated their names.

'May they rest in peace and rise in glory,' he prayed.

Sister Natasha asked why he'd wanted to pray for them when he didn't know them.

'Because I believe it's only through prayer that the evil and wickedness of this world will be overcome,' Cohen said.

'And love,' she answered, wiping away a tear from her face as she knelt beside him at the graves. She had brought two roses from the garden and laid them side by side on the tombs, praying softly in Russian.

As they walked back to the chapel, Cohen asked: 'Are you going to stay here? Did you ever consider being a wife, a mother?'

'Why do you ask such a question?' Sister Natasha frowned. 'I am a nun. I have taken my vows. Life is hard, but life is hard everywhere, even in Moscow. Wherever you go there is a cross to bear. I am happy here. I have the elderly nuns to look after. I have God, what more do I need?'

Cohen admired her courage and faith. He realised he had a long way to go before he could reach her spiritually. Being Jewish, he had an intuitive understanding of women. In many ways they were the stronger sex, and Sister Natasha had an inner strength. They were survivors. They kept the family together under extreme hardship, even in wars. Looking into Sister Natasha's dark brown eyes he felt that Russian women, too, were strong. They had suffered greatly in the Second World War, and some Russian women even fought on the front lines against the Nazis.

'You have family in Moscow,' said Cohen. 'Is there anything I can do?'

'They get by,' Sister Natasha said, holding back tears.

It was getting late and he felt he should be going. She walked him to the gates and said farewell by kissing him on the cheeks, as was the Russian custom. Cohen felt soft lips on his cheeks, his first kiss by a Russian nun.

'It was a pleasure to meet you sister,' Cohen said, 'although it was sad to visit the graves of the nuns. I shall pray for them at Vespers.'

'You must come and visit again sometime. We have Mass every morning,' she said smiling.

'I will,' he promised. Walking away, he turned and said, spontaneously: 'Sister Natasha, you're so graceful and beautiful.'

She half smiled and turned away in embarrassment, her cheeks blushing as she walked back to her convent.

'I've been kissed by a Russian nun. What man can say that?' said Cohen proudly, as he set off for the French monastery.

Back at the monastery, Father Samuel greeted him and asked if he had a driving licence.

'Yes, but it's British,' said Cohen, bemused.

'That's OK. You can drive in Israel with it,' said Father Samuel. 'The monastery dog has to be put down. You will have to take him to the vets the other side of town.'

The news saddened Cohen. He'd grown fond of the dog over the few weeks he'd been there and often took it for walks in the woods surrounding the monastery.

'Why has the dog got to be put down?' asked Cohen.

'He's got tumours,' replied Father Samuel.

'Can't they operate on him?'

'Too expensive,' said the priest. 'The monastery can't afford it.'

'I'll pay,' said Cohen.

'Waste of money, he's on his last legs,' said Father Samuel. 'Brother Paul is in charge. He's coming with you. Just make sure you bring the car back in one piece,' he demanded. 'One monk has already put a dent in the wing.'

Cohen and Brother Paul set off for the vet's surgery with the sick dog in the back seat. They drove through the West Jerusalem suburbs and into an affluent housing estate before pulling up outside the surgery.

The lady vet came out and Brother Paul asked if she could give the lethal injection in the car. The vet agreed, so the monk opened the car boot and got the dog and laid it on its side. Cohen refused to watch and walked away. He waited by a tree and could hear the dog howling as he was put down. They drove back with the dead dog in the boot.

Brother Paul, on seeing Cohen distressed by the incident, told him of how he once had to put down a donkey.

'I cut his throat,' said the monk, 'put him out of his suffering.'

He was upset by Brother Paul's ghastly experience. Cohen felt convinced that the French were no different to the Spanish in cruelty to their animals. That evening Cohen helped bury the dog in the garden next to its kennel. Alone in his cell, he prayed for the two dead nuns and the dog. He thought about his own death and how short life was. He remembered the words of Tolkien, who described death as an 'unacceptable violation', and thought how he too would be put into the ground like the dog and have earth shovelled over him.

Ashes to ashes, dust to dust. The sorrow of life and the injustice of death overwhelmed him. He wept into his pillow before going to sleep.

15

The following morning Sister Marie arrived from Bethlehem and Cohen felt the full force of her presence. Unknown to him she'd come with plans for her garden, and knew exactly where she wanted the earth dumped. 'Not over there, here,' she said, admonishing Cohen.

It was a sweltering day and after unloading four wheelbarrows of earth, he desperately asked for a cup of water.

'But you've had one already,' she said, in a matronly tone. She had obviously come from a remote region of Judea where water was scarce. Living as a hermit, one had to carry jugs long distances. Cohen felt it best not to argue over a cup of water. He'd rather go without it and keep the peace. But next time he'd bring a bottle of water with him. There was a steely toughness under Sister Marie's habit, no doubt acquired from her hermit life. Here was a frontier woman who knew how to take care of herself, and even though she was attacked by the Arab, she remained undaunted. She had the reputation of an iron fist in a velvet glove, and it crossed Cohen's mind that with her abrupt manner she may have provoked the stabbing incident in the first place.

One of the first tasks she ordered was to erect a huge fence around her trailer to prevent visitors wandering onto her property. 'I'm a recluse, and the public have no right to enter,' she said indignantly.

Despite all her years as a hermit, Sister Marie had much to learn about humility. He wondered whether she became a recluse to get away from people. Not the sort of charity one would expect from a consecrated nun. Then again, she had paid him for moving the earth, sending him money before she even arrived at the monastery. So there had to some good in her all the same, he thought. In fact, not long after settling into her hermitage, Sister Marie invited Cohen inside her trailer to look at some of her art. He expressed an interest in art and she showed him some of her icons.

'I've always painted icons. The money I get from my paintings means I can support myself without placing a burden on the church,' she said proudly.

Cohen admired her work. The icons were detailed, and vivid colours filled the whole of the canvas. He asked what medium she used. 'Egg mixed with oil,' Sister Marie said, 'a technique from the Russian icon masters.'

She was still painting an exquisite icon of Mary with the baby Jesus, and Cohen admired the technique. Icons were the most difficult form of painting and took patience and skill. She'd been painting much of her life and been schooled in Russian's icon painting. Cohen found his opinion of her changing as he delved into her background. She had an Interior Design degree and the trailer was spotless with icons displayed on the walls. Before leaving, he asked if he could buy one of her paintings.

Unfortunately, she said, she only worked on commission and was behind in her work, with all the upheaval leaving Bethlehem.

'I will consider it when I have settled in,' said Sister Marie thoughtfully.

The following day, Cohen met another artist in the community, Brother Jose. He'd been in the community for ten years but hadn't taken his final vows. One of the reasons he hadn't made a life-long commitment was because he was Mexican, not French. He had come to the Holy Land to be nearer to God.

Brother Jose's studio was next to the entrance to the monastery, above a workshop where Father Samuel made wooden crosses to sell to the tourists. He painted huge religious paintings, and Cohen was taken to a church where Brother Jose had a commission, a large painting of St. John the Baptist, above the altar. Cohen was awed by the sheer scale of the work. It was along the entire length of the wall, a backdrop to the altar, and vivid colours gave it life.

It was tempting for Cohen to stay at the monastery and be taught by these two icon painters, but he knew the Lord was calling him towards the greater use of his talents, a more radical direction – to bring the Jews to Christ.

Cohen spent an afternoon with Brother Jose in his studio, watching him at work and learning his technique. He felt he had something in common with the painter, not being accepted by the community, not being French. They were outsiders.

Cohen himself was becoming increasingly disillusioned in the monastery because he found it racist and self-serving, the very things Christ taught to overcome. Just how prejudiced the French were, and the Greeks also, he would find out to his peril.

But there was a monk who came to the monastery one day that changed his outlook. He was a Russian starets, Father Nicholas, a holy man in charge of a monastery near Moscow. He had come to Israel to help the thousands of Russians who had immigrated to the Holy Land. Within a year more than 10,000 Russian Jews had been allowed to settle in Israel.

Cohen met Father Nicholas in the refectory, sitting opposite him. While they were eating, they both looked at each other and the starets gave him a smile. He knew from those brown eyes that penetrated you that he was looking at a holy man. Staring into those mystical eyes, Cohen knew that he was like Jesus, radiating a pure love. He was forced to look away, for there was sin was in his heart.

On walking through the woods the next day he met the starets and greeted him with a holy kiss. They embraced each other and the love he gave was like the love King David had for Brother Jonathan, better than the love of a woman. He was sad to see the starets leave. For in the short time he'd been at the monastery, he'd radiated such love in the community, a spontaneous, natural love for one another, which the French monks lacked.

Having finished the backbreaking work in the garden, Cohen got permission to visit the village again. It was time to see Sister Natasha. At the convent it was a feast day for the one of Russia's greatest saints, St. Seraphim, a starets, who lived in the wilderness with wild animals he tamed.

He was much loved in Russia and died in a convent surrounded by devoted nuns.

After the mass, Cohen met Sister Natasha and told her of his discontent with the French monastery, that it was time for him to move on and serve the Lord in meaningful work. 'There is a home for handicapped children next to our convent,' said Sister Natasha. 'It is run by the St. Vincent de Paul nuns. They are always looking for volunteers. I'm sure the monastery would let you work a couple of days a week. It is the Lord's work.'

Cohen thought about her suggestion. It was time for him to go and he thanked her for helping him out. He kissed her on the cheeks and whispered: 'I'll miss you.' He walked back across the valley and decided he would volunteer to help the children. It would be a new experience for him, until he was certain of his mission. He'd had very little experience with handicapped children. It was important, especially for Christians, for Christ revered children, telling his disciples: '*Unless you become like of these children, you will not enter the Kingdom of God.*' It was important too, to spend more time with them and bring out the joy and spontaneity we often stifle in adulthood.

Father Samuel agreed that working part-time at the children's home was a blessing, and the next day Cohen made an appointment to see the nursing sister in charge.

Sister Norma was a Philippine nun in her late forties, who had joined the convent in her teens. Seven nuns from the St. Vincent de Paul, a Roman Catholic charity dedicated to the poor, ran the children's home. 'Have you worked with handicapped children before?' Sister Norma said. 'I ask because most of the children here are severely handicapped.'

'My cousin is disabled,' said Cohen. 'I can work with kids.'

Sister Norma, with dark brown eyes and high cheekbones, escorted Cohen on a tour of the three-storey home. He was shocked to see so many helpless young children in wheelchairs. They could barely move, having lost the use of their limbs, and spent the rest of the day in cots or in a chair. Most of the children suffered from cerebral palsy, a brain condition from birth. Many had been abandoned by their mothers because they couldn't cope. The experience of seeing such helpless children had a humbling effect on Cohen. Sarah, in her teens, was the only child who could walk, but the care home was short-staffed and had no-one to take her on walks. Sister Norma explained the girl needed regular exercise to strengthen her leg muscles otherwise they could atrophy.

Cohen immediately volunteered. At first, he took her round the grounds of the home and later into the village, where he would spoon-feed her ice cream, her favourite treat. She still had no control over her arms or facial muscles and occasionally would go into spasms.

At the restaurant Cohen met the Romanian waitress, Nina. She asked him if Sarah was his daughter, and whether he was married.

'No, Sarah lives in the children's home,' he explained. 'I'm just taking her for a walk.'

'Did you ring the consulate?' she asked anxiously.

'I did,' replied Cohen. 'I'm afraid I can't marry you. I would have to prove I could support you if we went back to England. I can't do that. I've packed in my job to come here.'

'That's a pity,' sighed Nina, 'I was looking forward to getting married. Thanks for trying. It's good you're looking after the children. You'll make a good father.'

Nina got up to leave and kissed Cohen goodbye. He felt sorry for the waitress and wished he could have helped her. But it would have been against his religion to go through an arranged marriage, for he firmly believed now that marriage was a sacred act before God, a sacrament of the church. So many people from poor countries were displaced, rootless and unhappy, even in Israel. All around him he witnessed so much suffering and sorrow.

Cohen took Sarah by the hand after she'd finished her ice cream, and led her up the hill toward the home. He stopped to wipe some ice cream from her mouth, and looked into her innocent eyes. She was beautiful, her red ruby lips and long black hair flowing down to her waist, her eyes crystal clear. But there was something missing in her life, this one imperfection tragically cutting her off from the world – she couldn't speak. She couldn't communicate or tell people how she felt. She could not express her inner pain.

Cohen felt sad for her. He felt the pain of isolation, the deep wound, and the hurt of being abandoned by one's parents. He picked her up and hugged her, carrying her up the hill as she lay quietly in his arms. In the few weeks he'd cared for her he never once heard her cry. At the top of the hill he took a rest in the field. He sat her down and looked into her deep brown eyes as she stared up at the sky. Cohen admired her beauty. He thought of Mary, the mother of Jesus, of how she would have looked at such a tender age. Sarah must be as beautiful as Mary. As she lay in the grass he watched her looking into his eyes, then leaned over to her and kissed her on the mouth, an innocent kiss, but one full of love. She looked into his eyes and tears welled up, the joy of a young girl being kissed for the first time. It made her feel loved and wanted and she smiled for the first time. She would raise her arms up and smile as he entered the ward, for he represented what little freedom there was to get away from the care home and go for a walk. Trapped as she was in her disabled body, her spirit would soar to the sun.

'You believe in God?' asked a young doctor who was visiting the care home. 'How can God allow this to happen to innocent children?'

Cohen, inspired by scripture, said: 'Their suffering will be turned into glory; they will reign in heaven with God's angels. There will be no suffering, no more tears; they will be with the angels. Death comes to us all. It is the sin of this world, ever since the Fall. But thanks be to God we can look forward to a new life, a life resurrected in Christ. These children will inherit everlasting life, and like the martyrs, they will be the first to enter heaven, for they have suffered as Christ suffered.'

The doctor stared at Cohen, shrugged, and walked away. Cohen could see the disbelief in his eyes, his lack of faith. Yet this doubting doctor would carry out mercy work in caring for these children. Perhaps one day the doctor would come to Christ, but like most Jews he regarded him as a minor prophet.

During his visit to Jerusalem he met an artist who invited him to see his studio and his paintings. He was elderly and content with life, for he had exhibitions all over the world. Cohen spent time looking round his studio, admiring the work, mostly large canvasses depicting Jewish life in the villages, where he often went to sketch.

His paintings reminded him of Marc Chagall, a Russian Jewish artist. He painted peasants at work, children at play, Jewish weddings, men praying at synagogues and women weeping at funerals. 'You have a love in your art,' said Cohen. 'Have you thought about death, your own death?'

'What is the point?' replied the artist. 'When you're dead, you're dead.'

'Then you don't believe in an afterlife?' Cohen asked.

'Nobody came back from the dead to tell us about it.'

'Jesus did,' said Cohen. 'He rose from the dead. He is alive.'

There was no response from the artist, though he added upon Cohen's departure that Jesus was a minor prophet.

Cohen had an hour in which to take Sarah back to the care home, so he decided to take her to visit the Russian convent further up the hill. Holding her hand he led her through the convent gate. As they walked along a path she let go of his hand and he continued towards the chapel. As he turned round he caught Sarah play-acting. She was bent upside down looking at him through her legs. It would have seemed comical but for her condition. He wondered if she would have performed such a feat had she been born normal. There was no doubt she got pleasure from looking at the world upside down. She was giggling.

Cohen smiled. It was the first time he'd seen her laugh, a blessed moment for a child who had suffered so much. Such was her joy that she couldn't resist performing another feat, this time in the chapel. It did not go down well with an old grumpy nun, face full of thunder. She grabbed Sarah's arm and started shaking and scolding her in Russian, which the poor child did not understand. Sarah started to cry. Cohen leapt to Sarah's defence. He was furious with the nun. He told her the girl was disabled and to leave her alone. Sister Natasha stepped into the fray and asked Cohen to take the girl outside for a while. She followed them outside the chapel and sat beside Cohen and the girl on the bench.

'Why were you upset with the elderly nun?' Sister Natasha asked.

'She shouldn't have a go at the girl. She's disabled,' remarked Cohen.

'What's wrong with her?'

'She suffered brain damage at birth. She can't talk, she got cerebral palsy.'

Sister Natasha admired Cohen for caring of the child. 'I see you love children. Would you like to have children one day?'

'Yes,' Cohen joked, 'with you.'

Sister Natasha, being Russian, did not share the sense of humour. She sprang to her feet, cheeks blushing and she yelled:

'I'm a nun! How dare you! I've made my vows,' said Sister Natasha, furiously.

Adjusting her habit, she stormed off back to the chapel.

Cohen looked at Sarah. She was bent over staring at the sky, upside down.

It was time to go and take Sarah home.

16

Cohen arrived at the French monastery to find Father Samuel admonishing Brother Jose for having been discourteous to Sister Maria. 'You must not speak to the sister like that again,' said Father Samuel sternly.

Brother Jose had a Mexican temper and Cohen quickly gained the sense that he had a distrust of women, especially in the religious community. He had a dislike of Sister Maria at the monastery. It was self-evident that he was a misogynist. 'Religious women are all crazy,' said Brother Jose. 'They should not be here. This is a monastery; women should be in a convent.'

Cohen was beginning to understand why Brother Jose had not yet taken his vows as a monk. Father Samuel had not asked him to take the vows, for he had doubts whether he would stay in the community. It was not long before the hot-bloodied Mexican lashed out at Cohen. It was over the new Alsatian the monastery had acquired after the old dog was put down. Cohen had taken the Alsatian out for walks, much to the anger of Brother Jose, who felt it his task to train the dog. He spotted Cohen out with the dog, straining at the collar, and was furious.

'You will not take the dog out again,' ordered the monk. 'The animal has to be trained properly,' he raged. Ripping a twig from a bush, he viciously whacked the dog on the nose, making it cower and whine in pain. 'That's how to stop it straining on the leash,' he shouted.

Cohen knew the Mexicans and Spanish had a reputation for mistreating animals. It was in their blood. He once witnessed bulls killed in a Barcelona bullfight. He'd never forgotten the cruel manner in which they were disposed of and how proud and arrogant the matadors stood in the ring after slaying the bulls, while they had been practically hacked to death by the picadors on horses.

Cohen felt a special bonding with the Alsatian by playing in the woods. He would throw the ball and have the dog return it for another throw. But that was a thing of a past. Now the dog had a new owner.

Brother Jose never spoke to Cohen again, nor Sister Marie. Cohen was given another job at the monastery, helping Father Samuel make wooden crosses, sold to tourists. He was assigned to a workbench next to the priest and had to sandpaper the crosses smooth and varnish them. One afternoon, as Cohen sanded down the crosses, Father Samuel told him that if he was going to stay at the monastery, he would have to learn French. Cohen had practised learning French, but Father Samuel gave up on the idea because of his lack of progress, being English, meant that languages were not his forte.

Father Samuel told him, that before he became a monk he was considering a religious life in his last year of school. 'When I told the teacher, girls started to cry,' chuckled the priest. There was no question that he would have broken a girl's heart by going into the monastery.

'I chose not to get married because if I had wanted one woman, I would have wanted them all,' he said, laughing. 'It's dangerous.'

But there was another side of Father Samuel that was not so humorous. Cohen discovered Brother Jose wasn't the only monk with a temper. Upon examining the crosses Cohen had produced one afternoon, Father Samuel flew into a rage because one of the crosses had not been finished properly, at least not according to his perfectionist standard. He later had the grace to apologise for his remark.

'Sorry, I should not have lost my temper. But the tourists spend a lot of money here and we have to make sure they are satisfied with what they buy. We don't want them to go away with an imperfect cross, you understand.'

It surprised Cohen just how humble some of the monks could be when they at fault, and how they would immediately apologise. He put it down to the grace of God, for in the monastery the monks would come together to confess what they called a Chapter of Faults, a sin could harm the community. Cohen knew that some of these faults people would hardly have given a thought to, least of all having caused offence, such as banging the door, ringing the bell late for the start of a service, and other innocuous sins.

The next day Father Samuel knocked on the cell door and asked if he would like to see the cave of St. John the Baptist. 'It's why this monastery was built as a shrine to John the Baptist.' said Father Samuel, smiling. 'He was a forerunner.'

Cohen followed the priest along a footpath and down a winding staircase by the side of the mountain. He came within a foot of the edge of the precipice, and several times he feared for his life, not having gotten over his vertigo. 'Here is the cave,' said Father Samuel, pointing in the direction, much to Cohen's relief. Cohen stood in awe at the entrance to cave where St. John the Baptist had prayed in the desert. He followed the priest inside and instantly felt the presence of the Holy Spirit. He fell to his knees, for he was in the holy place. He knelt in silence before God.

Then out of the cave came a voice calling him: 'Go out to my people and tell that about my son, called Jesus.' Cohen looked up and saw the body of Christ, at the far end of the cave, tortured and crucified. Was he redeeming the world through all its suffering, wars, and death?

Cohen remembered all those troops who fought in the Second World War and were never coming home. He knew that the German air force had bombed London by night and day in the Blitz and had dropped bombs on Buckingham Palace. On seeing the wreckage, King George VI and the Queen Mother walked with the wounded in the East End of London. Cohen thought suffering was everywhere, even in Russia, losing twenty-five million of their population in its war against Germany. History would never forget the bravery of the Russians forces in holding Stalingrad, the turning point of the war. More than 250,000 Germans were captured.

Like Napoleon, Hitler failed in invading Russia and had to abort the attack on England. He underestimated the harsh Russian winter and the German army had to withdraw. Thousands died on the march back to Berlin, as did Napoleon's troops on their retreat to France.

But the Russians, who had suffered so much death and destruction, did not learn from that experience. They inflicted the same horrific crimes on the Germans. The Germans were starved to death, and advancing Russian soldiers raped about 100,000 women in Berlin.

Suffering would continue to exist as long as man's inhumanity to man continued. Wars would happen unless man turned to God, to love his neighbour. Cohen prayed for peace and an end to wars. He called out for John the Baptist to come to his aid.

There was a moment of silence, and then a vision came to him, as if he was being transported to another place. At the end of the cave, sitting with his head in his hands, was the John the Baptist. He had long hair and beard and was wearing a camel skin coat and crying out to God.

And the Lord said: 'You are the chosen prophet and I am sending you out into the world to proclaim that Christ is the Saviour.' Falling on his hands and knees, John the Baptist cried out: 'Lord, do it unto me.' With that, John the Baptist disappeared.

Father Samuel looked at Cohen lying prostrate on the cave's floor, weeping like a child, and asked if he was all right.

'I saw John the Baptist.' Cohen exclaimed, pointing at the corner of the cave.

'We all have revelations,' Father Samuel explained. 'It's best you forget them,' he said indifferently.

Cohen knew in his heart he had seen John the Baptist and talked with him, an unforgettable vision. He questioned Father Samuel and why he was so sceptical of his revelation.

He got to his feet and followed the priest out of the cave and back up the mountain. As they reached the monastery Father Samuel told him that the brothers were few in numbers, and that he would like him to start cooking for the community.

'Brother Simon will show you how to cook for the French monks, but remember: it has to be perfect,' said Father Samuel.

Cohen did as he was told and entered the kitchen. Brother Simon was there, with a long beard and red hair, about to cut up the vegetables. He showed him how to prepare cooked snails, one thing the French loved, and how to make strawberry flans, another specialty. But Cohen was taken aback when the chef gave him the keys to the wine cellar and asked him to fetch four bottles of wine for supper. He took the keys and made his way to the cellar. It was stocked with the finest of French wines, and he chose the best wines from the top shelf and took them back to the kitchen. The chef complimented him on his choice.

The next day Cohen was alone in the kitchen. Brother Simon was off to Jerusalem and he would have to serve all the meals, dessert, and make the monks' coffee. It was a tall order.

Cohen decided that instead of the usual French cuisine he would serve the monks an English menu, with heaps of shepherd's pie with wine. He brought four bottles of wine from the cellar, and by lunch he had drunk a bottle all to himself. By pouring wine into the pie, he was sipping it all to himself.

That evening, as he was tipsily serenading himself in his cell to a tape of the monks chanting, all hell broke loose. Brother Simon with his red hair flaming burst into the cell snatched the tape recorder out of his hands and bellowed in French as he slammed the door.

In the morning, Father Samuel knocked on his door and asked Cohen to leave the monastery immediately. 'You're drunk, monks shouldn't behave like that' said Father Samuel, sternly.

He kissed Cohen on the cheek, in the way Judas kissed Jesus, gave him a reference for one of the monasteries, and bade him farewell.

Cohen considered it a blessing in disguise. He'd had enough of the French, their idiosyncratic ways and their dislike of the English. But being told to leave a second monastery, not long after being ejected from the first monastery, had a profound effect on Cohen. For Father Samuel had become a friend, taking him to Bethlehem and to the Chapel of the Nativity, where Christ was born in a stable. He felt not only rejected but deeply wounded. He packed his bag in disgust and left for Ein Karem, taking the robe with him.

Cohen wanted to say goodbye to Sister Norma and disabled Sarah, as he had plans to travel north. There was another reason for wanting to see the nun again. During the time he looked after the children, he'd been attracted to her. When seeing her he was sad to be leaving the village with such a heavy heart. He told her it was God's calling to leave Jerusalem and go to Galilee, where the Lord walked and prayed. He felt a desperate need for solitude. He wanted to go back into the wilderness and be with alone God, albeit for a short time.

Cohen knew he couldn't survive in the desert for too long, unlike the Jews of the past who spent forty years in the wilderness. God fed them manna's from heaven, and the odds of that happening to Cohen were a snowball's chance in hell.

On parting, Cohen kissed Sister Norma on her cheeks. Her dark eyes turned sad as he said farewell. He turned to Sarah, and smiled. 'Goodbye my little one,' he said, hugging her.

17

As Cohen left Ein Karem his heart was full of sadness. He thought he would never see Norma or Sarah or the village again. He took the bus to Jerusalem, intending to head for Nazareth and to spend time near the Sea of Galilee, to walk in the mountains as Jesus did before calling his disciples.

At Jerusalem bus station he waited in the queue for a bus to Nazareth, and there was a sudden deafening explosion. People screamed and dived for cover in all directions.

The bomb went off in a bus a few hundred yards away, but he was horrified by what had happened. Alarm bells sounded as ambulances and police screeched to a halt, attending to those in need. Cohen was unhurt. A bearded man in his eighties, directly in front of Cohen, began shouting: 'Let the Palestinians have what they want. Give them whatever they want just leave us alone in peace.'

The man was beside himself with grief, sobbing into his hands. The suffering was too much. He fell to his knees pleading with God to let the Jews live in peace.

A middle-aged woman helped him to his feet and scolded him. 'Get up and be a man. These terrorists can't destroy us. God put us here. It's our land.'

The bomb had almost deafened Cohen. He became disorientated and feared for the Jews. Women in the street were wailing.

It was carnage.

He wanted to help but he felt too shocked, appalled and disorientated to know what to do: and besides it was obvious that the emergency services were doing what needed doing.

So this was how God's chosen people were being forced to live tormented, persecuted, their children slaughtered before their very eyes, blown to bits, with suicide bombers sucking the blood and heart out of Israel?

Where was God's mercy in all this? Surely this was too much to bear for his chosen people? Yet still the bombings continued. Teenagers blown up at discos, the elderly bombed, weddings, children bombed on buses and in the marketplaces.

The slaughter of the innocents.

18

The shock and horror of the bomb made Cohen delay his trip to Nazareth.

He was fearful of travelling on the bus, as they had been subject to recent bombings. He walked out of the bus station, where the wounded were being taken to the ambulances, and headed for the Judean hills. He crossed into East Jerusalem and climbed to the top of Mount of Olives, where he spent a night in prayer.

Cohen was homeless and penniless again. He had given what money he had to the children's home. His only possession was the robe, along with a few socks. As he climbed the mountain discerning God's will, he heard a voice telling him to put the robe on and go preach the salvation of Christ to the Jews.

He remained on the mountain top praying until dawn broke. Convinced he was obeying God's will, he set out down the mountainside and headed back to Jerusalem, boldly wearing the Orthodox robe.

As he entered the Holy City his appearance caused commotion among the market traders. Arab youths taunted him, for Cohen was dishevelled, his hair and beard had grown considerably, instead of the neat bun tied behind his head, was left unkempt falling down over his shoulders. He looked like a wild prophet, a modern day John the Baptist, crying in the wilderness.

Cohen ignored the taunts and whistles as he walked past into West Jerusalem and into the Ben Yuhuda plaza, where

Jews were seated at tables celebrating the Shabbat, the Jewish Sabbath.

He noticed a man on crutches begging on the street. People ignored him as they passed by. He felt compassion for the beggar and approached him. The beggar told him he was a Jew who'd come to Israel from Canada, and that he had to get back to Vancouver for an operation on his legs. He'd been refused the operation in Israel because he couldn't afford it, but in Canada he had medical insurance. He needed the airfare to get back to Vancouver.

Cohen told him to trust in God, that if he prayed, the Lord would heal him. At this the beggar tore at his clothes, and foaming at the mouth, raised one of his clutches to strike a blow at Cohen.

'Missionaries,' he screamed, 'we don't want missionaries here. Get out.' His outburst caused a commotion in the plaza. People were gathering round the beggar asking if he was alright. Someone had called the police and Cohen was shoved against the wall. The policeman arrived and asked him for his I.D. He showed him his British passport. 'You're from England?' said the cop. 'You should know better than coming here and upsetting people.'

The policeman let him go but not without a warning. 'If we get another complaint about you you'll be arrested, you understand,' the policeman snarled.

Cohen left the plaza humbled and headed for the Old City. He realised his mistake in preaching to the beggar. Before setting out to preach, he should have received a blessing from God, crucial to his mission. He headed for the Holy Sepulchre, the tomb of Christ, the place where the Lord was crucified.

Here, at the holiest shrine for Christians, he hoped to receive a blessing. Journeying into the Christian quarter of Jerusalem, he mingled with hundreds of pilgrims making their way to the Holy Sepulchre. But on entering it he was taken aback by the lack of reverence. Few people got down on their knees and prayed. It was more like a museum full of tourists, arguing where to go next, to the Catholic shrines or the Greek ones, to the Coptic shrines or the Russian Orthodox icons.

Cohen experienced the mayhem that greeted Christ in the temple at Jerusalem, the bedlam of moneychangers, merchants selling doves, and traders peddling wares. Everywhere he turned there were trinkets, posters, beads, rosaries, books and candles for sale. It was in that synagogue, the holiest of holies, he understood Christ's anger and why he lashed out, upturning the tables and taking a whip to the merchants.

'Thou shall not turn my Father's house into a den of thieves.' said Jesus.

Deep down Cohen sensed the Lord's frustration. He felt there was only one to do – to give up all his possessions. He would obey the Commandment of Christ to give up everything and follow him. It was what Jesus told the rich man, who asked what he should do to inherit eternal life, even though he already obeyed all of the commandments.

'One thing more you must do, sell all you have and give it to the poor.' said Jesus. 'It is easier for a camel to pass through the eye of a needle than for a rich man to enter the Kingdom of God.' The rich man, on hearing it, walked away.

Cohen left his rucksack on the seat and went to pray in Christ's tomb. The rucksack contained all his worldly possessions: a few clothes, a flask, a hairbrush, his diary, his passport and socks. He joined the queue to enter the Holy Tomb, the place where

Christ was buried after He was taken down from the cross, the deposition. It was here that Mary Magdalene found the stone, which had been removed from the cave, and two angels sitting on either side of the resurrected Christ.

'He is Risen!' said one of the angels. She later found Jesus in the garden, mistaking Him for the gardener.

The Holy Tomb was concealed in a vault, and Cohen stooped low to enter. He knelt down before the marble tomb and prayed for God to bless his mission. The vault was so small that only one person could enter at a time, and he found himself alone beside the tomb of the Lord. He prayed in despair, for he felt the agony of Christ in his heart, the desolation He must have suffered on the cross that fateful Friday. But as he knelt and prayed, he suddenly felt the presence of God. The air that he breathed was the air God breathed. He felt not only one with God, but he was part of Him. There was no separation. His senses were suspended, as though there was no time. Cohen stood in the presence of the Lord. There was a profound silence in the tomb.

He experienced a deep peace in his heart, but the peace was broken moments later by anxious tourists urging him to move on, impatient at having queued up to enter the tomb.

Cohen got up and left the church, knowing what he had to do. Obeying Christ, he left behind his possessions in the rucksack on the bench in the Holy Sepulchre. Like Jesus, he now had no place to lay his head. He had renounced the world and all his possessions. He was a surrendered soul, putting his trust in God to provide for him, for he had not eaten for three days. Hunger pains were beginning to grow.

Cohen turned left out of the Holy Sepulchre and walked through the Old City. All he knew was that he was in the holy city and he'd received God's blessing to preach to the Jews.

As he passed the bazaars and the market traders, he spotted a sign: Monastery of the White Fathers.

Cohen did not particularly want to visit the monks, but hunger was getting the better of him. He rang the monastery bell and waited. They were Dominican monks, called after the White Fathers, missionaries to Africa. Natives named them that because of their white habits.

A tall imposing figure of a monk opened the door and impatiently asked what he wanted. Cohen explained he was in Jerusalem to serve Christ and he would grateful if he could have something to eat.

The monk looked down at him and, taking him for a tramp, reluctantly ordered him inside. He was told to sit on a bench while he fetched the abbot. Half an hour went by.

Cohen was about to leave when in walked the Superior, who asked him why he had come to the monastery. He explained that he was homeless and asked if he could stay at the monastery for a few days.

'The monastery does not accept guests unless by a prior arrangement,' said the Superior, 'but you would be welcome to have a meal, provided you eat alone from the brethren and leave soon afterward.'

Cohen was grateful for the meal but wondered if Jesus had been treated in the same abrupt manner. Monks were meant to show hospitality to a stranger and treat him like they would Jesus.

The monks left him alone to sit outside the refectory to eat his meal. It was a sumptuous dish, a three course dinner with ample helping of strawberries and cream for dessert.

After finishing his feast, he wondered how the monks lived so high on the hog simply on donations from the poor meant to help maintain the monastery.

Cohen left the White Fathers to their banquet. He would not be going back to the monastery. As he walked along the market, he realised that he'd left his passport in his rucksack. He scolded himself for such negligence. But as he headed back to the Holy Sepulchre he wondered whether perhaps the Lord was telling him that he didn't need a passport. For in Christ he had become a new creature, neither Jew nor Greek, neither male nor female. Taken on a new identity, he didn't need a passport after all. Nevertheless, he realised that if he ever wanted to leave Israel, God forbid, he would need his passport back. As he retraced his steps back to the Holy Sepulchre, Cohen prayed that his rucksack still be on the pew where he left it.

On returning there, he was in for the shock of his life.

Hundreds of people poured out of the church surrounded by policemen. One of them was holding the rucksack in the air and demanding to know who owned it.

Stepping out of the crowd, Cohen confessed it was his.

'Do you realise we had to evacuate the entire building?' the policeman reprimanded him. 'A bomb was reported in the church!'

Cohen stood open-mouthed, dumbstruck at what he was hearing. The rucksack was all that he had, with all his possessions that he had given away. The crowd was gathering round and cursing him for a terrorist.

Moments later the police had handcuffed him and took him away to headquarters where they interrogated him. He protested his innocence, telling the police he'd been sent to Jerusalem to convert the Jews to Christianity, that it was God's will that he had gone to the Holy Sepulchre.

'Why are you wearing a robe?' a policeman asked.

'Because I'm a Christian,' protested Cohen.

'And you're preaching Christianity to the Jews?'

'Yes, to save souls,' declared Cohen, 'especially the Jews, for I am one of them.'

'Next you'll be telling me you're Jesus Christ reborn, ha, ha,' roared the officer.

'He lives in me, as He does in all Christians. We are all little Christ's.'

'That's enough,' shouted the officer. 'Call a doctor.'

Cohen was escorted out and thrown into a prison cell to await a psychiatrist. When the doctor arrived he asked Cohen if he heard voices.

'Why, yes,' replied Cohen.

'And where do these voices come from?' asked the doctor.

'From God,' he declared, surprised at the psychiatrist's ignorance.

'And what do the voices say?'

'Save the Jews,' answered Cohen.

The doctor was surprised at Cohen's remark and asked him: 'Why the Jews?'

'Because our hearts are stubborn because we have ears to hear but we do not listen, we have eyes but we do not see. And you, blinded by science, know not what you ask.'

'Are you a prophet?' asked the doctor.

'I am a messenger.'

'A messenger from God?'

'It is as you say it is.'

'And God talks to you?' the doctor repeats.

Cohen did not answer. He remained silent, refusing to answer any more questions, for he could sense the doctor was not a spiritual person, more of an atheist, nor would he understand it if he explained it. Did Jesus not say you shouldn't cast pearls before swine?

The psychiatrist scribbled down notes and left the room abruptly.

Six hours later, not having had a drink of water or a bite to eat, a Cohen was handcuffed by a policeman and led to a van. Half an hour later he arrived at the Masada Mental Hospital and was taken to the psychiatric ward.

As he entered the ward a nurse escorted by two burly orderlies, ordered him to take some medication that she held in a glass.

'What's in it?' Cohen demanded.

'It's an anti-psychotic medicine,' the nurse said.

'No thanks,' he said. 'You take it.'

'If you don't we will have to make you take it,' the nurse threatened. Cohen looked at the two orderlies towering over him, and obediently swallowed the medication. After a few hours he was comatose. He lay back in his chair, the medication clouding his senses. He didn't know where he was or why he was there. His heightened spiritual awareness had all but deserted him. He felt drugged and disorientated, stupefied. He remained in this state for a week before he was to see the consultant psychiatrist, Dr. Feinstein.

'Do you know why you're here?' said the doctor.

'Why yes,' answered Cohen, 'I'm too drugged up to walk out of here.'

'Yes, well, we have diagnosed your condition,' said the doctor.

'Do tell,' said Cohen, sighing.

'The fact of the matter is you are suffering from a common complaint we have to deal with in Israel. Religious people come here on pilgrimage and fall under the spell of hallucinations.'

'What might that be?' queried Cohen.

'Jerusalem Syndrome,' pronounced the doctor, 'it's a common complaint, especially with religious fanatics such as yourself. The syndrome is prevalent mostly among people from the West who come here obsessed with God.'

'You say I'm a fanatic.' protested Cohen.

'You are suffering delusions,' said the psychiatrist. 'We have drugs to treat you, and then we will consider your discharge from hospital and return you to England. Are you in agreement with that?'

'Do I have any choice?' said Cohen.

'Not really,' said the doctor. 'We have many patients here suffering your complaint. You are not alone.'

Cohen was later transferred to a maximum security ward with a locked door which prevented patients leaving. Despite what the doctor said there was no other patient on the ward suffering from his condition. Most of them were clinically depressed, manic or plain suicidal.

It dawned on Cohen that he was in a position to help the other patients who were suffering from illnesses that were far more desperate than his. He was desperate too, for no one in his right mind could bear the suffering of being locked up in a madhouse for one's faith, a fate worse than death.

But Cohen saw it as God's will that he would help others by bringing Christ's love and healing to the ward.

In order to do that he came up with a way of hiding the pills, by holding them under his tongue, pretending in front of the nurse he was taking his medication. After doing this for a while, he could feel his senses coming back. The moment the nurse had gone he would spit out the pills and flush them down the toilet.

Day by day he became more alert and returned to his own self again. He spent much time talking with the patients and began to feel their pain and sorrow, for they had come mainly from broken homes and often been abused.

What Cohen had overlooked was that the hospital employed new nurses who mingled with patients, wearing no uniforms. It was while he was witnessing that one of the new nurses, whom he mistook for a fellow patient, reported him for preaching.

'Are you aware that proselytising is against the law?' the psychiatrist asked him.

'What does that mean?' asked Cohen.

'It means trying to convert Jews away from their faith,' said the doctor.

'But I don't do that,' he protested. 'I'm leading them into a deeper faith.'

Dr. Feinstein got out a dictionary and flipped through its pages. 'Do you understand what Jerusalem Syndrome is?' asked the doctor.

'Yes, it's something you invented.'

'Very funny, but something tells me you are not taking your treatment seriously, and for that reason I am recommending that you be sectioned under the Mental Health Act for six months, until we see signs of you responding to treatment. Do you understand?' warned the doctor.

'Six months!' he protested. 'You can't do that, it's against human rights. Is this country turning fascist? It was a fascist country that exterminated six million Jews.'

'There you go, you see what I mean. We try to help you and you have this totally irrational response as though we are your enemies,' said the doctor. 'We are here to help you get over your paranoia.'

'If you really wanted to help me then you'd let me leave.'

'Will you sign here?' said the doctor, 'It's an agreement for six months treatment, and then we can put you on a plane to England.'

'Over my dead body,' Cohen yelled.

'Then you give me no choice but to section you,' said the doctor. He pressed the alarm button and two burly orderlies appeared at the door in no time to drag Cohen upstairs and throw him into a padded cell.

Within minutes the nurse appeared. She injected a tranquilliser into his buttocks as the orderlies held him down. Cohen was beside himself with rage at the indignity of it all, but within a few seconds he was slipping into unconsciousness. He passed the night in complete oblivion such was the therapy of modern psychiatry. The following morning he awoke still suffering the effects of the injection. He was let back on to the ward and felt the best way to relieve his pain was to concern himself with the other patients' misery. One particular patient was an old man who sat in the corner not moving. He had a long beard and hair down to his waist and he called himself Moses. He believed he was a reincarnation of the ancient prophet. He would spend the day writing down the Ten

Commandments and distributing them to all the staff telling them to face the torments of hell unless they repented. Another patient, a middle-aged woman, claimed to be the Virgin Mary and kept lighting candles, much to the annoyance of the staff, who were convinced she was a pyromaniac intent on burning down the ward. Another man said he was John the Baptist and went round the ward trying to baptise everyone, throwing water over them and cursing anyone who resisted. But Cohen did manage to befriend one patient, a teenage girl who said she had been converted to Christianity while on holiday in Israel, but had got arrested in a restaurant for trying to turn water into wine.

On the following day, Cohen planned his escape. With military precision he monitored the nurses' shifts, what time they arrived and what time they finished their duties. He had planned to slip past security without being noticed.

All went to plan as he dashed for the exit door when the patient, the mad Mary yelled out: 'Don't leave me!' she screamed out loud, 'I need you! I want your baby! You're the Archangel Michael, come to set me free!'

Her desperate voice echoed throughout the ward, her pleas were a cry in the wilderness.

Cohen feared the commotion had foiled his escape, but the nurse on duty, after telling Mary to quiet down, closed the staff door and did not return. He seized his moment and climbed up onto the window, forcing it open, and climbed out onto the ledge. Steadying himself, he took a chance and jumped into the pitch-black darkness below, praying as he did so. He descended at such a rate that when he hit the ground he thought he'd broken both legs such was the pain that shot through his body.

But he was fortunate; the only injury he got was feeling winded, and he made his way down towards some woods.

Cohen was free at last, and knelt down beside a tree and thanked God for his freedom. He was exhausted, not from leaping from the window, but from the hangover of the hospital drugs, which he'd been forced to take. He lay down behind the tree and feared the police would come with their sniffer dogs. He got down on his knees and prayed. He felt as if he'd been in the Garden of Gethsemane, where Christ pleaded on his last night on earth. If there was any justice in the world then surely God would let him go, let him live in peace, rather than making him suffer any more persecutions and torments. The realisation that there was no peace in the material world came to him. Look what they did to Christ, who did no wrong and was without sin.

Cohen kept watch under the tree until dawn. He reached for his pocket and pulled out a Bible he'd managed to keep hold of. He opened it and read the first passage, a verse from Corinthians: 'You have called to be my servant but in serving me you must first learn to bear much suffering'.

On reading the words, Cohen fell to his knees and pleaded with God to take this cup of suffering from him. 'But I have suffered enough,' he cried.

A few moments later, as the sun was coming up over the hills, he heard a small voice within saying: 'Let my will be done.'

The sun was now shining through the trees and in the distance he could hear a young girl walking in the woods. He approached her and said he was going to the monastery, asking if he was going the right way. 'You have to go that way, bearing right,' she smiled.

Her smile comforted him. He had been locked up in the hospital for a month, almost as though in prison. He looked at her blond hair and fine figure. He was tempted to embrace her and kiss her, but instead looked into her clear blue eyes and asked: 'Are you a Christian?'

'Yes, I'm off to church,' said the girl.

'Bless you. I'm on my way to the monastery,' said Cohen, disgusted at his lustful thoughts. He remembered that the devil roamed around in secrecy devouring young converts. Cohen marched on over the steep hill. In the distance he could see the outline of the hospital. Much to his relief he could see no sign of the police or dogs. But as a precaution against being arrested and taken to the madhouse he decided he would change his appearance. He took off his robe, taking a razor out of his holdall. He shaved off the beard and cut his hair, feeling like a new man.

On setting out for Ein Karem he noticed a boy crying by the wayside. 'What's the matter?' said Cohen. 'Be not afraid. I know you're hurting.'

'How do you know?' asked the boy.

'By your eyes which are full of sorrow, my son,' Cohen said.

'I have leukaemia and not long to live,' said the boy, breaking into sobs.

'Have faith, my child. Pray to God and he will heal you,' said Cohen.

'I do, but nothing happens,' he answered.

'Come, we shall pray together,' said Cohen, sitting down next to the boy.

He laid his hands on him, calling down the Holy Spirit to heal him. The boy knelt beside Cohen and he continued to pray in tongues, in Aramaic, the language that Jesus spoke. The boy closed his eyes and felt a deep warmth surge through his entire body.

'I feel better now,' said the boy. He went away with renewed joy.

Cohen made his way to Ein Karem. On his way to the monastery he called in at the care home to see Sarah and Sister Norma, whom he had affection for. On arriving at the children's home a French nun, Sister Claire, approached Cohen admonishingly and said: 'Why do you want to take Sarah out?' There was a look of distrust in her eyes. 'There are boys who need looking after. Why don't you take them out instead?'

'But she's the only one who can walk, and she likes going out,' said Cohen.

'She's not supposed to be taken out of the hospital grounds,' the sister insisted. 'If anything happened to her, the hospital would be responsible. In the future you can take out the boys.'

'Where's Sarah?' asked Cohen.

'Her mother has her for the weekend. Look after one of the boys,' she said sternly, staring at him with beady eyes.

Cohen wondered if she'd seen him kiss Sarah from her window. But if she had seen it, then it was clear from her steely-eyed expression and the anger in her voice, she disapproved. He began to regret having kissed Sarah's innocent lips.

Cohen set out to find Sister Norma. She was in her office, standing on the footstool and reaching for a book. He went up to her and put his hands gently round her waist to steady her balance. She turned with her face beaming and allowed him to lift her down from the stool. 'Michael, where have you been?' Sister Norma asked.

As he lifted her down she held onto him, her arms draped round his broad shoulders. 'My, you are strong,' she admired.

Cohen looked into her dark brown eyes, her golden skin in contrast to her white habit, as he felt her breasts against him. He looked at her beautiful lips enticing him and kissed them so passionately as if it were his first ever kiss.

He was expecting her to push him away, but to his surprise she responded. Her lips felt soft and warm as she fell limp into his arms, their tongues entwined in a moment of ecstasy. No longer able to restrain himself, he gently fondled her breasts.

'Oh, Michael,' she sighed.

He was beside himself with passion and pressed her petite body against his. He held her against the desk and stroked her soft nylon tights, moving his hand between her slender thighs and touching her intimately. She sighed again clinging to him with all the passion of a celibate nun denied the embrace of a man.

Seizing the moment, Cohen got hold of her hand and placed it on his manhood. The touch of nun's hand made him feel hard and rampant, as if he was about to come there and then. Then, for some odd reason, he felt himself cursing the inventor of women's tights. He wanted her, but the tights protected her from impure advances, as the habit and veil protected her from the world. As he groped helplessly at her body, she shouted: 'The door, it's unlocked.'

'I'll lock it,' said Cohen, urgently.

'No, if someone comes they'll wonder what's going on,' she said. 'You realise I'll have to go to confession after this.'

'It's me that will go to confession,' Cohen said. 'I'm sorry if I got carried away, but you're so beautiful, and to think you never married! Are you a virgin?'

Sister Norma looked away, blushing. Cohen guessed that she was about fifty years old. He assumed she'd found her vocation when she was in her early teenage years and so had never had a boyfriend.

'You're the first man I've ever kissed,' she confessed, blushing again. So I was right, thought Cohen. He kissed her again on her cheek.

'Please, no more,' she said, pushing him away.

Cohen let go of her and said he had something to confess. 'I kissed Sarah,' he said, 'an innocent kiss. Sister Claire, the French nun, said I couldn't see the girl again, but that I should take out the boys. What nerve!'

'Are you in any trouble?' Sister Norma asked.

'What do you mean?'

'The police came here yesterday asking about you,' warned Sister Norma.

'What did you tell them?' asked Cohen, curious.

'Only that I hadn't seen you for a long time, that you had gone away. Is it Sarah?' she asked.

'It's not about Sarah. The police had me arrested for preaching, but I escaped.'

'What will you do? You cannot stay in the Ein Karem. The police will come back.'

'I don't know. I'm running out of monasteries,' Cohen said forlornly.

'There is one I know,' said Sister Norma reassuringly. 'It's near Nazareth. You'd like it there. It's near the Sea of Galilee. They won't come looking for you there. It's in Arab territory.'

Cohen, feeling hopeful, kissed her. 'If you hadn't become a nun, I would have married you. You're the most beautiful woman I've ever kissed.'

'Thank you,' she said, 'but go now, before somebody comes. I don't want you to get in more trouble.'

'I understand,' he said, stroking her veil.

'Please write to me, Michael,' she insisted. 'Do you need money?'

'The Lord will provide,' said Cohen, hopefully.

Sister Norma reached into a drawer and took out $50. 'This will get you to Nazareth and food on the way.'

She asked him to promise not tell a soul of their embrace, holding tightly a crucifix. 'Go with God,' she said, blowing him a kiss. She waved goodbye and went her office.

She sat down at her desk and tried to concentrate on her work, but it was impossible. Her body was aroused to the point that she felt compelled to go back her cell and take out a picture of him. Lying on the bed she removed her tights and touched herself intimately. The veil had slipped from her head. Knowing he was gone for good, and that she'd never see him again, she cried into her pillow.

Cohen went away with mixed feelings. Having kissed such a beautiful woman, he now felt guilt-ridden for having caressed a nun. He knew that, having given into temptation, he would suffer the consequences. Although Jesus came to save sinners, God chastised those who fell from grace. He had only himself to blame.

It was too dangerous for a man leading a spiritual life to be alone with a woman, no matter how enlightened he was. He had sinned against God and against a nun, of all people, yet the more he wrestled with his conscience, the more he pictured Sister Norma in his embrace, her soft, virginal lips wanting to be kissed.

Cohen made his way to the bus stop for the service to Jerusalem. While waiting for the bus, he remembered a prayer from St. Augustine's Confessions:

'Lord, make me chaste, but not yet.'

Knowing he was human after all, just like any other man, raised his spirits. His fall from grace had humbled him. St. Augustine's struggle with chastity was very much Cohen's own cross, a struggle that would continue the rest of his life.

He realised that to become a committed Christian with one's whole heart and soul was, in many ways, a contradiction of all that the world meant to him.

It was a call to separate oneself from the world and all its distractions, namely power, money, property and possessions. It was a call to love God, to be detached from the world, to give up attachment to the opposite sex, and love Him first.

For Jesus said: 'He who leaves his mother, father, brother, sister, wife and children for the sake of the Kingdom of God, shall inherit a hundred fold, and in the world to come, eternal life.'

Christ was calling upon men to detach from the world, to love God first and foremost. That's why He called fishermen away from their homes and families to live a life dedicated to the Lord, to become his Apostles. Cohen knew he was struggling with his sensuality, his love of women, yet his rejection of them contradicted his desire to meet someone special, a wife. In fact, Cohen's dissatisfaction came from copulation, for it was over in a few minutes, after which the body would die, but the soul was immortal. He realised that one could only truly give one's heart to the Lord, and certainly not to a woman. Such was his dilemma, to practise detachment or allow one's own fleshly appetites to become trapped by the female sex and suffer the consequences – attachments, families, worldly possessions, pride and greed and ultimately death. The soul was made for union with God, to remain in its childhood state of innocence and purity, not to be corrupted by the world and sin, which would lead to death. The longer man lived, the more he was corrupted by the world and the more he was prone to sin. When a child died it was an innocent death and its soul was transported by an angel to heaven.

It was clear to Cohen that humanity had lost its way that people no longer worshipped their Creator, but themselves, the works of their own hands, even gold and silver and idols, as the Jews did in the wilderness when they turned against Jehovah and worshipped the golden calf. Such was Moses' wrath he destroyed the Tablets bearing the Ten Commandments, hurling them from Mount Sinai to the Hebrews below as they revelled in their orgies.

Little had changed over the centuries. Man had not learned his lesson from history. He turned his back on what was spiritual to pursue materialism and his own vanity. But God was patient with us, for he was a loving God and wants to love Him above all else.

Cohen was deep in thought as he caught the bus to Jerusalem. He vowed never again to be alone with a woman, no matter how holy and virtuous she was.

In fact, all the more reason for not being alone with a woman. Many a saint's fall from grace with a pious woman had been their downfall, not to mention a few Popes he had read about in libraries.

Cohen enjoyed the time spent in the libraries, especially reading the biographies and lives of the saints. He would read avidly about their suffering. In them he found inspiration to persevere in the search to find God.

He became acutely aware of their inner grief, their torments and temptations, and how God would intercede on their behalf and raise them up as saints. Many such saints lived in the wilderness in rocks and caves to be nearer to God. They were ascetics, hermits, able to bare not only the hardships of the desert, but the fiercest winters. They were strong, tough and brave, for they were tested severely under the harshest conditions. Yet their hearts never hardened. The more they suffered, the humbler they became, the purer. They would feed animals before taking food such was their humility and love of God's creatures. Cohen knew that two such Russian saints were St. Seraphim and St. Sophrony.

St. Sophrony left Russia to suffer the rigours and hardships of Mount Athos in a monastery. Hundreds of monks, both Russian and Greeks, still lived on Mount Athos, a Greek peninsula south of Thessalonika.

Women are banned from Mt. Athos, but it hadn't stopped women baring their breasts from the boats sailing past the monastery.

Some of the monks had never seen a woman before, let alone topless – such wanton temptation! Monks put it down to the fallen Eve, tempting monks to copulate.

Father Sophrony had spent his life at the monastery, giving to the Russian church much of the Orthodox liturgy they sung today. He often taught Russian monks harmony and counterpoint he'd learnt from the Greek liturgy. He never went back to Russia, and later in life he founded the monastery of St. John the Baptist at Tolleshunt Knights, Malden, Essex.

On his journey he visited the Monastery of the Servants of God in Crawley, Sussex, and wrote:

'Revelation, the joy of discovering the depths of asceticism in England, so congenial to the asceticism of Mount Athos.'

Father Sophrony had died in 1993 and was buried in the tomb at the Monastery of St. John the Baptist, Essex. Later Cohen went there and prayed at Father Sophrony's grave.

Cohen began humming Russian chants as the bus entered Jerusalem. The memory of the nuns singing in the Orthodox chapel came flooding back to him. Suddenly, as he was getting off the bus, a bomb went off.

A loud explosion ripped apart the far end of the bus station and sent passengers fleeing for their lives. Pandemonium broke out and people rushed past Cohen, knocking him to the ground. As he lay prostrate, people trampled close by him.

It was clear that a bus had been blown up as it left the station. Women screamed as mangled bodies were strewn throughout the station. Carnage had come to the streets of Jerusalem once again. It was the second time in a week the bus station had been targeted and he vowed never to catch another bus.

Cohen began walking back to the relative safety of Ein Karem. He was still in fear of being recognised by the police and taken back to the asylum. He had nowhere to stay that night. He couldn't go back to the friars or the French monastery, both of which had asked him to leave. There was only one option: he would spend the night sleeping rough, on the hillside near the village.

When he reached the village, he climbed a hill and made a camp bed. But it was the middle of the hottest month in the summer and he couldn't sleep. The mosquitoes were attacking him all night. Much as he tried to protect himself with a T-shirt over his head, they bit him on his face and arms all through the night. When he woke up at the break of dawn, his arms had welled up, and he scratched at the bites, making them bleed. Only Sister Norma would make them better.

On climbing the hill, he entered the grounds of the children's hospital and went up to the ward. Sister Norma was in the pharmacy room when he entered. She was shocked to see him as she'd been to confession. The priest told her not to see Cohen again, and if she did, never to be alone with him. Such was the authority of priests over religious women.

When he asked to talk with her in her office, she recoiled, her eyes no longer tender and loving but full of fear. However, she had compassion when she saw Cohen was badly bitten. She went to the medicine cabinet and rubbed disinfectant on both arms. Her hands were soft and smooth and the ointment began to sooth his skin. He felt her warmth but there was an element of detachment in her. 'I've been to confession, you understand,' said Sister Norma with conviction in her voice. 'I'm a nun'.

It was as if their moment of embrace, their passion, never existed. Her stern attitude surprised him, for she had been always gentle with him, a woman full of love and grace, with a profound love for humanity, never a woman full of fear. He looked into her dark brown eyes, the eyes of the woman who'd loved him so affectionately, but they had grown cold. He did not feel the love he once had. There was no warmth, no affection in her eyes anymore. She was not the same woman who had held him intimately, but a woman who did not want to be with him anymore, let alone touch her.

Sister Norma had the fear of God in her eyes, and he realised for the first time what it meant to offend the nun. She had spurned Cohen in the name of God and her undying faith. Of course, he understood her faith and love of the commandments, understood her religious devotion and commitment to her vows, her desire to live for the Lord. It dawned on him that she was a devoted nun, consecrated to God and her vows of poverty, obedience and chastity. He was guilty of tempting her to sin and making her impure and unchaste.

Cohen had come between her and God. And he felt wretched, torn with guilt and self-loathing. But what if he had met her before she became a nun? Would it have been different? Could they have become lovers and married? He doubted it. He was not a good provider for a start, barely able to look after himself let alone provide security for a wife and kids. In any case, he had no interest in material comforts. Money and power were not his aim in life.

He wanted God.

Cohen had tried being close to God, living in monasteries, and even thought of taking the vows she'd taken, including chastity. But he knew how hard and austere religious life was. The early rising before dawn, working in the fields all day, the constant praying, standing in the choir six times a day, and fasting. It all took its toll on the body.

Cohen thought there was still be a chance he and Sister Norma could be together, maybe sometime in the future, and that she would come away with him. They could travel north and go on a pilgrimage together and get married.

Sister Norma looked at Cohen with tears in her eyes, as if she was reading his thoughts. He knew deep down he was in love with a consecrated nun, and that despite all his romantic longings, she would never be his. She was a dedicated nun and nurse and he knew that she would stay with the children she cared and loved. He would have to forget her, to leave the children's home for good. It would be good for Sarah too, since Sister Claire had sensed Cohen's attraction to the girl.

Cohen took Sister Norma into his arms and hugged her for a brief moment. Her confessor had a lot to answer for. He had made her frightened of the very thing her body craved – love, and the enjoyment of sex. But he realised this was all a romantic fantasy and he would have to forget her, for her sake, for her own spiritual well being, for he was always attracted to pious and religious women, for they were good souls, like his mother.

'Why did you come back to Ein Karem?' Sister Norma asked, finishing applying the ointment. 'I thought you were going to Nazareth.'

'I was, but a bus had been blown up just as I got to the station,' said Cohen.

'You weren't hurt?'

'No, just shaken up because of you,' he joked. He kissed her on the lips for the last time and said goodbye. As he walked down to the gates, she called to him.

'Here, take this,' she said, offering some money. 'You might need it.'

Cohen thanked her, for he was broke. Sister Norma was a true Christian, always concerned for others. She would leave a lasting impression on Cohen, one of holiness and stability in the face of suffering, such was her faith. He began to view woman differently: no longer a temptress like Eve, out to beguile man, but now Mary the Mother of God, a maternal being, *Ave Maria*.

He left Sister Norma looking after the fifty children she cared for.

On his way out of the grounds, Cohen made one last visit to the Russian convent. It was getting late and he asked Sister Natasha where he might spend the night. He had just missed the last bus. 'Have you tried the Christian lodgings further up the hill,' she said. 'There are some Christians living there. They might put you up.'

After lighting a candle in the chapel, he thanked her and made his way up the hill toward the mansion, a white building with four storeys and a gateway.

It was a steep climb and at the top of the hill he was confronted by an iron gate with fencing around it. He rang the bell and dogs began to bark. He began to wonder what kind of Christian community it was and whether or not it was a sect or a cult. The dogs were howling for several minutes when the gate was opened by a smartly-dressed American pastor. He looked at Cohen, still in his shabby robe with long hair and beard, and invited him in after hearing his English accent.

The American took him inside the vast mansion, with marbled floors and winding staircases, through to the lounge and introduced his secretary, a blond with a revealing dress. Cohen admired the huge house, his secretary, and the spacious garden surrounding its outdoor pool.

'My, you do like to live well,' said Cohen, glancing at his secretary with a smile.

'This house was the formerly the Anglican bishop's residence, and we purchased it to form a new Christian community,' said the American pastor, a Jew by the name of Simon. He converted to Christianity and left the United States to preach the good news of Christ to the Jews of Israel.

Cohen explained that he was a Jew, too, and had come to Israel to write about the new Jewish temple, and while here had become a Christian and gone to live in monasteries and became a missionary, preaching to the Jews.

'Are you still preaching?' asked Simon.

'Not now, after what I've gone through,' said Cohen, aggrieved. 'I was arrested for preaching Christ to the Jews – they call it proselytising. They threw me in a mental ward, accused me of having 'Jerusalem Syndrome'. Right now I'm just trying to keep out of trouble and stay alive.'

The secretary came over and kissed Cohen on the cheek. 'You are very brave,' she said, bending over to reveal her breasts.

'Thanks,' said Cohen, consoled by a kiss.

'Our mission too has been persecuted,' said Pastor Simon. 'Even with a regular congregation it is still a struggle to preach. We meet every Sunday in Jerusalem, mostly Jews who have converted to the faith. The Lord is blessing us with more converts every week. You must come to one of our services.'

Cohen warmed to Pastor Simon and his blond secretary. He was a genuine, sincere Christian, an evangelical who took the word of God to heart. He was thankful to meet another Messianic Jew, a fellow convert who would let him stay overnight. Before going to bed, Cohen went to the bathroom, and there was the blond secretary alone naked. He looked at her, with her voluptuous figure with huge breasts. She walked past and smiled.

Temptation was everywhere, even in the Christian Jewish community.

At breakfast Simon asked him his plans and how he would go about serving the Lord.

'I try to serve wherever I am,' said Cohen, looking at his secretary as she waltzed by, revealing her cleavage. 'Right now, I've been trying to get to Nazareth, but the terrorists are bombing the buses.'

'What will you do in Nazareth?' asked Simon.

'I'll visit Lake Galilee and the monastery nearby.'

'Aren't no women there?' asked the secretary, giving a glimpse of more cleavage.

'I don't know, not having been there yet,' Cohen said. 'And what will you be doing, spreading the Good News?' turning to Simon.

'We'll continue preaching, bringing the saving message of Jesus to our Jewish brothers and sisters,' said Simon. 'They are not so removed, you know, from Christ. God came to the Jews first, and He wants them all to be saved. As Jews we are duty bound to tell them about Jesus, the Messiah they've been waiting for, ever since the prophets foretold he was coming.'

Pastor Simon then invited Cohen to pray with him before leaving. He was not used to praying out loud and he stumbled over his words, praying for the disabled children and the monasteries and for Pastor Simon's work in the Jewish community. 'Go with God,' said Simon. 'Take this, you might need it.'

He gave Cohen 500 shekels. Cohen bade farewell to Simon and his blond secretary, whose name he never got to know, made his way down the steep hill and caught the next bus to Jerusalem. As he waited there for the bus to Nazareth he peered nervously over his shoulder, looking out for signs of another bomb blast, but there was no terrorist to be seen. He also looked around for any policeman, who might want to take him back to the asylum, but there weren't any, and he safely boarded the bus bound for Nazareth.

He looked out the window as the bus took him out of the city into the vast desert beyond. In the distance there were Bedouin tents, men riding camels, women washing and children playing in the sand. He envied their simplicity of life, the few remaining nomadic tribes. Arriving in Nazareth, he was greeted by a barefoot Arab girl wearing a headscarf and begging in the street. She offered him some peanuts wrapped in newspaper and he handed her some shekels. She smiled and said goodbye as she walked out of the bus station.

On the journey to the monastery Cohen thought of Mary, the Mother of Jesus, how she could have been that girl at the bus station, begging for money to feed her family. The bus took him on a winding journey through the desert and mountains, until he arrived at the outskirts of Lake Galilee. He was hoping to find someone who could give him directions to the monastery when he was approached by a group of young Arabs. He was apprehensive, with night closing in, as there were several of them. But unlike the youths in the Jerusalem, they greeted him in a friendly manner and agreed to show him the way.

Cohen was startled to see that one of the Arabs was an albino. His skin was white and his eyes pink, he was devoid of skin pigment, the result of inbreeding. It was not unusual for Arabs to marry within their families, mostly cousins, so that the land and property could be kept in the family for generations.

'You can get to the monastery following this path,' said the albino boy. It was later he was told he'd worked at the monastery before.

Cohen set out for the monastery, hoping that this monastery would be the last.

19

Crossing the valley Cohen glanced nervously up at the mountain, a formidable 5,200 feet high. He passed the last row of houses and set out up a winding path at the foot of the mountain. It was a steep climb and half way up he took a rest. Cohen gazed at the stars overhead and wondered whether or not he could reach the top, as its peak seemed almost to touch the stars from where he was lying. Night had fallen when he continued his climb and lost his path and found himself stumbling through undergrowth in the pitch black. As he clambered up the side of the mountain, struggling to maintain his footing, he suddenly heard a deep growl among the bushes. He froze, riveted to the spot. The beast growled again, more fiercely this time, ready to attack him.

Cohen picked up a large stone and waited for the beast to attack, his body trembling with fear. It may have been a wolf on the prowl or perhaps a big cat hunting for prey. Fearing the most, he threw a stone at the bushes, which the beast let out a howl. In a flash, the animal was scurrying away.

Relieved, he felt safe enough to continue his climb up the mountain. In the distance he could see the faint glimmer of a light at the top of the summit. Could it be the monastery? Or was it a small hut, for the light appeared too dim for a building? In the pitch black, he wandered far from the mountain path and had to grope his way through thick undergrowth, until he reached a large wooden hut perched on the side of the mountain.

Cohen knocked on the door, and a voice asked him to enter. Seated round a long wooden table were monks eating supper. They looked up indignantly, not wishing to be disturbed during supper. One monk, a frail old man with a white beard, beckoned him to join them for food.

He was Father Joseph, the Father Superior. Cohen showed him a letter of recommendation from the French monastery, which briefly stated that he was interested in a monastery life.

Father Joseph was from Holland and had founded the monastery about twenty years ago with Father Colin, an American monk, in order to set up a community of monks in Israel. The only member to join the monastery so far was an Argentinean monk, Brother Carlos, a dark stocky man with a black beard, the only monk who had befriended Cohen.

Another monk, Brother Benjamin from the Netherlands, was completing his novitiate and had brought a skill to the monastery, one which Cohen admired – brewing home-made beer.

The others seated at the table were guests on retreats, including one woman, Lydia, also Dutch, who had been staying at the monastery for several months. She had an air of superiority about her, having admired the abbot since her childhood. She looked dismissively at Cohen as he was introduced.

The American monk, renowned for speaking his mind like all Americans, asked Cohen a lot of personal questions, like such as his age, why he'd come to Israel and why he wanted to join a monastery, especially at his age. 'You want to be a monk at your age,' scoffed the American. 'It gets harder the older you get.'

'Why should it be harder?' Cohen asked.

'Because older people are stubborn,' Father Colin said, sarcastically. 'They can't adapt, too rigid in their ways to accept change.'

Lydia looked contemptuously at Cohen, as if she seen him before.

'There some exceptions,' Cohen objected, 'like St. Francis who converted later in life.'

'Quite so,' agreed Father Joseph. 'I myself didn't come to the priesthood till later in life. How was your journey here?' he asked, tactfully changing the subject.

'It was fine, until I was attacked by a wolf on my way up the mountain.' He showed his arm full of scratches.

'Ha, ha,' laughed the American. 'There are no wolves on this mountain, just wild dogs.'

'Scared the hell out of me,' Cohen said.

'An Englishman scared of dogs?' Lydia smirked.

Cohen felt tension in the air, a sense of rivalry, the same kind of anti-English discrimination he felt back at the French monastery. The Dutch had been envious of the English throughout history, ever since the Second World War when the British threw out the Nazis.

Father Joseph leaned back in his chair, took a puff of his pipe and began to reminisce about the monastery. 'We had a Jewish boy living here not so long ago, couldn't get along with anyone so he went to live in a cave not far from here. We took him some food and books. Poor man, he had other problems too. He was the only Jew living here.'

'Why did he come to the monastery?' asked Cohen.

'Beats me,' Father Colin answered.

'He didn't stay long,' Father Joseph recalled. 'He went off and married a girl in the village. Best thing that could have happened to him.'

'Was it the Jewish village?' Cohen asked.

'Yes. He settled down and had a family,' Father Joseph said matter-of-factly.

'He could have been so different if was a monk,' remarked Cohen, feeling the man may have been hard done by being a Jew.

'He didn't stick it out,' said Father Joseph. 'In fact, no-one has come for years since we founded the monastery, except Brother Carlos.'

'Are you sad about the monastery not recruiting?' Cohen asked.

'But of course,' said Father Joseph. 'It was the main reason for starting a monastery, to try and bring Jews and Arabs together and reconcile their differences. The young men, Arab and Jew, would come and stay with us.

'In time, they would have become monks living alongside one another as brothers. That was our goal...' his words tapered off.

'It wouldn't have worked,' said Father Colin dismissively.

'I'm a Jew,' said Cohen, proudly. 'I'm here.'

'Are you really a Jew?' asked Father Colin, taken aback.

'Yes, I am,' said Cohen. 'It can work, for are we not one body in Christ?'

'Indeed we are,' said Father Joseph, brightening up. 'It may happen here. That is our hope. Let us not forget, our Lord works in mysterious ways. Jews have come to know us well. They often come to see us. You'll see for yourself tomorrow, it being the Sabbath. The young men from the Jewish villages come for lunch.'

Father Joseph offered Cohen some wine. He was wary of drinking again but thought it impolite to refuse, especially on his first night at the monastery. Father Joseph said there was an empty guest room next to the refectory where Cohen could stay in the meantime. In the morning he would show him the chapel and they'd have a chat in his office.

'It's time for bed,' said the Father Superior, getting slowly to his feet. He said goodnight, leaving Cohen to spend the rest of the evening with the monks, and a few bottles of wine. Cohen resisted the temptation to drink. He was too tired from his journey. The hike up the mountain had exhausted him.

Brother Benjamin, the guest master, showed him to his room. He collapsed on his bed and fell asleep instantly.

The sound of the chapel bell ringing at 4am from the top of the mountain woke him abruptly. He staggered out of bed and into a dark foggy night, making his way past the hermitages and huts where the guests were sleeping soundly.

Cohen approached the tiny chapel on the top of the mountain and stepped nervously inside. The monks stood in a circle around the altar and had begun chanting psalms, first in English, then in Hebrew. It was the first time he'd heard Hebrew spoken in a monastery and it raised his spirits. Cohen joined the monks round the altar, listening intently to the Hebrew verses, as they sung in harmony.

After a few minutes he became distracted, and glancing out of the window he was suddenly taken aback by the giant sun looming up over the chapel. It was stupendous, making its dawn appearance over the crest of the mountainside. It hovered in the sky like an orange ball, so close that he could almost reach out and touch it. The contrast of being in the dark one moment and the dazzling light the next felt as though it had partially blinded him.

The monks followed the Eastern Orthodox rite. It was neither Greek nor Russian but an order of the Melokites, part of the Coptic tradition. The Melokites had been broken away from the Roman tradition and incorporated Middle Eastern traditions into their worship, including Hebrew music.

Father Joseph was the only one injecting any Hebrew tradition into his chanting of the psalms. The variety of such liturgy, although confusing to Cohen at first, added richness and depth to the worship. As the sun continued to rise above the mountain, Cohen could see in the far distance the lake that Jesus walked upon. It was Lake Galilee. And glancing south, he could see yet another Biblical landmark, Mount Tabor, the very mountain on which Jesus was transfigured in glory. He vowed to make a pilgrimage to both the holy sites as soon as it was possible.

After matins the monks filed out of the chapel and made their way back to the refectory for breakfast, which consisted of herbal tea and bread. At breakfast times Father Joseph assigned each monk duties for the day. There was no such thing as a daily roster. Cohen, along with a Dutch guest, Boris, was given the unenviable task of cleaning out cistern a water storage tank more than twenty feet deep in mud.

It was a mammoth task which would take them several days to do, the mud having to be hauled to the surface by buckets. It was more than an initiation for Cohen, for the monks put off for cleaning the cistern for years.

Cohen found Boris easy to get along with, though he later turned out to suffer from mood swings, which Cohen put down to being Dutch. He had a drug problem and had come to the monastery to try and kick his habit.

Ignoring his anti-English jibes Cohen got on with his work, although it was impossible not to hear his derisory comment about Holland knocking England out of the European football championship.

It took them most of the week to clear the cistern. The tank had not been cleaned for several years and the mud was nearly waist high when they started. Cohen did not begrudge the work, for he did not mind getting his hands dirty for the Lord. In fact he enjoyed it, for toiling the earth by the sweat of his brow had the effect of purging his soul. They took it in turns to haul the buckets to the surface and by the end of the week they had hauled more than fifty buckets. They disposed of the mud, pouring it down the side of the mountain. Caked in mud from head to toe they looked like Neanderthal cavemen, much to the hilarity of the guests.

After work, Cohen asked Boris if he went to church.

'No, I don't go to church,' answered Boris, irritated. 'Religion is for the weak.'

'Why do you come to the monastery?' Cohen asked, surprisingly.

'I have Dutch friends here, and I like Israel.'

'You're not a believer then, not a Christian?' queried Cohen.

'I believe in life. My religion is football, and Holland beat you in the Euros,' Boris smirked.

'Is that all you care about, football?'

'Who are you to judge?' said Boris defensively. 'I find most Christians hypocrites. They say one thing and do another.'

'We are all sinners,' confessed Cohen, 'but God forgives us.'

'Don't talk about forgiveness,' answered Boris aggressively. 'Why does God allow all these wars? How many died in the Second World War, fifty million? Where was God in all of that?'

'Without faith you cannot go to heaven,' said Cohen imploringly.

'There you go, judging again. You've no right to judge.'

'It is not my judgement, it is God's,' Cohen replied.

'And you speak for him, is that it?'

'No,' answered Cohen, 'it is the Gospel.'

'Sanctimonious,' scoffed Boris, turning in disgust and walking back to the monastery.

Cohen stood there feeling embarrassed for having brought the matter up. He had no right to judge, unless of course you witness for the Lord. But those who do not want to hear about salvation, it's best not to argue with. Let God deal with them. It was clear, in some way God had called Boris to the monastery, even if he wasn't aware of it. But it still puzzled Cohen why he should come to the monastery when he could have gone to the rehab centre, or kibbutz, for Boris never bothered attending the chapel or any services.

Dripping in mud, Cohen headed back to the monastery desperate to take a shower. It was more like a medieval monastery, in line with the monks' Spartan existence. There was no telephone, no electricity and had to use oil lamps. It was a hard existence, one designed to test a monk's endurance and character, to teach him self-sufficiency and how to live off the land.

When he got to the shower he opened the cubicle, thinking that it was empty. To his surprise, he saw a statuesque blond woman, in her late twenties, and wearing a blue towel around her body about to step into the shower. 'I'm so sorry,' Cohen said. 'I thought there was no-one in here.'

'Oh, please don't worry,' she said. 'I'm as quiet as a mouse, and that's why you didn't hear me!' She smiled. Her eyes were a lighter hue of blue than her towel and her teeth were perfect.

'I'll leave you be then,' Cohen said, feeling embarrassed.

'No, it's alright. I've only just arrived here. I'm Bridget, from Stockholm. I'm here with my boyfriend. By the way, would it be alright for my boyfriend to stay in my room? We live together in Sweden. I know that this is a monastery, but do guests share a room?'

Cohen smiled. 'I'm not really the person you should be asking, but I'd just tell him to spend the night with you. I don't think anyone would mind.'

'You're very kind,' she said. 'So are you a monk yourself?'

'No, just a postulant, but I do intend to become a monk.'

She smiled flirtatiously at him. 'So, do you think you could live without women?'

Cohen smiled. 'Probably not,' he said.

Heaven exists, he thought, so does Hell.

20

The next morning Bridget arrived late for breakfast as Cohen was about to clear the table in the refectory.

'You're only just in time,' pointed out Cohen.

'I just want some coffee,' smiled Bridget. 'I just wanted to say thanks for being OK about letting my boyfriend stay over. If there is anything you want, please let me know.'

'What do you mean anything?' asked Cohen.

'Doing you a favour in return,' she kept her voice down. 'For example, would you like to make love to me?'

Cohen was surprised but not amazed. He had already noticed that Bridget liked him, and that she was rather broad-minded. 'Wouldn't your boyfriend disapprove?' asked Cohen. He thought about the time of seeing the naked woman in the tent, and how she'd French-kissed him and driven almost out of his mind with excitement.

'My boyfriend taught me free love,' answered Bridget. 'It's about sharing.'

'Is that so?' said Cohen. 'Well, I'll think about it. I'm off to a meeting in a chapel, but I'll catch up with you later.'

Upon leaving her in the refectory, Cohen made his way to the chapel in turmoil. He was about to meet with the monks, but Bridget tempting him like this was enough to make him walk out of the monastery and flee to the village. How could anyone in their right mind allow such an incredibly beautiful woman as Bridget to come to the monastery in the first place, when the monastery was for celibate monks? But, after all, she was a guest and known Father Joseph for some time. With such torment, he walked out of the chapel and went to his room. He lay on his bed thinking about Bridget, her vivacious, mesmerising smile and inviting lips and what she wanted to do with him. What she said about free love ran contrary to what the monastery was all about, preserving one's self control, an inner belief in one's chastity, a calling from God. The community did not work in the afternoons because of the heat, so Cohen decided to spend the rest of the day reading and praying for a blessing for his weekend pilgrimage to Lake Galilee and Mount Tabor.

That evening after supper, drinks began to flow. The conversation turned to Boris who had been lamenting his life as a single man. Bridget was there too, with her boyfriend.

'Maybe we should find you a wife in the village?' suggested Father Joseph.

'A Jewish wife, or an Arab wife?' Boris joked.

'In your case you'd be lucky to get either,' chortled Father Colin.

'What do I want a wife for?' asked Boris. 'They only give you trouble.'

'That's a sexist remark,' snapped Lydia, turning away in disgust.

Changing the subject, Cohen asked Father Joseph: 'I noticed a cemetery on the top of the mountain. Are there any monks buried there?'

'Not yet, but I'll be there in time,' chuckled Father Joseph. 'There is a man buried there, not a monk. He had been staying at the convent in Bethlehem helping out the nuns in the garden, but then he was taken ill and the nuns asked if we could take him in. Within a few months he died and we buried him in the cemetery. I expect I'll be joining him shortly.'

'I don't think so, father,' said Brother Ben. 'You'll live to the age of Moses.'

'If I live till that age, the brothers will have to carry me to the chapel, God forbid,' exclaimed Father Joseph, lighting his pipe. Nonetheless, Father Joseph was getting frailer each day. He could no longer walk up the mountain as he had done. When he wanted to go into the village, or to Nazareth to visit the dentist, one of the monks would drive him in the monastery jeep.

Cohen looked across at Lydia, the Dutch girl, who had ignored him when he first arrived at the monastery. He was convinced he had seen her somewhere before. 'Weren't you at the French monastery in Ein Karem? he asked.

'Yes, for a few weeks. Why?' she asked, abruptly.

'I thought I had seen you before,' said Cohen. 'You didn't want to speak to me then,' he said.

'I was on retreat.' said Lydia coldly. Brother Ben passed the beer he got from the cellar and asked Cohen how long he would be staying.

'I'm hoping to join the community,' Cohen replied.

'You'd make a good monk, I think,' said Bridget.

'Thanks,' said Cohen. He wondered how serious she'd been about offering to let him make love to her.

'I think we'll sort out the duties now rather than in the morning,' said Father Joseph. 'I am going to Nazareth to see my dentist. Have you worked with goats before?' he asked, turning to Cohen.

'No, only those in the congregation,' quipped Cohen. His joke fell flat. Sadly, the monks did not have a sense of humour.

'Well,' said Father Joseph, 'there's always a first time.' And turning to Brother Ben he asked him to show Cohen the goats.

Cohen was not used to animals and so it was with trepidation he set out with Brother Ben in the morning to the goat shed. Brother Ben opened the gate and shooed away a goat to stop it escaping. 'Goats are like people,' said Brother Ben, annoyed that another goat was trying to get past the gate. 'They need a leader. Before you take them out, you must find the lead goat or all hell will break loose. You get him in front with a stick and the others will follow. He will lead the goats to the feeding ground.'

'Where is the feeding ground?' asked Cohen.

'The other side of the mountain, I will show you. They feed on green leaves on bushes.'

Brother Ben raised his stick and hustled the lead goat out of the pen, followed closely by eleven other goats jostling for position as they brushed past.

'They know where they are going,' remarked Cohen.

'Not if you don't get in front of the lead goat,' said Brother Ben. 'You have to be a shepherd leading them down the mountain. I thought you English knew about farming?' said the monk, laughing.

'Not really, we are more a nation of shopkeepers. That was how Napoleon described us,' Cohen chuckled.

Cohen walked ahead of the lead goat, but within a few metres the goat had suddenly stopped dead in its tracks and refused to go any further. The goats followed got lost and confused, bunching up with nowhere to go.

'What now?' Cohen yelled to Brother Ben, for the goats had no intention of following him down the mountain, but instead had begun to turn and head back to the safety of the stable. Brother Ben strode forward and raised his stick and gave the lead goat a whack. It darted forward and the rest of the herd followed in hot pursuit down the mountain. Within minutes the goats had reached their feeding ground and started eating the leaves of the bushes and shrubs that dotted the mountainside.

'I will leave you now,' Brother Ben called out. 'I'll trust you to bring the goats safely back and make sure the gate locked.'

Cohen looked on aghast. He was not expecting to be left alone with wild goats on his first outing. What if they escaped and fled down the mountain? Brother Ben turned and said: 'When you want their attention, just whistle. You need to shout as well.'

Cohen sat on a rock and watched the goats graze. They had voracious appetites and within minutes they had shredded most of the leaves, even though the bushes had thorns. He marvelled at their digestive system, how they could possibly digest thorns and not suffer. The lead goat, having stripped several bushes of leaves, suddenly decided to leave Cohen and took off up the mountain in search of new pastures. The other goats followed him and Cohen found himself scurrying up the mountain yelling at them to halt, all to no avail. He rushed after the herd, his heart pounding for fear of losing them for he had strict instructions to bring them all back safely. If he lost one he would have to go and search for it, like Jesus did for a lost sheep, except it was a goat.

When Cohen finally caught up with the goats, he resigned himself to the fact that they were in charge, and they knew it.

The goats had climbed up another peak, grazing in the grass, as they did before in the past when King David was a shepherd. He sat down on the stone and studied the animals, looking into their slit yellow eyes, and the calm way they grazed without a thought for the morrow.

But it wouldn't last long. The deafening roar F-15 fighter jets resounded through the mountainside, so low that Cohen could see the pilots in their cockpits as they swooped overhead. The roar of the engines scattered the goats in all directions. Cohen fell flat on his face and covered his head, for he was convinced that the monastery was under attack.

He got slowly to his feet, shaken and partially deafened by the roar. The jets roared past over the mountain and into the distance, leaving vapour trails behind. He figured the planes were out on exercises, monitoring the border between Israel and Syria. The monastery was not far from the Golan Heights, a territory seized by Israel after Syria sent tanks across the border in the '67 war. Bullet holes could be seen to this day in the walls of the monastery. It was a war in which Israelis were convinced that God was on their side, for no sooner had the Syrian tanks crossed the Golan Heights that they stopped suddenly, having got stuck in the sand.

Cohen rounded up the goats with a whistle he'd taught from Brother Ben. He lay down on the slope staring up at the sky, and wondered if Israel would be gearing up for another war. Why, with God on their side, would Israel need to defend itself with jet fighters and nuclear bombs? Were the Jews afraid of another Holocaust? If they simply obeyed and trusted in God, they would not need all these weapons of mass destruction.

Did not King David, as a boy trusting in God, slay the mighty Goliath!

The problem for the Jews was that they were living by the law of the Old Testament, which meant an eye for an eye and a tooth for a tooth, as opposed to the Christian belief of mercy.

If they had accepted Christ as their Messiah they would not live by the law, but by faith.

The Law of Moses would have damned the woman caught engaging in adultery to be stoned to death, but Jesus did not condemn her. Instead, he asked those who were without sin to cast the first stone. Jesus taught the way of love.

Cohen led the goats safely back to their pen, counting the exact number as they entered the gate. The goats scurried past and went in the shed, climbing upon the bales of hay, staring down at Cohen as though he was personally responsible for frightening them with fighter jets. Relieved he had the goats safely home Cohen went to his room and tried to calm his shattered nerves. Jets soaring over the monastery had unnerved him. He swigged a bottle of beer he had brought from the evening before. He felt the need to get away, to roam the hills again in solitude, to rediscover the peace of God.

That night after finishing his beer, he packed his rucksack determined to leave the monastery in the morning and head out on his pilgrimage to Lake Galilee. His soul was in need in refreshment, to be restored beside still waters.

At first light, while the monks were at matins, he left a note for Father Joseph explaining his need for solitude and that he would spend the night on Mount Tabor, where Jesus was transfigured. He set out as the sun rose, with clear blue skies overhead, intent on reaching the lake by the evening. From the monastery the lake did not appear too far away, but distances could be deceptive and the journey took him twice as long as he'd expected. There was no direct road leading to the lake and he was forced to cut across fields. By midday the sun was beating down on him mercilessly, and he was running out of water.

He started to get anxious, for he was still some distance from the lake and had forgotten to bring with him any head protection. He began to feel dizzy in the heat and decided to rest up for awhile. He lay down and prayed. He must have fallen asleep for a bird overhead startled him, letting out a squawk as if to warm him of the dangers of lying down in the desert. Cohen got up slowly to his feet and continued his journey. By late evening he had reached his destination, the shores of Lake Galilee, and falling to his knees he gave thanks to God for having reached the lake. He dipped his hands in the water, his parched lips quivering as he quenched his thirst. Looking up, he saw fishermen casting their nets, as the men had done before Jesus called them to be disciples, fishers of men.

He gazed across Lake Galilee, recalling how the disciples abandoned their nets and left everything to follow Jesus: their homes, wives and children. He lacked the courage of those men and wished he had their faith.

Cohen gulped the water back. He was drinking the very water Jesus walked on all those years ago, the very water Peter tried to walk on when Jesus called him. It was while meditating on these events he suddenly heard a voice from behind ordering him to get up.

'What are you doing here?' said the officer. It was an Israeli policeman, one of secret servicemen on patrol.

'I was just thirsty and having a drink,' replied Cohen, fearing the police were still on his trail and would want to send him back to the asylum.

'This is a restricted area, for military purposes only,' warned the policeman. 'Show me your I.D.'

'I left it behind at the monastery.' Cohen pointed eagerly at the mountain. 'That's where I'm staying. I'm here on pilgrimage to visit the holy lake.'

'If I were you, I'd get back to the monastery before you get arrested,' snapped the cop.

Cohen shrugged and walked slowly away, back towards the monastery. He was not going to argue with the policeman, or give him any reason to check his identity. He felt aggrieved though that his pilgrimage had ended so abruptly, that the law of the land had come between him and God. Such was the way of this world.

But he had no intention of going back to the monastery just yet, for his heart was set on climbing Mt. Tabor. He glanced nervously over his shoulder as he struck out for the mountain, making sure the policeman wasn't following him, for the last thing he wanted was to be arrested and taken to the nuthouse.

Cohen headed out to the desert again and could see Mount Tabor rising majestically in the distance, its peak pointing to heaven like a spiritual beacon lighting the path to paradise.

A few hours later he reached the foot of the mountain and kissed the ground, for he knew he was on holy ground, the very mountain on which Christ was transfigured in His glory. He trembled as he took his first step up the mountain, recalling the very same journey disciples took with Jesus, climbing to the summit and falling on their hands and knees as Christ became transfigured, appearing with Moses and Elijah.

As Cohen reached the summit, a dazzling light shone down, partially blinding him. He fell to his knees in fear and trembling, not daring to look up. As he lay on the ground, a voice called out: 'Be not afraid.'

Cohen looked up into the blinding light and saw a figure appear, an angel adorned in white, with such beauty and grace. He thought he must be hallucinating, but all the same he cried out with fear: 'Who are you?'

'I am a messenger of the Lord Most High,' the angel said. 'The Lord has blessed you. Go unto His people the Israelites and tell them to repent of their sins and turn to Christ. Counsel women not to rebel against the Lord, nor their husbands. As Christ is the head of the Church, so husbands are the head of the home. Implore them to follow Mary, the Mother of God, in all humility. Tell husbands to love their wives, as Christ loves the Church, and to follow his teaching, for in his suffering is their salvation.'

'Why ask this of me?' begged Cohen. 'I am nothing but a wretched sinner.'

'The Lord in His mercy has taken pity on you. Obey His commandments and sin no more.'

The angel departed and so did the dazzling light. Cohen rose slowly to his feet, an overwhelming sense of peace and love filled his heart. He took a deep breath and gazed out into the wilderness beyond, sweat pouring from his brow, his body shaking from the experience. He repeated the words the angel had said to go to the Jews and tell them about Jesus. His calling was a divine calling to witness to the Jews.

But Satan was forever on the prowl, and anxious to destroy the very seeds of godliness, to put doubts in Cohen's heart and make lose faith. He feared being locked up again in asylum with Jerusalem Syndrome, in exile and tormented. What more does God want to put him through?

The Jews were not interested in him. They didn't want to hear about Jesus. He was just a minor prophet. Yet who but

Christ and the Holy Spirit could bring peace to Israel? For Israel had become one of the most formidable states in the world materially, putting its hopes in its army, fighter jets and nuclear bombs – and forgetting God. Cohen knelt down and cried out: 'Where can I go from your Spirit?' He prayed for strength to resist the devil and all his temptations, to be given courage to fulfil his mission and to be empowered with the Holy Spirit. He prayed for Jews to renounce their sins and repent and turn to Christ, their Saviour. With renewed hope in his heart he set off down the mountain to return to the monastery, glancing back over his shoulder to see if he could catch one last glimpse of the angel, but he had gone back to heaven.

Cohen adjusted his rucksack, he returned from his pilgrimage. When he finally got back to the monastery the monks chastised him for being late. He had been assigned to cook supper. It was evident that Father Joseph had not got his note for the priest was away that day. 'You'd better get a move on,' urged Brother Ben. 'You've only got an hour to serve it up.'

Cohen looked at him aghast. With new guests arriving, the number of people in the community had risen to seventeen, and he had never cooked for that many before.

He fled to the kitchen in a state of panic and filled the saucepans with rice and vegetables. There was no time to consider anything appetising, least of all the French cuisine he'd been taught to cook at the French monastery. It would have to be a plain, simple meal, but seeing a bottle of wine in the kitchen he decided to add this to it for flavour. Despite his anxiety he managed to serve the meal on time, a vegetarian dish cooked with a bottle of wine, thanks to his experience of being a cook at the French monastery. During the supper he was surprised to receive compliments on his cooking from several of the guests, most of whom were partial to fine wine.

'Is that something you learned at the French monastery?' Father Joseph asked. 'We'll have no wine left in the cellar at this rate.'

'Can you cook for us again tomorrow?' Bridget asked.

The monks sat in silence and Father Colin looked at Cohen and asked sternly: 'You must come to the kitchen on time. Why did you come to Israel to be a monk? Why didn't you go to a monastery in England?'

'I'm a Jew,' Cohen replied. 'I didn't become a Christian until I came to Israel.'

'Is that right?' remarked Father Joseph, surprised. 'Tell me, what work did you do?'

'I was a journalist,' said Cohen.

Father Joseph seemed somewhat impressed. 'In that case, I have some work for you. I need typing done, and we need a librarian. I'll show you the library in the morning.'

Cohen wished he'd kept his mouth shut. His disastrous experience in the Franciscan library was still on his mind. He feared the new library was in a similar state of disorder. 'I'll come and help you,' offered Bridget, leaning across the table with her breasts exposed as she helped herself to more wine.

'That's kind of you but I think I'll be able to manage,' replied Cohen, resisting temptation.

'You'll be glad to hear you can move out of your cramped quarters,' said Father Joseph. 'There's a bedroom next to the library. You'll have bit more peace and quiet there.'

The next day, Father Joseph led Cohen across the mountain to an isolated building at the far end of the monastery grounds, close to the cemetery. He showed him his new quarters, a stark room overlooking a valley, equipped with a bed, table and chair, a typewriter and an oil heater. It was an ideal hermitage, far removed from the noisy guesthouse where he was woken up most nights by revelling guests. Father Joseph then took him into the library, the adjoining building. It was a brick building and the only one of its kind, for all the other buildings in the monastery were made of wood. Cohen was surprised to discover the library was in reasonable order and most of the books were indexed. But then Father Joseph pointed to a pile of books in a corner, all of which had to be filed and indexed in their proper order. Cohen studied the shelves. The majority of the books were religious of course: Bibles, lives of saints, even a section in Hebrew, including ancient copies of the Torah. In a separate storeroom books were piled on the floor in complete disarray. Father Joseph told him not to bother with that just now, for the books were secular books, mostly left by the guests. He then told Cohen he wanted the library index brought up to date, as the monks had difficulty finding books.

Cohen was curious about the building and asked why it was the only one to have been built from bricks.

'It came about purely by chance,' Father Joseph explained. 'We had bricks donated by the village. But we were thankful we built the library because we were forced to use it as shelter when Syria invaded. The shells from their tanks were pummelling the mountain and I doubt we would be here today but for the bricks. The building protected us from shrapnel and we were forced to sleep here for several nights before the bombardment stopped. It was a frightening experience, especially for the younger brothers. Thank God for His intervention, for the tanks got stuck in the sand and had to retreat.'

'So it's a fortress as well as a place of prayer,' Cohen quipped, 'heaven and hell.'

Father Joseph chuckled. 'Well, its time I left you to find your way around. I'll bring you some typing tomorrow so I'll have to change the liturgy.'

Cohen moved his belongings into the new room before taking on his library duties. He looked around the room and peered through the window. He could see the Golan Heights in the distance and Syria beyond. He wondered if the Syrians would attack again. He wouldn't stay in the library; that was for sure. He would flee to the nearest village. One shell would have blown the building to bits.

The following day was the Sabbath, and Cohen made his way across the mountain to the chapel. But on his arrival he was surprised to see that the monks were not there. It was the Sabbath and he had forgotten that the service would be held in the main chapel, which had been built underground in the mountain, carved out of chalk. The main chapel would be ideal for the monks and guests, for it had only been built recently. After descending several steps he was surprised to find how huge the main chapel was. It extended all the way across and up to the altar on the other side. The monks were praying at the altar, along with a few guests. Bridget was among those, gazing at admiringly at the priests.

The service lasted more than two hours, and after the Mass Cohen retreated to his new quarters to spend the rest of the day in peace and quiet.

The next day a German woman, a stunning brunette called Margaret, in her late-twenties, came on retreat. She was staying with nuns in Jerusalem and had come to the Holy Land to be closer to God. Cohen warmed to her straight away. She was quiet and unassuming, and very beautiful. In the evening after supper, he stoutly defended her when one of the Dutch guests called Stefan began berating her for being German. It was the same man who declared that on previous retreats he'd made several conquests of females at the monastery. After being told Cohen was the librarian, Margaret approached him about taking out some books, asking if he could recommend some spiritual reading.

'I'll show you where the library is tomorrow,' said Cohen, cheering up.

It was a warm sultry afternoon when he and Margaret walked to the library. On the way he noticed that her blouse was partly undone. He looked again at this Bavarian beauty and saw that her nipple was showing.

'Let me show you round the library,' said Cohen, holding the door open and allowing her to pass in front of him so he could take a second look. After showing her around the library and selecting a couple of books, he asked if she'd like to see his room. She followed him demurely and he invited her to sit at his desk. He told her that sometimes did some writing and that she was welcome to come and use the typewriter anytime.

'You write?' she inquired, looking at some manuscripts. 'That's a wonderful gift you have, especially if you're trying to live the solitary life.'

Cohen stood behind her as she leaned over his desk, looking out of the window. 'What a lovely view,' she said, gazing into the distance.

Margaret was unlike most Germans he'd met. She was a sensitive soul, warm and responsive. He sensed she had a liking for him as an Englishman and felt a warm friendship between herself and him, a welcome relief from the hostility of the

Dutch guests. He admired her for long brunette hair, which flowed down to her shoulders. He placed his hand on her shoulder and began to caress her neck, yielding to temptation.

'I think I'd best be getting back,' said Margaret, getting up from the chair.

'No, don't go just yet,' protested Cohen. 'Let me make you a cup of tea.'

'Some other time,' said Margaret, adjusting her hair.

In a moment of passion he reached out for her and kissed her on the lips.

'What are you doing?' protested Margaret. 'Aren't you training to be a monk?'

'Yes, but temptation overcame me,' said Cohen. 'Let me kiss you?'

'Please don't,' she moaned, 'I don't want to go to confession again.'

'Again?' inquired Cohen.

'Yes, it happened the day after I arrived in Israel. A priest seduced me in the laundry room, so much for priestly vows.'

'A priest!' exclaimed Cohen, jumping up. 'How could you let him do that to you, in a convent of all places?'

'He was too strong,' wiping a tear from her eye. 'He asked me to do his washing and then followed me in to the laundry room. What could I do?'

Doing up her blouse, Cohen meekly apologised. 'I don't know what came over me.'

'Men are all the same,' said Margaret resignedly. 'One would have thought a priest would set an example.'

'You're quite right, sister, and that's why I don't think I'm suited to being a monk. It's too stressful, all this self-denial.'

'Are you going to marry then?' asked Margaret.

'That's even more stressful,' said Cohen despondently.

'Don't tell me: you can't live with a woman and can't live without them,' she joked. 'Do you want to remain a bachelor all your life?'

'Such is the power women have over men,' shrugged Cohen.

'But you managed to stop,' she insisted. 'And I don't think I could have denied you. Women have needs too, you know.'

Cohen pulled her next to him and kissed her on the mouth. 'You're a remarkable woman, Margaret, but I don't think you'd feel the same if I told you I was Jewish.'

'You're a Jew?' she said, alarmed. 'Oh my God...'

'See what I mean,' shrugged Cohen.

'No, you misunderstand,' she said. 'I love that you're Jewish. It's just all my life I've been brought up to bear the terrible guilt for what the Nazis did to your people. How can we possibly put that right? How can I, a German woman brought up during the war, reconcile all that mass murder in the concentration camps?'

'You can't,' Cohen reassured her. 'Don't blame yourself, Margaret. You were just a child when all this happened. It had nothing to do with you.'

'Michael, please let me offer you some comfort,' said Margaret. 'Your family must have suffered terribly.'

'They did, but all that suffering is consumed by Christ now,' said Cohen. 'There is no more bitterness, no more hatred, not on my account.'

'You can forgive my people, and want to make love to me, a German woman?' she asked, incredulously. She called Cohen to sit beside her, offering herself to him as she lay beside him.

'I don't want your pity,' protested Cohen.

'It's not pity; it's compassion,' she said. 'Come here and make love to me,' she insisted.

Cohen's weakness, his love of beautiful women, just like King Solomon's, who had a thousand concubines in his harem, overcame him and he fell into her tempting arms.

'You want me – a Jew?' he asked in disbelief, as he began kissing her with renewed enthusiasm.

'Yes, I want you,' said Margaret, lifting up her skirt. Cohen was about to possess her when suddenly he heard a knock on his door.

It was Bridget. 'I need some books,' she said.

'Just coming,' cried Cohen, pulling up his trousers.

'Oh, it's you,' said Bridget, smiling. 'I didn't know you were in charge of the library,' she said, peering round the door.

'I'm the librarian,' Cohen said. He closed the door behind her and went to fetch her books. 'These are the ones, I'll see you at supper,' he said, abruptly.

Bridget, noticing Margaret, turned to Cohen and said: 'Be good.'

Cohen, all flustered, turned to Margaret and apologised: 'It's one of the drawbacks of being a librarian: people come by all hours of the day. Women seem to follow me around. It's such a beautiful day, why not come with me into the village? I have to go and pick up the mail for the monastery.'

Margaret paused as she held the door. 'What about the library?' she inquired.

'I'll leave the key at the monastery. Come and let me show you round the village. You'll enjoy the trip,' said Cohen.

She looked nervously at her watch. 'I guess we have time. Supper isn't until five o'clock. But I'd like to change first into something more comfortable than this skirt,' she said, embarrassed at her behaviour. She had, after all, come to the monastery to go on a spiritual retreat, not to indulge passionately with a man training to be a monk.

Cohen followed her along the footpath to the guest rooms. She unlocked her door and invited him in. Her room was Spartan, with just a single bed, desk and chair. But in her short stay at the monastery she had already added a feminine touch. On her table were some freshly cut tulips which Cohen recognised as those that grew on the mountainside when he took out the goats. Margaret had brought along her own photographs and displayed them proudly. There was a large icon of the Virgin Mary beside photos of Gandhi and Elvis, and the far wall a portrait of Adolf Hitler.

Cohen stood in front of the picture gobsmacked. He turned to Margaret, his voice trembling in rage: 'How could you do that?'

'Do what?' asked Margaret as she unzipped her skirt.

'That picture of Hitler! How can you have a picture of Hitler on your wall?' demanded Cohen.

'Oh, that. It was given to me by my father,' she said, matter-of-factly. 'I'll explain later. Let's go into the village, and let's not spoil the afternoon. Let's not argue about the past. It's all history.'

Cohen looked away from the portrait, and there stood Margaret, naked, deciding on which knickers to wear. He looked at her beautiful body, forgetting all about Hitler. She had quite large breasts, a narrow waist and long legs. He reached out and tried to kiss her. 'Stop it,' she insisted.

'You know I want you,' demanded Cohen.

'You can't do this,' she protested. 'You're wearing a monk's robe.'

'I borrowed it,' Cohen confessed, attempting to touch her breasts.

'I presume that in fact you stole it,' said Margaret, pushing his hand away.

'I borrowed it from another monastery.'

'Get off me,' she yelled. 'You're despicable, just like that priest.'

'I want to make love to you,' said Cohen, frustrated.

'What is wrong with you? You stole that robe and now you're pretending to be a monk, seducing a woman in it!' she protested. 'Are you no different from the priest who raped me?' she said, glaring at Cohen with all the anger of a woman defiled.

Cohen stared at her in disbelief. How could she ask him such a question? Was she really the kind of cold-blooded woman the Germans were renowned for? Whose side was she on? Was it Hitler and the portrait? Cohen felt confused and anxious.

He turned to her and grabbed her by the arms. He held her tightly and kissed her on the lips, undoing her bra.

'You've done this many times before,' she moaned.

'Done what?'

'Undone a woman's bra,' she protested. 'You did it so quickly, faster than any man who's ever undone my bra.'

'If I didn't know you were German, I could have sworn you were Irish,' said Cohen.

'Why do you think I'm Irish?' said Margaret.

'Because there is an Irish charm in you mixed with madness.'

'You think I'm mad?' she scoffed, pulling away abruptly. She stood back with sudden petulance. 'Anyone who dresses like a monk and ravishes women has to be mad. Who do you think you are – Rasputin?'

'You think I'm like Rasputin?' Cohen said, aghast at her comments.

'I'm a woman. I don't make judgements. We just know what is right,' said Margaret, matter-of-factly.

'Are you saying women are instinctive creatures, slaves to their moods and emotions?' Cohen asked sarcastically. 'Women are emotional. That's what makes them women.'

'You don't understand women,' protested Margaret. 'Women know when something's wrong. You are a Christian and trying to be a monk. Get a grip, Michael. Stop molesting me and let's go to the village in peace, as sister and brother.'

'You assume too much, Margaret. You think I want you all the time that I'm lusting for your body, especially when you undress?'

'So, what happened in the library was all in my imagination, the ravings of a mad woman – is that what you're suggesting?' said Margaret.

'You misunderstand me, as all women do when they pigeonhole me and set out to change me. I'm simply saying that all men have a weakness for the fairer sex, but there are some who don't, like gays. Others have been blessed with celibacy, like asexual. For a heterosexual person to practise celibacy is a struggle. Men are human, so are women, and they have their weaknesses too.'

'Oh, and what are they?' queried Margaret.

'I've told you. You want to change men instead of letting them live their lives their own way.'

'And men don't do that to women?' questioned Margaret.

'Women are in control,' exclaimed Cohen.

'At last you have come to your senses,' said Margaret, disdainfully. 'Then in future when a woman says no she means exactly that.'

'Then why did you undress in front of me?' asked Cohen, perplexed.

'Where else could I change but in my room?' she said.

'But in front of me? You could have asked me to wait outside, but you invited me in.'

'I didn't want people seeing you wait outside my door. What would they have thought? Besides, it's Christian to invite people in. It's called hospitality – in case you'd forgotten – not an invitation to jump on me and molest me!' she said indignantly.

'You're quite right,' he confessed, 'but there's no need to go about it by nagging.'

Offended by his remark, Margaret raised her chin in the air and stormed off in the direction of the village. Cohen caught up with her. 'You're going the wrong way,' he pointed out.

'I can see the village below, how can I get lost?'

'Carry on then. It'll take you twice as long and you'll end up in the bushes with thorns. Not a pleasant sight, I can assure you.'

'Typical man, always wanting to be in charge,' fumed Margaret.

'That's how it should be,' he said, matter-of-factly.

'Says who?' she asked.

'The Bible,' said Cohen. 'Adam came first and Eve second, to seduce him. Man is the head of the house, for man was created first and then a wife, to obey her husband. It is God's will.'

'And where in the Bible, pray tell, does it say that?' queried Margaret.

'In St. Paul's letter,' he said.

'What did he know?' scoffed Margaret. 'He was a misogynist.'

'He was an Apostle to the Gentiles, filled with the Holy Spirit.'

'I'm a Lutheran,' she said. 'We do not accept everything Paul says as Gospel, but every word that the Lord Himself says is true.'

'You're a Protestant?' Cohen asked.

'Yes,' said Margaret proudly, 'but its different now. We pray for church unity. Lutherans are closer now to Roman Catholics than the Church of England.'

'Why?' asked Cohen

'The Church of England has ordained women priests and women bishops too.'

Cohen laughed out loud. 'I thought you were all for women's rights. I could have sworn you were a feminist?'

'I'm not a feminist,' said Margaret, 'I believe in women's rights, but not ordination. You're right; women should not lord it over men as bishops. Only men can be ordained. It has been going on for 2,000 years. What right does the Church of England have to change all that?'

Cohen was beside himself. 'I can't believe what I'm hearing. It's you that's come to your senses.'

Margaret leaned against a tree coquettishly, placing her hands seductively on her hips. 'What do you think of my figure?'

'Gorgeous.' he exclaimed, admiring her breasts.

'And what do think of my waist?' she asked, precociously.

'Magnificent,' Cohen said, admiring her body.

'Let's go now,' she insisted, letting go of her seductive pose and striding down the mountain ahead of him. Cohen realised he had a woman of substance on his hands, was not only strong, but also a temptress, a child full of passion, a woman who wanted a man but only on her terms – a holy *femme fatale*.

'Shall we lie down here?' Cohen suggested after they had come to a green pasture shaded by olive trees.

'Why here?' asked Margaret. 'Are you suggesting something?' she said with a wry smile.

'Only to rest,' Cohen said, 'and share the chocolate I brought.'

'Chocolate!' she exclaimed. 'You obviously know what chocolate does to a woman...'

'It turns you on?' said Cohen suggestively.

'Maybe,' she said, lying down in the grass, arms over her head so that she revealed her breasts. Lying in the grass like that, she was the spitting image of the Danish girl he'd met at the fountain, wanton and ravenous.

'Margaret, there's something I have to tell you,' said Cohen, seriously.

'Don't tell me you're married?' she laughed.

'No,' said Cohen, blushing, 'I'm not a virgin, but I've not had as many women in my life as you seem to think. And for me, each of those relationships has been sacred.'

'You're serious?' she said.

'Yes,' he said, emphatically.

'Well, let's be sacred then,' said Margaret, lifting her skirt, about to consummate the affair. Cohen admired her ample figure and long legs. He began kissing her as they laid together in the olive groves, her legs akimbo, when suddenly a bell rang out, getting louder as it echoed across the mountains.

Cohen's amorousness seemed to wither away all at once. 'It sounds like the bell announcing Judgment Day,' he exclaimed.

'For God's sake,' exclaimed Margaret, 'it's only the monastery bell.'

'The monastery bell?' he said, perplexed. 'Are you sure?'

He looked at Margaret standing over him, his knees shaking and his manhood shrivelled. 'Are you a man or a mouse?' she asked.

'Sorry,' he apologised. 'I've never heard bells like that before. There must have been an echo.'

'Oh my God, let's go,' she said, frustrated, and pulled up her knickers. She marched on ahead of him down the mountain. Cohen caught up with her and they walked to the village when a voice called out. It was an Arab woman inviting them to her house for a coffee.

'It's the Arab custom to invite people in,' Cohen said. 'She's asking us in because you're a woman. If you don't accept it will offend her. If I was alone she wouldn't invite me in; her husband wouldn't approve,' he said. 'Arab women are very hospitable to Western women. I guess it's how women are with each other, which ever country they're in. They like to share their suffering.'

'What suffering?' Margaret asked.

'Like giving birth, being a mother, losing a child, that sort of thing.'

'You have a feminine side,' she said. 'Are you gay?'

'If I was gay, I wouldn't have tried to seduce you, would I?'

'It's you that needs seducing,' she scoffed. 'Alright, so you're not a virgin, but I think sex with a woman terrifies you. That's why you resisted when the bell rang.'

'Not so.' protested Cohen. 'I heard the sound and thought Judgement Day had come.'

'Making love to me is a sin; is that what you're saying?' asked Margaret incredulously.

'Well, Eve sure messed up Adam,' said Cohen.

'You men are so pathetic,' said Margaret. 'Adam allowed himself to be seduced. It was his own fault.'

'Who tempted him?' asked Cohen.

'Eve, of course.'

'And why she did seduce him?' asked Cohen.

'She's a woman, that's why, to procreate life,' said Margaret.

'She corrupted Adam. He was happy in Paradise until she came along.'

'Then why did God say it's not good for a man to live alone?' asked Margaret. 'And who gave birth to the Son of God – a woman!'

Cohen had no answer. Margaret looked at him compassionately. She wanted him to be at peace. She knew he was struggling to make love to a woman. She felt somehow that he must have been denied love as a child, and sought desperately to compensate for an emotional deprivation by clutching at women and causing conflict. He must have been a victim of his Jewish upbringing, most likely an overbearing mother.

Cohen followed her across the cobbled street where the Arab woman lived, beckoning them to come inside for a coffee. On entering they were greeted by a brood of children, about seven of them, from a young baby to a teenage boy.

'You have children?' asked the Arab mother. 'I have seven children; the eighth is on its way.'

'I'm single,' said Margaret.

'No husband, no children?' asked the mother, surprised.

'I haven't found the right person,' said Margaret.

As they resumed climbing the mountain, Cohen reached out and held her hand to lift her up over a rock. 'Can we lie down and have a rest?' asked Margaret, getting her breath back.

Cohen led her to an olive grove and sat down in the grass out of the sun.

'You won't hear the bells from here?' she said, lying down in the grass.

'What are you suggesting?' asked Cohen.

'I know what I need,' she said. 'Come here.'

'I thought you wanted a brother and sister relationship?' he queried, lying down beside her.

'That was then,' said Margaret. 'This is now.' Cohen leaned across her heaving breasts and kissed her on the mouth. Her lips were soft and warm, quivering with anticipation.

He lifted up her skirt and noticed she was wearing blue knickers.

'They're my university colours,' he said, laughing.

'For heaven's sake, get on with it!' she moaned.

Cohen needed no further prompting, ignoring the fact that at Matins he'd promised to stay celibate. He pulled down her panties and studied her pussy as she lay spread-eagled in the grass.

'What are you doing?' she asked.

'I was just curious,' Cohen said. 'Wondering why boys come out of there and spend the rest of their lives trying to get back in.'

'Are you staring at my vagina?' she asked, alarmed.

'Just coming to terms with it, your sacred cup, your sacred vessel,' he said smiling.

'Here, let me show you.' She grabbed his manhood.

He was in the very act of possessing her when he suddenly heard footsteps approaching.

Cohen immediately jumped off her. Looking up into the intruder's face, he recognised who it was. It was the albino boy.

'Have you been following us?' demanded Cohen.

The boy stared at the naked Margaret and grinned. 'I'm going to the monastery and do some work.' the boy said.

Margaret covered herself up and railed at Cohen. 'What's wrong with you?' she shouted, and stormed off up the hill with the Albino boy.

Cohen reached the monastery later, exhausted from the day's upheavals. He went to his room depressed, and fell asleep.

21

Cohen awoke to the sound of Father Colin banging on his door. He had slept in, missing the morning chapel and breakfast, and was wanted in the kitchen to do the washing up. 'There's no peace for the wicked,' groaned Cohen, turning over in his bed. He was hung-over and barely remembered the night before, not to mention the events of the day. But he was soon to be reminded, and it came as a shock to him.

At midday prayers Margaret suddenly burst into tears and ran out of the chapel. Father Joseph, in alarm, dashed out after her. She seemed to be having a crisis of conscience, if not a nervous breakdown over what happened on the mountain.

Why allow neurotic women into monasteries in the first place? Cohen asked. It was bound to end in tears. He went back to the library and got on with his duties, forgetting Margaret.

Within the hour Father Joseph appeared at the library. 'I've just heard some disturbing news about what happened yesterday on the mountain,' said Father Joseph.

'What's wrong?' asked Cohen, innocently looking up from his typewriter.

'Our German guest, Margaret, was molested on the mountain. Do you know anything about it?' asked Father Joseph. 'You were with her that day.'

'No Padre, she wanted to come back alone,' said Cohen.

'This would be a scandal for the monastery if it got out,' said Father Joseph. 'Is there a possibility she is making this up? Are you sure you didn't see anything?'

'She's a bit unstable,' said Cohen, 'like a lot of women who come to the monastery.'

'Yes, yes,' said Father Joseph, impatiently, 'but you must not mention this to anyone else. It would be most detrimental to the monastery, you understand. I've managed to calm her down, and she's said she won't complain to the authorities But if the news got back to the village the police could get involved, and the monastery's reputation would suffer.'

'I won't mention it father,' said Cohen. 'Women are trouble, perhaps more so when they come to a monastery.'

'Even so we must show compassion to the weaker sex. But I can't understand why she's making this accusation. She's been to the monastery before and been no trouble,' said Father Joseph.

'Did she say anything about me?' asked Cohen, apprehensively. 'I mean, regarding yesterday.'

'Just that she went to the village with you and you came back alone.'

Cohen was thankful to Margaret for not getting him in trouble. Was there anything between Margaret and the Albino boy? She'd gone ahead before Cohen and remarked that she had a maternal longing for the boy.

The following day it was community washing day when everyone helped out. The hardest task was putting to the clothes into cold water and rinsing them, for there wasn't sufficient hot water for this. This had to be done in freezing water, numbing the hands.

It was now December, and the frost was beginning to show on the mountain. Margaret was washing the women's underwear, keeping her distance. She did not want to socialise with anybody, but as she passed by to fetch more clothes,

Cohen teased her with a smack on the behind. She ignored him and walked back to washing.

After supper he went to her room to thank her, but she was gone. He would never see her again. She had left the monastery without saying goodbye. She was booked in at the monastery for Christmas, but never returned. Cohen felt sad because Margaret was his one true friend at the monastery. He busied himself in the library, reorganising the filing and index systems and rearranging the bookshelves. The work not only took his mind off the past few days but was also fulfilling and enjoying, as opposed to the hassle of women.

But now he had the energy to serve the Lord. In between times spent organising the library, he had started to paint again. He had been looking through some icons of saints when he came across one saint, Saint Rita, an Arab woman who had been born in Palestine, much revered for her works of charity. After copying an icon of her, Cohen took it to the village and presented it to the minister of his local church. The priest recognised the saint immediately and said the icon should be paraded through the streets of the village and preserved in the church.

The priest insisted Cohen be part of the procession before it was hung permanently near the altar. He was later feted throughout the village as the Painter of Saints and enjoyed the freedom of the village, including being invited to the join the mayor at a banquet in his honour.

Cohen had been at the monastery for three months. It was Advent and the monks were preparing for Christmas. He wondered how they would celebrate the birth of Christ.

One thing was for sure, they wouldn't run out of alcohol. On entering the store, he was surprised to find cases of wines and spirits sent to the monastery as gifts from the village. In addition, Brother Ben would be brewing up some special beer for Christmas Day, as well as bringing several bottles of vintage wine for the occasion. 'Last Christmas a woman got so drunk at the party,' roared Brother Ben, 'that she lost her way to the guesthouse and I found her asleep in my bed!'

'What happened?' asked Cohen. 'Did you kick her out?'

'Of course!' he chuckled, a cheeky grin on his face. 'Where's Margaret, I thought she was staying for Christmas? '

'She left,' replied Cohen. 'Could be back in Germany for all I know.'

'I think she'd taken a shine to you,' said Ben, winking.

'Who can fathom a woman's heart?' asked Cohen, getting up.

He said goodnight and went back to his room, having sneaked a bottle of spirit from the storehouse. He was feeling down about Margaret so decided to get the festive season underway and opened the bottle. After a few glasses he went into the library in search of a book on carols. Whether it was the alcohol or his new filing system, try as he may he couldn't find one. In the morning he tried to remember some of the carols he'd heard in England, where pony-tailed girls in white socks and frilly blouses sang at Christmas carol concerts. By the time he'd finished the bottle, he could remember half a dozen carols, including Hark the Herald Angel Sing, Ding Dong Merrily on High and Away in the Manger.

On Christmas Day he went into the refectory singing a solo performance of carols, fortified by Brother Ben's special brew. As the singing went on he found that the more he drank the fewer carols he remembered, until the final Gloria refrain went on and on – and the monks left.

It was time to say goodnight.

22

After Christmas life at the monastery became difficult for Cohen. He had been drinking too much and his relationship with Margaret had given him serious doubts about becoming a monk.

He realised after he woke up with a hang-over that it was time to move on. Alcohol was a problem and matters weren't helped by his inappropriate behaviour with women, not what was expected of a monk. He decided to see Father Joseph and explain his dilemma, and needed cash as he was broke and had no money for his journey. His journey was further south, to Sinai, for he had got it into his mind to visit the oldest monastery in Christendom, the Orthodox Greek Monastery of St. Catherine, dating back to the fourth century. It was a long journey. He'd read about it and seen photographs of the monastery perched high upon Mount Sinai, surrounded by ancient fortress walls built to keep out Muslim invaders.

Here was his last chance to become a monk, for women were not allowed in the Monastery and guesthouses remained outside the fortified walls.

During the time of King Constantine, Muslims invaded the monastery and built a minaret where it still stood today. On hearing the news the King sent an army to recapture the monastery.

The thought of Cohen becoming a monk in the oldest monastery, built on the same mountain as Moses was given the Ten Commandments, fuelled his imagination to flee the monastery and head for Sinai.

He decided to swap his choir robe for an Orthodox robe hanging in the cloister. This would be more suitable to wear in the Orthodox monastery. You had special permission to be near the monks' cells, let alone live with them.

'You want to leave,' asked Father Joseph, 'and to go to St. Catherine's?'

'I don't feel like I fit in here anymore,' said Cohen regretfully.

'You'll find it even more difficult there. The monks have to deal with constant tourists. The worship is hard to maintain and the Greeks don't want to take in outsiders,' said Father Joseph, dismayed at his leaving. He reached into his drawer and handed Cohen enough money to get to Mount Sinai.

'I sorry you want to leave. I thought you were coping quite well, apart from women.'

'What you do mean?' asked Cohen, raising his eyebrows innocently.

'I can understand you've had difficulty with women. Some monks have difficulty when women are constantly around. You must learn to treat them with respect, as mothers and sisters, and to show them the love of Christ,' he said.

'At St. Catherine's women aren't allowed to mingle with monks,' said Cohen matter-of-factly.

'That's so. Well, when you get to my age, it's easier. The urge goes away,' said Father Joseph. 'Go in peace, and God bless your journey.'

Cohen thanked him, went back to the library and packed his rucksack. He stuffed the Orthodox robe in the bag, making sure he left the choir robe in the same place he had taken the Orthodox one from, on the back of the library door. He took one last look at the room, where he first met Margaret, then headed down the mountain into the village to catch a bus into Jerusalem. He felt a sense of relief at leaving the Dutch monastery, especially at getting away from women and the constant criticism of the English. But he was sad to leave Father Joseph, for the padre had been good to him. He'd shown him compassion and love. He also sensed that Father Joseph, now in his eighties, had not much longer to live. But Cohen made a point of writing to him to thank him. He later received a reply saying that he would be welcome at the monastery, but could no longer be considered for a monk in view of his 'inappropriate behaviour' with female guests.

As he waited for the bus to Jerusalem, the albino approached him and asked where his woman was.

'She's left, gone back to Germany,' he said, feeling miffed by the boy.

The albino boy, sensing that Cohen was upset, offered him another woman, only younger.

'She is very beautiful,' said the boy, 'only 100 shekels.'

'No thanks,' said Cohen. 'I've had enough of women.'

'She likes English,' said the boy, putting his fingers in his mouth and whistling across the street. Moments later a stunning girl appeared, dark and voluptuous. Cohen couldn't believe that this beautiful girl would sell herself for money. It was Palestine after all, and people were living hand to mouth.

'Is she your sister?' asked Cohen.

'No, my girlfriend,' said the albino. 'You like?'

'It's your girlfriend?' Cohen said, aghast. 'Why would you want to sell your girlfriend? She's beautiful.'

'We need money to go to America,' said the boy. 'No work here, nothing.'

Flashing her long dark eyelashes, the woman came up to Cohen. 'Come with me. I can give you what you want,' said the girl.

Cohen looked into her dark brown eyes and, overcome with lust, reached for his pocket. But the thought of becoming a monk and getting to the Sinai monastery got the better of him.

'I'm training to be a monk,' said Cohen, putting his money away.

'A monk?' the girl gasped, turning to her boyfriend furiously. 'Why you bring to me a monk, shame on you!'

'I didn't know he was a monk. I thought he was visiting the monastery.'

Cohen was relieved to see the bus for Jerusalem arriving. He left the couple arguing as he climbed on board. The albino boy waved him goodbye, a wry grin on his face, as the girlfriend continued to harangue him.

On the journey Cohen reminisced about his stay at the monastery. He had respect for Father Joseph, even though he was against him being a monk. For twenty-five years the padre had had the courage to reconcile Jews and Arabs to Christ on the mountain. Yet not one person from either village had joined the monastery. Father Joseph's life had been one of trials and perseverance, but in the end it bore no fruit, save only the seeds of Christ he planted in the hearts of the guests who came and went. No monks ever joined. Once he foretold what was coming in the afterlife. 'I don't think we can imagine being without a body in the next life,' he said 'we are so used to it.'

His remarks echoed what Cohen heard on a visit to Canterbury Cathedral by the then Dean, Dr. John Simpson, an Oxford theologian: 'For God created us; it is inconceivable that our consciousness would not continue after the body dies.'

Cohen often thought about his own death, his mortality and how people would all die. If people had one thing in common it was death, the Grim Reaper. But Christ had given him faith by resurrection, a life after death where the body could change from a corruptible body into an incorruptible body, a spiritual body.

As Cohen passed through Palestinian villages he witnessed poverty and oppression, suffering brought by the killing of Arabs by Jews in the name of Jehovah, Arabs killing Jews in the name of Allah, in the so-called Holy Land. Where was Christ in all this? Cohen asked. Just then he heard a small voice saying: *On the Cross.*

To this day the Jews would not understand. They rejected their Messiah, their own flesh and blood and crucified him, calling out: 'Let his blood be upon our heads.' Cohen felt disappointed at seeing the state of Israel and he feared for its future. He picked up the newspaper and glanced at the front page. To his shock and horror it was the prophecy he had predicted: RIOTS OVER TEMPLE BUILDING. The Jerusalem Post said that riots had broken out in the streets of the Old City over the building of the new temple. More than fifty people had been killed after builders had begun laying the foundations at the site in the Muslim Quarter.

Although initially shocked he wasn't surprised that riots had taken place after all the research he'd done on the re-building of the temple. Blood was flowing on the streets of Jerusalem again, and this time he was going to be caught up in the middle of it. He could not avoid it. There was no other way of getting to Sinai other than a bus from Jerusalem.

Would peace ever come to the holy city? He doubted it, not in his lifetime. He was now of the firm conviction that peace would not come until the Second Coming, which would last for a thousand years, according to the scriptures.

In the meantime he read what was actually happening in Jerusalem. Arabs in the Muslim Quarter had attacked Jewish builders laying foundations for the rebuilding of the temple next to the Dome of the Rock, and then all hell broke loose.

Several builders and Israeli soldiers had been killed, some stoned to death, as Muslims had stormed to defend their holy shrine.

It was anarchy in the holy city again, and the Israelis responded by sending in troops with riot gear, firing at will on the protesters. It snowballed out of control as the army and fighter planes attacked the West Bank and the Gaza strip.

Cohen's heart sank as he finished reading the shocking news. He recalled the prophecy that the Messiah would come when the temple was restored. Could riots caused by the devil to prevent the Second Coming, the return of Jesus Christ?

Yet other prophecies told of Satan setting up his throne in the new temple, marked with the sign of the beast, before the Second Coming of Christ.

Could Satan, the prince of darkness, come in person as an angel of light to deceive the world? Which prophecy was correct – that the Messiah would come when the temple was restored, or the Book of Revelation, which said Satan would set himself up in the temple in the last days?

Cohen pondered the mystery as the bus neared the outskirts of Jerusalem. In the distance he could see flames shooting above the Moslem quarter. He had only one intention – to get out of the city. He would not play the martyr, or risk entering the Muslim Quarter, even though work on the temple had begun.

His intention was to flee Israel, just as Joseph and Mary had done with the baby Jesus 2,000 years ago.

Chaos greeted him at the bus station as throngs of people crowded around with the same intention. Soldiers and tanks rolled past, heading for the Old City. It was like Armageddon, a mass build up of troops with artillery heading for the final conflict in the holy city. Fearing a mass exodus – ingrained into the Jewish people from time of Moses – extra buses were diverted to the city, amid chaos and confusion.

Cohen despaired of his chances of getting a ticket for Elat, the southern port of Israel on the border with Sinai, as Jews besieged the station carrying whatever possessions they could manage. Women and children were being crushed in the panic to board the buses.

Fearing for his life, Cohen fled the bus station and began walking towards Ein Karem. He could stay in the village just for a few days until the rioting had calmed down. He would not be welcome at the Franciscan monastery, or the French monastery, but he hoped the Catholic nuns would put him up, if he offered to work for his upkeep.

As he headed out of Jerusalem he could hear the sound of shelling in the distance. He turned and looked at the fire and brimstone raging down on the Muslim Quarter, just like Lot had done when fleeing Sodom and Gomorrah in the old days. His wife turned back and was transformed into a pillar of salt for defying God.

Cohen stood in shock and disbelief as he witnessed the horror of Jerusalem being ravaged by war. Death pervaded the air. The very life force had been drained out of him, as if he was dead. He forced himself to continue the march back to Ein

Karem, as the roads were jammed with traffic leaving the city, most bound for Ben Gurion airport in Tel Aviv.

Once again the Jews were caught up in a mass exodus, but this time there was no Moses to lead them to the promised land of Israel. This time they were fleeing it.

Cohen was relieved when he arrived at the village, for there remained a sense of calm and order. No one was panicking or making frantic phone calls to leave, despite what they'd heard on the news.

He walked through the village and made his way to the convent and rang the bell, just as he had when he'd entered the village with no place to stay. He waited patiently for a nun to appear, hoping they would put him up.

It was Sister Sharon who opened the gate, a broad smile spreading across her face as she recognised him. 'We thought you'd gone back to England,' she said, greeting him warmly.

'I was hoping you might have a room for a couple of nights?' he asked. 'All hell's is breaking out in Jerusalem, but let me not concern you with that just now,' he said, wanting to spare her feelings. 'Suffice to say that it's a sad world we live in, sister.'

'It certainly is,' replied Sister Sharon. 'Do come in. We have a spare room for you as we're not very busy this time of the year.'

'I'm afraid I haven't any money, but I'm willing to work for my keep,' he said.

'Don't be worrying about that, our Lord didn't have money either,' she said, closing the gate. She took him to the same room he had when he first stayed, with its sparse furniture and a solitary crucifix hanging over the bed.

As he sat on his bed, peace pervaded the room, a sense of timelessness even though war was breaking out in Jerusalem.

After all his travelling, his restlessness and pursuit of peace, Cohen could understand why the nuns chose to live in a convent, with the stability and order it gave even though the confining walls of a monastery were not for him. As he lay down he thanked God for all the peace and quiet of the convent, even though it would not last long. What was happening in Jerusalem was beyond comprehension. He wondered if the nuns had heard of the fighting. Feeling hungry, Cohen went into the refectory. He asked one of the nuns if she had a radio. She looked at him aghast.

'Heavens no!' said the nun indignantly. 'This is a convent.'

'You're not concerned that Jerusalem is burning?' said Cohen incredulously.

'Jerusalem has always suffered,' the nun said.

Cohen did not wish to argue with her and walked out into the garden for some fresh air. He felt the urge to leave the convent and headed for the bar. When he arrived a group of men were crowded round the TV shouting and waving their hands in the air. It was clear the riots in the Muslim Quarter had been crushed, dealt with by the army. The rebuilding of the temple would start the next day.

Cohen was relieved to be able to leave the troubled city for the most revered monastery in all Christendom, the St Catherine Monastery of Mount Sinai.

It was his last call to be a monk.

23

Cohen said farewell to the sisters and kissed Sister Sharon on her cheek, knowing that he wouldn't see her again. He had grown fond of her coming into his room and bringing the breakfast. Parting was such sweet sorrow.

He caught the bus into Jerusalem and was tempted to go and see whether building work had resumed on the temple. But he thought best he didn't, for fear of the Muslims rioting.

Instead he went to the ticket office and caught the next bus to Elat, the holiday resort and southernmost port of Israel.

It was a long journey as the bus stopped at several locations to pick up passengers and make rest stops, one of them Massada, where exiled Jews fought the Romans. One thousand Jews held out against the Roman army for three years on the top of a mountain. It took the Romans two years to build a ramp for them to besiege the mountain summit. When they attacked, all the Jews were dead, dying by their own swords rather than surrender to slavery.

Cohen got out of the bus and stared up at the mountain, a flat plateau where the Jews had lived in harmony until the Romans came. He was astonished at how the Jews managed to scale the mountain in the first place, let alone survive in the harshest desert for so long. He imagined the Jews suffering alone in the desert, exiled from their own country, standing up to the might of the Roman army. He admired their courage in choosing to perish by their own hand rather than execution, for it must have taken a great deal of bravery to die that way, especially for the women and children.

Cohen took one last look at the mountain, which gleam almost the colour of blood in the midday sun. Wiping a tear from his eye, he went to the bus and headed for Elat.

After a few hours, he arrived in Elat, the border with Egypt and the Sinai desert, land captured by Israeli in the 1967 war but given back to the Egypt under the subsequent peace deal. Egyptian border officials seemed over-cautious when checking Cohen's passport and visa. They were suspicious of any Jew entering Egypt. Finally he was allowed to pass through the Egyptian border and get on a bus to take him to St. Catherine's Monastery in Sinai. As the bus was letting passengers on board an English girl in her early twenties was struggling to lift her suitcase onto an overhead rack. She was wearing a see-through blouse and Cohen noticed that she wasn't a wearing a bra. Her breasts swung like pendulums in front of him as she reached over. He got up to help her with the case, but like most girls in the West, she insisted on doing it herself, preferring independence.

Her stunning figure distracted him for the most of the journey until the bus stopped at a resort, Dassa sur Salem in the Sinai Peninsula, where she promptly got off. It was late in the evening and Cohen decided to stay in the resort overnight and continue his journey in the morning. He thought no more about the girl until, when looking for a bar, he saw her sitting alone at a table outside the restaurant.

Cohen asked her politely if he could join her. Her name was Helen. She made no objection and they fell into animated conversation about her Greek journey, with her telling him about an amazing Greek lover she'd had.

Cohen noticed her beauty, which made him envious of her Greek lover. Why English girls gave themselves so readily to foreigners was beyond him. 'What made him a good lover?' he asked.

'He was very experienced. He touched me in all the right places, you know what I mean.' Helen giggled.

'Aren't you afraid of travelling alone?' Cohen asked, concerned.

'What's there to be afraid of? If someone rapes me there's not much I can do about it,' she said matter-of-factly.

'Where are you staying tonight?' he asked, anxious for her safety. 'In Arabia white girls have been kidnapped and put in harems.'

'I haven't the faintest idea,' said Helen, stretching her arms. 'I'll look round for a room or sleep on the beach.'

'I'm staying overnight,' said Cohen. 'We can look for a place together.'

'OK,' she said, nonchalantly, getting up from the table. 'All I know is how important it is to get a good night's sleep, after all that travelling,' said Helen, yawning.

They left the restaurant and walked along the shore where they came to a seaside hotel. She marched ahead of him into the reception and asked if they had any rooms available. She was shocked at the price.

'We can share a room if you like,' suggested Cohen. 'It will be cheaper. You've got nothing to worry about.'

She gave him a suspicious look. He blamed his feeble attempt to allay her fears when it came to sharing a room with a stranger. The truth was he wanted to be with her that night, but his ploy backfired. Picking up her suitcase she marched out of the hotel and headed along the beach in the direction of a holiday camp the receptionist recommended.

It was a sultry night. The moon reflected its rays on the water and the warmth of the sea air embraced them. Helen strode energetically ahead of him, anxious to find a bed for the night as it was getting late. Cohen struggled to keep up with her and before they were halfway there, he was out of breath.

'Hold on a minute.' he shouted after her.

Helen turned and walked back to him. 'What's the matter? We're nearly there.'

'I just a bit of rest to catch my breath,' he panted. He sat down on the sand and stared out to sea. 'It's a beautiful night. Just look at the moon. It's awesome.'

She sat down next to him and looked at the moon, all amber.

'It's so romantic,' she said softly, raising Cohen's hopes and dashing them in the next breath: 'I wish my Greek lover was here.'

She lay down in the sand, resting on his rucksack. Cohen looked down at her as she invited him to come closer and the waves rolled gently onto the shore. He leaned across her and looked into her deep blue eyes and could see the reflection of the moon rays in her pupils. 'You're so beautiful,' he whispered. He edged closer to her and moved his hand slowly up her blouse and fondled her breasts. The thrill of the soft flesh gave him aroused, and he was about to seduce her when she suddenly said:

'Have you never made love to a woman before?'

'Yes, but never very well,' he said panting.

'I'll show you,' said Helen, lifting her skirt.

'What about your Greek lover?' Cohen asked.

'I'm not in Greece now,' she said, opening her legs. Cohen laid between her gaping thighs in a state of ecstasy, not believing his luck that such a beautiful creature would give herself so willingly to him, a stranger she'd just met. He was about to possess her when suddenly a wave broke upon the shore and poured all over him.

'Don't stop,' she moaned.

'But I'm soaked. Look at my jeans!' yelled Cohen, jumping off her.

'Bugger your jeans,' she hollered. 'You've gone and spoiled everything.'

She instantly pulled up her skirt and strode off into the distance, leaving him soaked to the skin and bemoaning his fate with women. He vowed to never make love to a woman again as long as he lived.

When he arrived at the camp exhausted and bedraggled Helen was nowhere to be seen. The cabins, nothing more than makeshift huts of bamboo, were all booked. Cohen made his way to the reception and he was told that a girl had just booked the last room and there were no spare beds for the night. 'You can sleep in the porch until we find a room for tomorrow,' said the receptionist.

Picking up his rucksack he headed for the porch and tried to get some sleep, with his sleeping bag soaked through. In the morning he found Helen asleep in the cabin a few blocks away. She was fast asleep and nestled in her warm sleeping bag, which was zipped up only halfway. As she lay on her side, Cohen noticed one of her breasts was exposed. Tempted to go and cover her up in case some stranger came into her hut and molested her, but fearing he might disturb her and cause her to scream, he turned away never to see Helen again.

Cohen made his way back to town and waited for the bus. He had a half-hour wait for the next bus to arrive, so he went to the washroom to change into the robe he'd taken from the monastery. With his long beard and long hair tied back, the robe not only gave him the appearance of an Orthodox monk, but would protect him from the wiles of women.

As he looked out across the wilderness Cohen realised he'd had no idea of the vastness of the Sinai desert. In the distance he marvelled at the mountains as they came into view and it was the first time he'd seen a herd of wild camels roaming through the desert plain.

There was an overnight stop before journeying on to St. Catherine's, where he stayed with some Bedouins, enjoying their hospitality around a camp fire.

That night he made his way to the beach for some solitude and walked barefoot along the sand in his robe, with not a soul in sight. He relished the peace and quiet by the sea as the stars stretched endlessly in the night. Looking up to heaven he felt the presence of God. In awe he stood alone, in perfect peace. But that was not to last long, for troubling thoughts arose. His conscience pricked him, for once again he had yielded to temptations of the flesh while on a pilgrimage to one of the holiest shrines, the sacred mountain where God appeared to Moses, Mount Sinai. Stricken to his heart, Cohen fell to his knees and prayed.

Tears of penance welled up inside as though his soul was wounded, and suddenly, without warning, a feeling of joy overwhelmed him, one he'd not experienced since he confessed his sins after his baptism.

In the morning he set out on his last journey, to St. Catherine's. He was apprehensive about his chances of gaining access to the monastery as a postulant monk, for the monastery had a reputation as one of the stricter communities, not letting anyone in without the full authority of the bishop. He feared the bishop would find out how sinful he was and banish him.

He arrived at St. Catherine's monastery wearing the Orthodox robe, his beard fully grown out with his hair back, looking every bit an Orthodox monk. Cohen's appearance was so indistinguishable from the Greek monks that on his arrival one of the monks there asked him which monastery he had come from.

'I was at the monastery near Nazareth,' he said. 'I've come to join your community.'

Cohen had always sensed he had been Orthodox ever since hearing about St. Catherine's. The size of the monastery with its towering fortress walls overwhelmed him. It was built halfway up Mount Sinai and protected by a vast range of mountains. To protect the sanctity of the monastery guests were not allowed in the enclosure, but there were several guesthouses outside the grounds.

Cohen had no money to give for the guesthouse, which he'd spent on bus fares and meals on his journey. He asked the monk if he could stay at the monastery.

'You'll have to ask the bishop,' said the monk. 'But you can stay in the guesthouse free,' he said, looking at Cohen's tattered robe and taking a closer inspection. 'Are you Orthodox?' queried the monk, a puzzled look on his face.

'Anglo-Orthodox,' said Cohen.

He spent an anxious night in the guesthouse, not knowing whether he would be allowed to live inside the monastery, for if he was refused he had no money to pay for lodgings.

In the morning the monk returned and beckoned to follow him into the monastery to meet the bishop. He entered the cloisters through a narrow arched doorway, so small he had to crouch down to pass through. It was built in the times when men were short, although it had a humbling effect when you entered. In fact that was the reason for the narrow doorway.

A humbled Cohen thus entered the cloister, and was surprised at how many buildings of all shapes and sizes and colours were scattered around the monastery. The buildings were haphazardly built. The only semblance of planning seemed to be the monks' cloisters, high up on the east side, with a veranda running the length of the monastery.

In the middle of the monastery stood the last remnant of the Muslim invasion, an Islamic prayer tower, a minaret, which towered above the other buildings, even the chapel. Cohen was surprised it hadn't been demolished centuries ago, but it stood there to appease the Muslims who were still working there to this day.

The Greek monk took Cohen to the chapel and asked him to wait for the bishop.

The chapel was breathtaking, decorated in the Orthodox tradition with hanging lamps and beautiful icons on every wall. Rows of endless candles were lit before each icon and the overwhelming presence of God filled the frankincense air.

Cohen stood in one of the pews that rested upright against the wall, and meditated on the holiness of the sanctuary. Monks had been there since the fourth century. It was the oldest monastery in Christendom and Cohen stood transfixed, in awe of its splendour and place in history.

After a short time praying, he walked around the chapel studying the icons and admiring the architecture. At the rear of the chapel, placed in a darkened alcove for protection from the light, he discovered the oldest preserved icon, the Madonna and Child, a Greek painting dating back to the seventh century.

The icon was of exceptional beauty, painted with divine skill and holy inspiration. Cohen went back into the chapel to light a candle in front of the icon of St. Catherine when he saw the imposing figure of the Greek bishop, a portly man dressed in a monk's habit wearing a veiled hat. The Greek Orthodox Church only appointed bishops to run their monasteries. He struggled to sit in his special chair, the bishop's throne, and summoned Cohen before him.

'Are you a monk?' asked the bishop, abruptly.

'I'm training to be a monk, your grace,' said Cohen, handing him a letter, a reference from one of the monasteries.

The bishop had forgotten his glasses and pressed his nose impatiently to the letter. 'But you're not an Orthodox monk?' he asked, peering at his robe.

'I was a Roman Catholic, your grace, but I'm willing to convert.'

'You'll have to be baptised, and that will take six months,' said the bishop.

'But I've already been baptised,' replied Cohen, startled at the bishop's request.

'That does not count, it's not Orthodox Church,' said the bishop gruffly. 'If you're willing to be baptised into the Orthodox faith you can stay. We have a monk here from England, Brother Paul. He will show you to your cell.'

Cohen felt confused about having to be baptised again, but immense relief at having been accepted, for this was no ordinary monastery and had strict rules on accepting postulants. He was also relieved because he had no money, and had the Bishop refused him entrance he would starve in the Sinai desert.

Brother Paul appeared and led him out of the chapel across a courtyard and up several flights of stairs until he reached the cloisters. At the end of the veranda the monk unlocked the door and welcomed him to his new cell.

'I hope you'll find it comfortable,' said Brother Paul. 'There's an electric fire if you need it, although the monks don't use them.'

'Were you a monk in England?' Cohen asked.

'Yes, I stayed at an Orthodox monastery in Essex for a year, and the Abbot suggested I come here. I was thinking about going to Mount Athos, but he said this monastery would suit me better. Which monastery are you from?'

'I was with the Franciscans in Jerusalem,' said Cohen, 'then went to a French monastery in the Judean desert. I've just come from a monastery in Nazareth.'

'You've been around then. Are you thinking of converting?'

'Yes, I feel Orthodoxy is the only tradition that's remained unchanged,' said Cohen. 'It hasn't allowed itself to become worldly.'

'You realise you won't be allowed to take Communion for six months, and the library is out of bounds until you're baptised?' Paul remarked, closing the door.

Cohen lay down on his bed and pondered his fate. It didn't make any sense, he thought, being baptised again. It was as though the Orthodox Church was telling him that there was only one baptism and it had to be in the Orthodox Church, as though as other faiths didn't exist and that baptism outside the Orthodox Church was invalid and non-sacramental.

He felt uncomfortable in his new surroundings. He felt an air of distrust, a feeling of not belonging, as if he was an outsider. His discomfort and apparent isolation was no figment of his imagination, as he was to discover a few days later when he was taken ill.

He had attended Mass, and stood in one of the pews in front of a monk who did nothing but cough all over him the whole time. The following day Cohen was struck down with flu so serious that he couldn't get out of bed for a whole week. The electric fire was on all that time. No one came to see him or offer food. Brother Paul must have known something was wrong as Cohen hadn't attended the services or eaten any meals in the refectory all that time. For the entire week he lay in bed sick as a dog, his temperature soaring and without medication to relieve his suffering. What he didn't know at that time was that there was a resident doctor in the monastery held surgeries most mornings, mostly seeing the wives of Bedouins, who worked as porters and labourers.

Cohen felt completely let down by the community as he stared out of his window to see a group of Bedouin women queuing up outside the surgery. Some of them were beautiful, wearing long Sari dresses and with their hair plaited. He felt the need for spiritual nourishment and after a week's unnecessary fasting. He headed down to the chapel, lined up with monks and guests. As he waited the receive the Eucharist, all of a sudden Brother Paul, his eyes blazing, rushed up to him and forcibly removed him from the queue.

'You're not allowed to take Communion,' said the monk, angrily.

Cohen, still reeling from his illness, looked up in disbelief. He was dumbfounded at such aggressive behaviour by the monk in front of the altar and the bishop. This rejection in front of the whole community pierced his soul like a sword. He staggered out of the chapel and went back to his cell and prayed. After several hours in prayer he began to realise that he was in the wrong place, that he shouldn't be cooped up in an

Orthodox monastery with Greek monks who couldn't care less about him.

Cohen's mission was to be out in the world witnessing to fellow Jews. However, he had come to the monastery with good intentions. He wanted to prepare himself for his ministry and enter the Christian faith more deeply.

Did not Jesus prepare himself for his ministry by going into the wilderness for forty days? And should man not live by bread alone, by every word of God? Maybe his sickness and involuntary fasting was God's mysterious way of preparing him for his calling, of refining his spirit in the depths of suffering.

He recalled the sufferings of St. John of the Cross, the torments he went through in the monastery, his Dark Night of the Soul, his rejection by his brethren. St. John was evicted from the monastery and forced to live in the desert where he nearly died. Cohen feared a similar fate. His spirit was crushed by the confines of a monastery that didn't seem to care whether he was alive or dead.

Not having eaten for a week, Cohen made the effort to go to the refectory, but he was too late and the monks had already eaten. There was no food left. He would have to wait for supper. A monk on kitchen duty offered him a piece of bread, urging him not to tell anyone as the monks were not allowed to eat between meals. But Cohen declined, not wishing to get the monk into any trouble. It seemed as if his life at St. Catherine's couldn't any bleaker. It was a disappointment to him after having read so much about the history of the monastery and its place in Christendom.

But within a few days the atmosphere had changed. It was January, the Orthodox Christmas. Cohen was going to celebrate Christmas all over again, having celebrated it only two weeks before at the Dutch monastery. But the Gregorian calendar had always celebrated January 6th as the feast of the birth of Christ, as opposed to the rest of the churches which celebrated it on December 25th. It would at least bring a little cheer to the monastery, he hoped.

Cohen was still feeling weak from his confinement and the next morning went to the doctor. The surgery was on the ground floor below his cell and when he arrived there was a queue of more than a dozen Bedouin women. He turned away, feeling the women needed the doctor more than him, and went back to his cell.

In the afternoon, when the women had left the monastery, he returned and knocked on the surgery door. The doctor, a bespectacled young Greek, told him that the surgery was closed in the afternoons, but then took one look at him and beckoned him inside.

'You should have come to me sooner,' said the doctor, examining his chest and handing him some medication afterwards.

'I was in bed for a week,' said Cohen, noticing the chess set on the table in the surgery. 'Do you play chess?

'I do, but the monks don't approve,' said the doctor.

'I will play you,' said Cohen. They set up the pieces and within a few moves Cohen had checkmated him.

'You play well,' said the doctor, congratulating him. 'We must play another time.'

'Can I ask you a personal question?' asked Cohen. 'The Bedouin women that come to see you, do they let you examine them intimately?'

'Why do you ask?' queried the doctor.

'It's just that Muslims are very protective of their women, like Hindus. They usually prefer a female doctor.'

'You have studied other religions, I see,' said the doctor, 'Seeing as I am the only doctor in Sinai, the women have little choice. But to answer your question, no, they don't object. Whether their husbands object, I have no idea.'

Cohen went back to his cell and took his medication. He realised later that he had got his facts wrong about the Hindus. Doctors are allowed to examine women intimately, providing their bodies are covered with a sheet and a hole so as to facilitate the examination and not to cause embarrassment. On the other hand, Muslims feel that their women give rise to impurity if they are intimately examined by male doctors.

In England, a white male doctor once examined a Muslim women and the angry husband and went to the hospital complaining, whereupon two doctors colluded to put the man in mental hospital – all because of religion. In another case, a male doctor intimately examined a wife in maternity. On hearing the news the upset husband took an overdose and was sectioned to the mental ward.

The doctor blamed the husband's overdose for him not wanting a baby, but the husband was overwhelmed by his son birth. The truth is that the husband was a religious man and he wanted a female doctor.

Cohen spent the rest of the day recuperating in his cell reading the life of St. Catherine, a chaste virgin. He was curious as to why the monastery had changed its name from the Transfiguration of Jesus to St. Catherine almost three centuries ago.

According to the legends, three monks guided by a dream discovered the body of St. Catherine on Mount Sinai and dedicated the monastery to her name. They believed her body had miraculously appeared on the mountain, having flown from Alexandria. Needless to say, there was no aircraft in those days.

St. Catherine's life was no less remarkable. In 305 A.D, at eighteen years of age, she was kidnapped in Alexandria by the Emperor Maxentius. She had studied much and was a devout Christian. The Emperor brought fifty philosophers to try and persuade her that belief in Christianity was foolish. She convinced them her faith was real and converted them all to Christianity. Emperor was enraged at hearing the news and he had them put to death. Because she refused to marry him, the Greeks called her Aei Katharina, meaning 'ever pure'. The Emperor put her in a dungeon and ordered her to be executed. She was tied to a wheel adorned with razors but instead of cutting her to pieces, the wheel broke and the Catherine Wheel, the firework, took its name from her attempted execution. She was later beheaded. How her body could fly from Alexandria to Mount Sinai baffled Cohen completely. But then again, God could do anything – even raise the dead!

The next day Cohen felt well again and decided to visit the Bedouin village near the monastery. His spirits lifted as the sun beamed down and he walked to the village. He sat down in a café and ordered a cup of coffee.

Two Bedouin boys, noticing his robe, came and sat with Cohen. They were comfortable in his presence, knowing that he was from the monastery.

One of the boys, called Ali, pointed at Cohen's watch. It was a cheap toy watch made of plastic which he had found in a field at the Dutch monastery. Ali liked the watch so much because it sparkled, Cohen gave it to him.

Just then an Arab walked in carrying a huge bird of prey, its talons bound by leather straps. He placed it on the table and ordered a drink.

'What's that bird?' asked Cohen, upset that it was tied up.

'It's an eagle,' said the Arab.

'Why have you tied it up?' he asked, perplexed. 'What are you going to do with it?'

'Going to sell it,' said the owner. 'You want it?'

'You should let it go,' urged Cohen. 'Birds like that shouldn't be sold.'

'You pay me and I'll let it go,' said the Arab, laughing.

Cohen had no money to buy the bird's freedom and left the café disgusted. He couldn't bear seeing birds caged, let alone an eagle, the very bird he spotted at the French monastery soaring high and free above the ravine.

On the outskirts of the village he came across a Bedouin with a camel for hire. On seeing his monastery robe, he let Cohen ride it for free. The Bedouin instructed his son to help Cohen mount the frisky beast, for he'd never ridden a camel before. He'd never felt so awkward and cumbersome. The camel groaned as it got up off its front legs, sending Cohen rocking backwards and forward. He feared being thrown off. He was told by the boy to ride with one leg over the other, and holding the reins tightly he managed to steady himself and set out upon the open desert. He spent an hour on the beast and vowed to stick to horses in the future. Never had he experienced such an unnerving and precarious journey. It made him feel travel sick.

Upon his return, the Bedouin chief invited Cohen to his home, a two-room shack on the outskirts of the village. He was introduced to his wife and daughter, a beautiful girl with long dark hair and a full figure. The women made fun of Cohen's robe, touching it to feel the material, as they joked among themselves how bland it was compared to their colourful costumes. It intrigued him why they wore so many gold coins, jewellery and chains. It was their culture to dress the women with all their wealth on their bodies.

Cohen sat on the floor, as was the custom, and thanked the chief for the camel ride and the coffee, even though he felt seasick. The Bedouin chief then surprised Cohen by offering him his daughter. The girl smiled at Cohen. She was striking beautiful, her long raven hair and dark eyelids flashing.

He wondered if he was the first man who had been offered the girl. She looked like an innocent child, a chaste virgin. 'Very pretty, you like?' asked the Bedouin, thrusting the daughter in front of Cohen.

'She is charming, but I am just a poor monk and we are not allowed to go with women, you understand?' said Cohen apologetically, for he did not want to offend the chief's hospitality.

'I want my daughter married. You marry her and leave this monastery. It's not good for you,' said the Bedouin, seeing the sadness in Cohen's eyes.

Cohen thanked him for the offering and turned to kiss the girl and stroked her long dark hair. 'Sorry to part with such beauty,' he said. 'She will marry soon enough. Men will be fighting over her. You'll see.' Shaking the chief's hand and waving goodbye, he left for the monastery.

It was Christmas at St. Catherine's monastery and the monks were preparing for the night Mass. Shortly before the service started, he spent some time in prayer at the Shrine of the Burning Bush. It was here on this very spot that God spoke to Moses and gave him the Ten Commandments.

Cohen wept as he prayed, not out of self-pity for his suffering at the monastery, but out of joy for having prayed at such a holy shrine a miserable sinner like him. Such was the overwhelming compassion of God that Christ died on the cross for him for his wretched sins. He recalled a prayer of St. John of the Ladder, who wrote The Ladder of Ascent here at St. Catherine's, where he spent his entire life in devotion:

'I am a wretch, broken by my distractions, a sinner through and through. My only help is in God's mercy. That is why I am a Christian, for the Lord Himself came down from heaven and was crucified on the cross, a sacrifice for my sins. All men are sinners in the eyes of God, but when they truly repent and amend their lives, then the mercy of God, His forgiveness and blessings come and His Grace, the Holy Spirit comes and dwells within. Such is the overwhelming love of God for mankind.'

Cohen lit a candle and placed it next to the shrine. He knelt before the Burning Bush and went back into the Chapel where the Christmas Mass had begun.

The chapel was rapidly filling up with guests from all over the world, some from Europe, the United States and even South America. Monks had flown in especially from Mount Athos to join the choir and celebrate the holy feast. The chanting was divine, far surpassing the choir of the French monastery. Cohen managed to find a pew as the chapel filled up. An elderly monk stood beside him with a walking stick and Cohen offered the man seat. The monk, full of vigour in his old age, took offence at Cohen, saying he was strong enough to stand with anybody. Orthodox monks were able to stand for the entire length of the service, even Christmas Mass.

The Mass began at midnight and did not finish until six o'clock in the morning. Cohen was completely exhausted when it was ended, but deeply wounded by the fact that he was not given Communion – thanks to Brother Paul. He wanted to go back to his cell and sleep, but was there was a Christmas party at the Bishop's residence and everyone was required to attend.

Cohen, tired out, took a seat at the back and listened to the obese Bishop, sitting on his throne handing out presents like Father Christmas, rambling on in Greek for what felt like at least two hours. He then started tucking in to his turkey and Cohen wondered how spiritual he really was for large amounts of wine bishop's drank as he jeered and laughed. He made the sinful monks look like saints. Disgusted with the Bishop's behaviour, Cohen walked out. He was not to be perturbed by the bishop's ranting, for he had already celebrated Christmas at the previous monastery, the proper time to do it.

The following day, a group of monks were standing around an American guest, a professor of ancient Hebrew Scriptures. He had been invited there to decipher some of the Dead Sea Scrolls, which had been discovered by an archaeological expedition.

Some of the monks were hanging on every word that the professor said as he expounded on ancient history in that annoying brash American manner. Cohen later met with the professor in the guesthouse and was introduced to his research assistant, an attractive raven-haired Canadian called Scarlet. They were sharing a room together in the guesthouse, but because of the VIP status the bishop had invited the professor to stay at the monastery, a rare invitation for a guest. Cohen sensed a certain intimacy between the couple and he was not surprised when the professor, Dr. Alan Greenberg, declined the invitation as his assistant would not be allowed to stay overnight in the monastery.

Dr. Greenberg asked Cohen what a Jewish Englishman was doing in a Greek Orthodox monastery. He explained as best he could, but made the fatal mistake of airing his complaint of the bishop who had made him think about leaving the monastery. The professor told him that he would be driving with his assistant back to Elat the next day. Cohen, having no money, asked if he could catch a ride. But the American had not planned for a party of three, for he had intended to go there on a romantic trip, an intimate drive across the desert, with no room for a monk.

Scarlet had other ideas. She had taken to Cohen, with his long hair and beard and Jewish origins. She tried to cajole her academic lover into taking him along. But the professor was having none of it. He noticed his assistant found Cohen attractive, and they'd developed a rapport which made him uncomfortable. He insisted to Cohen that the car was full up with luggage and equipment and abruptly got up and left, demanding that Scarlet follow him. While the professor was away talking to the bishop, Cohen felt the need to ask Scarlet if she would run away with him if he was to leave the monastery. She was indeed very beautiful, with a vivacious smile, fine figure and long legs. He needed an ideal woman who would fulfil his dreams, leave him happy, and rid him of all the tensions and upheavals of the monastery. He was looking for his soul mate. Scarlet turned to Cohen and smiled, before taking one last look at him and leaving with the professor.

That afternoon, Cohen was summoned to the bishop's office. After a long pause, the bishop said: 'I'm going to have to ask you to leave the monastery. I can't give you a reason, so don't ask.'

It came as no surprise to Cohen, given how many services he'd missed when he was ill, but he didn't expect to be evicted so soon. He had been at the monastery barely a month. He felt at a loss again, with no money and no place to go. If this were to be the pattern of his experience in monasteries, then he'd never set foot in one again.

Monasteries had caused him so much anguish and suffering that he'd be better off living in the desert with a woman. At least that way he would be looked after.

'But why?' asked Cohen, ignoring the bishop's request, for he wanted to know.

'If you insist...' sighed the bishop, 'you tried to take Eucharist before your baptism. It's a sacrilege, and I've heard that you not content at the monastery anyway and plan to leave. I don't think you are suited to this life, so you'd be better off in England.'

'I have no money to get back to Israel, let alone England,' Cohen said.

'I'll see that you have money,' said the bishop. 'It's a hard life,' he added, lighting another cigarette. 'You'd be best off with your own people.'

Cohen agreed, said farewell to the bishop and went back to his cell for the last time. He was furious with the mad professor for betraying his trust. He sensed a jealous streak in him which explained everything. For he had not realised that Scarlet was the one who'd betrayed him.

Cohen that afternoon went to the monk in charge to get his money. The monk, who was fat and bald, was livid about Cohen's expulsion and ordered him to return in the afternoon. In the meantime, Cohen visited the aged monk he met in the chapel who'd refused his offer of a seat. He was the oldest and longest serving monk, having been at the monastery for nigh on seventy years. Cohen knocked on the cell door. He was sitting on his bed meditating on the rosary. When Cohen walked in his eyes lit up like those of a child.

'Sit down,' said Brother John. 'How many languages do you speak?'

'Just English and Hebrew and a bit of French,' Cohen said.

'I speak seven languages,' said the old monk proudly. 'I've been here for nearly seventy years, came as a boy, never wanted to go anywhere else. You want to stay here?'

'I don't think I'm cut out to be a monk,' admitted Cohen. 'I need to be out in the world, just like Jesus was.'

'Dangerous place,' warned the monk. 'What job did you do before?'

'I was a journalist,' he confessed.

'Never read newspapers,' scoffed the old man.

'Were you ever tempted to leave the monastery?' asked Cohen, finding it difficult to understand why the old man had spent all his life in his cell.

'There is nothing out there,' said the monk.

'Well, there are people; we're all God's creations.'

'The world is going to hell,' lamented the monk.

'What should people do to be saved?' enquired Cohen.

'Repent,' he said, banging his fist on the table, 'in sackcloth and ashes,' abruptly ending the conversation.

Cohen got up and thanked him for his time and left. Walking past another cell, he could hear a monk chanting psalms, calling out to God to have mercy on this fallen world. He walked dejected to his cell and packed his rucksack and notebooks. He took one last look at his room, one of the few comforts during his stay. It had nursed him back to health with the electrical fire and blanket and solitude. It had been his sanctuary throughout his month-long ordeal at St. Catherine's. There was no one he wanted to say goodbye to, not even the English monk, Brother Paul, who'd reported him to the bishop when he wanted to take the Eucharist. He knew deep down in his heart that he wanted to forgive Brother Paul, but being reported to the bishop over Communion was unforgivable.

It was incidents like this that not only wounded him, but made him aware of the divisions in the Western Church, for the church was meant to be Christ body on earth, yet the separate churches were crucifying Jesus all over again with constant rivalry and in-fighting. The churches no longer practised what the Gospel taught – that we are one body in Christ.

Picking up his rucksack, Cohen headed back along the veranda, taking one last look at the chapel below, the row of monks' cells above and the refectory at the end of the cloisters. He turned towards the minaret, the infamous tower of Babel in the middle of the courtyard, a stark reminder of past atrocities. Crossing the courtyard he was approached by the guest master, who handed him a brown envelope.

'The bishop asked me to give you this,' said the monk, staring accusingly at Cohen. He took the brown envelope and turned away and headed for the gate, jostling past the tourists who just got off the coach. It came as no surprise that the worship was compromised, what with all the invading tourists mentioned by Fr. Joseph. Any piety or holiness of the monastery had gone.

It was a sad indictment of how so-called progress with tourism and leisure and computerised technology had replaced the love of God. The monastery was now so affluent and worldly it had even installed the latest IBM Computer which let the monks go online and produce their own web pages.

The monastery had once been revered as one of the most sacred sites in Christendom, a place of worship by monks, and a sanctuary for the pilgrims who for centuries had braved the perilous journey across the Sinai desert.

Alas, not so today. St. Catherine's had been raped by progress, its towering walls, once a fortress, has been breached by hordes of tourists viewing the monastery as little more than a museum.

It was with great relief that Cohen walked out of St. Catherine's monastery through the narrow gate for the last time. He turned and looked up at Mount Sinai and wondered what Moses would do if he was alive now. No doubt he would have done the same thing as when he witnessed the debauchery and idol-worship of the Israelites all those centuries ago. He would have sent the stone tablets crashing down upon Mount Sinai again in rage.

Cohen in his disgust left the monastery and walked into the village to the bus station. He opened the brown envelope from the bishop and counted the money. He had enough for a bus to Elat. After that, he would be on his own, impoverished again and making his way across the Sinai desert to reach Jerusalem.

Before the bus left, he had time to go into the station washroom, shave off his beard and remove his robe. If he was going to be a missionary, he wanted to be anonymous, indistinguishable from the crowd, to be a humble disciple, not parading around in robes like a proud Pharisee.

After a long and uneventful journey, Cohen arrived in Elat late in the evening. He had a few shekels left and headed for the bar on the marina. He sat down in the bar wonder where he would spend the night when in walked a couple arm-in-arm. He couldn't believe his eyes. In strolled the mad professor and Scarlet, his girlfriend. She totally blanked him, like women do when they feel wronged. Sticking her nose in the air, she walked past him. The professor burst out laughing upon seeing Cohen, robe-less and beardless, sitting on a bar stool drinking.

Cohen waited a few moments before turning around to see which table they had taken, but he was not surprised to see them carry on straight through the exit door. No doubt they feared a confrontation over Cohen's dismissal from the monastery.

They had good reason to fear, for he was angry over Scarlet betrayal. He wanted to go after them and demand an explanation, but there seemed little point. They had ridiculed him for leaving the monastery. Such was the way of the people who mocked the Lord.

With nowhere to go, not even a hotel room for the night, he had no choice but to spend the night on the beach hoping he'd get some sleep. A few hours later he was abruptly woken by a policeman, poking him with a stick. The prod in the ribs felt to him like being stabbed, but he breathed a sigh of relief when the cop told him to move on. The thought of being taken back to the asylum terrified him. Cohen did as he was told and left the beach, exhausted from not having slept enough.

He walked out of Elat and began to hitchhike along the main highway to Massada. It was on this highway that a Jewish couple hitchhiking had been shot recently. They were picked up an Arab man and the boyfriend was shot in the back when the driver told him to put their luggage in the boot. He then raped the woman, who survived after being shot in the face. Fortunately for Cohen he was picked up by an Israeli businessman who drove him to Massada. The Israeli offered a sandwich, for he hadn't eaten for two days. The driver took a turn off from the highway and left Cohen stranded in the middle of the desert.

He stood for several hours without getting a lift and so he walked all night, as it was getting cold. He felt like he'd been walking forever when he collapsed on a bench at the bus shelter, where he spent an uncomfortable night getting little sleep.

At the break of dawn he set out for Jerusalem, cold and hungry. Several hours passed before he finally got a ride, again from an Israeli who took him all the way to Jerusalem. After dropping off Cohen he generously handed him fifty shekels, taking pity on his destitution. He offered to pay the man back but the Jew declined. It was one of few acts of kindness Cohen had experienced in Israel, which restored his faith in the Jews. It was an act of charity he would never forget. So exhausted by the lack of sleep and starvation, Cohen thought he would not make it back to Jerusalem, but instead die in the desert, forgotten and destitute. He tried to return the Israeli's charity by witnessing for Jesus, but the driver wasn't interested in religion. It created wars, he said, and all he could do was look after his family and do good towards his neighbour and treat others how he would want to be treated. If the rest of mankind behaved like that there would be no wars, thought Cohen.

When he finally arrived in Jerusalem he was relieved to discover the rioting had stopped and that peace and order had been restored. With the money he'd been given he treated himself to a meal and a few beers. He strolled along the beach where a few Israelis were gathered and, encouraged by the alcohol, told them he was a missionary sent by God and that Jesus was their Messiah. They looked at him blank.

Cohen turned away and caught the bus to Ein Karem, where he once again took refuge in the convent with the

Catholic nuns. But on this occasion, they weren't so charitable. They made him dig the garden and wash dishes for his food and board. He welcomed the physical exercise for the outdoor work, which not only made him fit and healthy again but refreshed his mind and invigorated his soul. He stayed with the nuns for two weeks until the Mother Superior asked him to leave the convent, for it was fully booked on account of the upcoming Easter festivities. Cohen left the nuns with a heavy heart with nowhere to go and lay his head. He went out to the Judean hills and slept out under the stars until Easter came to the Holy Land.

24

It was Palm Sunday, one of the holiest days in the Christian calendar, and Cohen left the desert hills to go into Jerusalem.

Thousands of Christians from all over the world had flocked to the Mount of Olives to celebrate Christ's triumphant return to the Holy City. He joined the throng of pilgrims paying homage to the Lord, waving palm trees and chanting 'Hosanna, Son of David, hosanna, hosanna, Christ our King.' Hoards of pilgrims rejoiced as they proceeded down the mountain spreading palm leaves along the way, the very path Christ he took to Jerusalem on a donkey.

Cohen noticed one girl in the crowd. She had enormous breasts and he looked away, for it was a holy day, not one for temptation. The procession wound its way slowly down the Mount of Olives, past the Jewish cemetery where the prophets lay buried, and past the Garden of Gethsemane where Christ was arrested. Never before had he witnessed such a joyous occasion as the pilgrims worshipping God, singing psalms and exalting the name of Jesus.

Arab merchants, eager to cash in on the occasion, lined the route with their market stalls selling beads, incense and cards of Jerusalem and souvenirs. As Cohen passed the stalls he thought of Jesus taking a whip to the merchants, turning over the stalls in righteous anger for denigrating the temple into a marketplace.

On several occasions Cohen was pestered by merchants selling their goods. One even insisting he buy some worthless coins. But having experience of poverty in Israel he bore no grudge. They had families to feed, hungry children. He left the procession and purchased a rosary at one of the stalls. It would feed the hungry children. The procession reached the foot of the Mount of Olives and passed through the valley of Gethsemane, where Christ had prayed out loud 'Thy Will Be Done' on the night he was arrested. The people made their way up a steep incline before entering the Holy City.

Passing through the Lion's Gate where Cohen first witnessed the shooting of an Arab boy, the procession then wound its way through an archway into the courtyard, where the sick were healed in the bathing pools. It was here in the Bethesda pool that Christ healed the cripple. On entering the courtyard Cohen went across to the bathing pool and peered down into the baths, large rectangular trenches cut deep into the earth several metres below. It was a breathtaking sight. Cohen pictured the crippled and lame crying out to the Lord to be healed. He wondered how he, a sinner, could bring that same healing power of Christ to a fallen world, namely to Jews who didn't believe in Jesus. He went back dejected to the courtyard where the Mass was being held. It was the first Mass he'd attended outdoors and it lifted his spirits. The congregation, all those who proceeded down the mountain in Christ's footsteps, were about to say a general confession. Cohen lowered his head and recalled his sins, in particular the sin of staring at the buxom girl during the procession. The conviction in his heart made him call to mind his Lord's admonishment:

'Whoever looks upon a woman with lust in his heart commits adultery'.

After making his confession and asking forgiveness, Cohen wondered whether or not Christ's condemnation was meant for married men, for only married men could commit adultery. He was single.

After the Mass, the congregation dispersed and went their own ways. Cohen was left to ponder his fate and where to go next. Before leaving the city he would go and see what progress, if any, had been made on the new temple. The site was only a few blocks away and when he entered the Muslim Quarter he was astonished at the view. In the few months since he last visited, builders had not just completed the foundation but built the surroundings walls. It was a spectacular sight, the new temple walls towering into the sky, built faithfully according to the architect's plans, the very plans he'd seen in Ein Karem when he first came to Israel, an exact replica of the original temple built by King Solomon.

Cohen approached the temple in awe and appreciation and knelt down on the steps leading to the sanctuary. It wouldn't be long now before the roof was completed and the new temple finally restored as he prophesised. Then the worship and animal sacrifices could begin and the Jews would pray for the coming of the Messiah. Cohen wiped a tear from his eye.

If only they knew, if only they had faith that the Lord Jesus Christ was their Messiah that he had died for their sins, Israel would be free and could live in peace with its neighbours.

As he knelt on the steps it dawned on him the awesome responsibility of taking the Gospel message to the Jews.

Despite the setbacks he suffered in the monasteries, he had been well trained for the task. He had received the Holy Spirit and put on the full armour of Christ, the helmet of salvation, the shield of faith, the breastplate of righteousness, and had taken up the sword, the word of God.

All that was left to fulfil his mission was to go out to the Jews. But how could he get the Jews to listen? Maybe they would simply cast him out, like they did Christ.

Cohen spent a month preaching the Gospel in the streets and marketplaces in Jerusalem. But his teachings fell on deaf ears. Some few would stop and listen, but then walk away, with others calling him a traitor and telling him to get out and go back to England. Despite being hungry and exhausted and sleeping rough in the cemetery, he refused to accept any assistance from monasteries or convents. He put his trust in God. He would provide sustenance, to keep body and soul together as he carried out the call to spread the Good News.

It was while he was sleeping one night in the cemetery that the police came and arrested him in the middle of the night, like they did Christ. They had received a number of complaints of him preaching, disturbing the peace, proselytising to the Jews, and vagrancy.

The police took him away, like Jesus, and placed him in a cell.

When Cohen appeared in court the next day he was convicted of the crimes listed. The court was told he had been previously been sectioned under the Mental Health Act and incarcerated at the Massada Mental Hospital with Jerusalem Syndrome, whence he escaped.

After finding him guilty the magistrates sentenced him to an indefinite period in a psychiatric hospital. Upon his admission the doctors treated him again for Jerusalem Syndrome, forcefully injecting him with anti-psychotic drugs and tranquillisers. When he refused to respond to the treatment, the doctors and the Israeli authorities ordered him deported back to England.

25

Cohen remained true to his faith, living the rest of his life away from women as a hermit on Holy Island, off the northeast of England. Occasionally, he set out on a pilgrimage to the shrine of Our Lady of Walsingham, where he prayed for the salvation of the Jews, asking Mary, the Mother of God, to intercede for them now and at the hour of their deaths.

Alone in his cell, in periods of quiet recollection, he thought back on his life and reminisced about all the women he'd met.

Most of all, he never forgot the beautiful woman who kissed him in the tent all those years ago.

Ave Maria.

THE END

Acknowledgements

My sincere thanks to my editor and publisher James Essinger and to Joseph Mooney for additional editorial help.

My thanks also to my dear wife Sharon, and also to Margaret Dowley for her work on the formatting and to Charlotte Mouncey for her help with the book's cover.